The Wrath of Moses

John Sturgeon

BLACK ROSE writing™

ISBN: 978-1-61296-549-9

PUBLISHED BY BLACK ROSE WRITING

www.blackrosewriting.com

Printed in the United States of America

Suggested retail price $17.95

The Wrath of Moses is printed in Palatino Linotype

To my children, John, Allie and Matt. Always follow your dreams.

Author Photo by Mary Sturgeon.

The Wrath of Moses

Prologue

Murderer! When my eyes popped open the day after Christmas that was the first word that came into my mind. As much as I believed in the system that provided justice in our country, I had taken it upon myself to become judge, jury and executioner in dealing with my father in the alley behind Freiburg's Dance Hall. Don't get me wrong. I knew what my father was, and I wasn't sure I knew everything about him. I could have probably gotten past the underage girls that were working the bar and perhaps him calling my mother a whore, but it was the smug look and those beady eyes that showed absolutely no warmth, not a care. His only worry, his only concern in the world, was turning a dollar. People, human beings, were just like the liquor he sold, just stock in some store.

Immediately after the shooting, I seemed to enter a hazy state. I felt nothing, but a calm sweep over me. I walked out of the alley as my father lay in the dirt, his blood seeping out of him, and a light snow falling about me. There was no panic in me, no increased heart rate. I didn't see anyone. I didn't hear anything. There were signs of Christmas everywhere, twinkling lights, big wreaths and colorful bows, but none of it registered with me. I walked out of the alley and went straight to Coopers. There was a small crowd dining and I know some people acknowledged me, but I don't remember who. I ordered a steak and a beer. I may have had another beer, but I don't recall. It wasn't late when I finished, maybe seven, seven-thirty, but I left the bar and walked home, undressed and crawled into bed. I slept as well as I had in a long time; there were no demons, no Kluge, no one pounding on my door. I needed the sleep. I was bruised, mentally and physically. My actions of the night before proved I was damaged, but none of that mattered at the time, but it hit me when I awoke.

What kind of a world did we live in? The past two weeks had proven to me that all of the wild animals of the world were not safely locked up. I was living amongst them; I may be becoming one of them. Who keeps women locked and trapped, drugging them and turning them into prostitutes? Who murders people in their sleep? Who kills half blind people and cuts their dog's throat? Who slashes prostitutes and leaves them lying in the cold snow to bleed out? These were the worst of things I'd seen in the past two weeks and that hadn't covered it all. The Field case still had my head ringing. Why hadn't Field let me arrest Major Thorsen? Did Thorsen turn himself in? I hadn't heard.

After my first thought, condemning myself as a killer, I considered my next move. Would the next sound at my door be the officers coming to arrest me? I didn't think so. Should I turn myself in? No. I felt I had done the world a good turn. If they came for me, I would answer the charges, but I wasn't going to give myself up. I didn't think I'd done anything that terribly wrong, although criminal. So what was my next move? Someone murdered the Harts, Mary Hastings and Louie Pagano. Sam Walker was working those cases. Someone beat up Gunter and I'm not even sure that was being investigated. Horace Langley had tried to murder me and Gunter had shot him dead. Who was Horace working for? Where was Gussie Black and how was he connected to all of this? Who was the blonde, mute man who seemed to be working for Colosimo?

Was he tied into any of the murders? He seemed strongly tied to the white slaving. What was the white slaving all about? We had seen those shackled girls out in Blue Island, but the prostitutes we'd talked to in the Levee insisted nothing was amiss. Very bizarre indeed. Lastly, the image of Eleanor lying in that dirty snow by Bubbly Creek, holding my locket, made my heart lurch. I felt I hadn't done enough to keep her safe. We had executed Kluge and then a murder that mirrored his crimes had occurred. Was he back, as Gunter said? I smiled. That thought was ludicrous, but someone was killing again and had left me some reminders on my doorstep. Our supposed mistake that Kluge was acting alone had gotten Eleanor murdered. There was just too much going on and I was still on medical leave, but this needed to change. I needed to get back to work.

• • •

With little else to do, I checked on my new friend, Major Thorsen. The man who Marshall Field had called a man of honor, was supposed to turn himself in the day after our encounter in Field's office. I checked with some people I knew at headquarters. No one named Thorsen, or Major anybody, as a matter of fact, had turned themselves in. I found out where Thorsen resided, a cozy apartment house on Dearborn, close to the river. I took a carriage to the building and, after showing my badge, got the landlord to let me into Thorsen's flat. I was not surprised, nor was I that upset, when I found the place abandoned of all of Thorsen's personal effects. The man had disappeared. I stared out the window, wondering where he had gone. I laughed. Field had wanted the case solved, wanted to know what had happened to his son. When I solved it, when we found that Thorsen had been the one to shoot Marshall, Jr., Field had given Thorsen a pass. He hadn't really wanted justice. He just wanted the truth. I wondered, besides Thorsen, the old man and me, who would ever know the real story. I doubted very many. What the world knew today was that Marshall, Jr. had shot himself accidentally while cleaning his gun for a hunting trip, the story Marshall, Sr. made sure the papers got when the incident occurred. That was how Field wanted everyone to remember how his son had died.

. . .

With the date approaching for my father's funeral, I noticed a tension settle into me. I had never liked, loved or even respected the man. I found him to be vile. The thought of attending his funeral was making me physically sick. I wasn't good about dealing with death to begin with. Father Luigi had only been gone a couple of weeks and I'd struggled at his funeral. This would be my second in a very short time. When my wife and two children were burned beyond any recognition at the great Iroquois Theatre fire, I was able to view their dead, blackened bodies at the morgue. I knew they had died in that inferno. Seeing them in that morgue, lying on the cold floor, was my final farewell to them. No emotional, Catholic funeral was going to bring about any change for them or for me. I was very upset with God. He had taken my life from me. If there is a God, how did he let all of those people, a large percentage of them children, die in that cauldron? I stayed away from the funeral and I stayed away from the church for a long while. Quite a few people, particularly my wife's family, chastised me for not attending, but they would never understand. I had been an orphan with no real family until I'd married and we'd had children. The only one who could understand how I grieved their loss was me.

. . .

My father's funeral took place four days after I shot him in the alley. I had never been in a synagogue, but Temple Beth Shalom was packed with mourners as the rabbi read from the Torah and most people in the crowded space probably couldn't understand a word that was said. I played my part as well as I could, taking a place near the front of the room, maintaining a grim face and shaking hands and accepting condolences from all that offered them. Of course, Coughlin and Kenna came by to shake my hand and tell me how sorry they were and what a great man my father was. I immediately felt a need to wash my hands or be sick to my stomach, but I managed to make it through. The synagogue was also overcrowded with most of the leading pimps and madams from the ward. The Everleigh sisters were there, looking very somber. Big Jim Colosimo, all dressed in a white suit, was there, but he was smiling. I saw Captain Morgan, but really no one else from the department. I looked all over, but Gunter was not present. I wasn't sure he'd been released from Mercy. I hadn't seen him since my visit before Christmas. Thankfully, Margaret was also not present.

The crowd thinned considerably as the service moved to the Hebrew Benevolent Society Cemetery, a slow, monotonous ride. The weather for late December was warm and there was dirty snow and slush everywhere. Once again I was forced to maintain my solemn appearance as the rabbi read more prayers and finally good old dad was lowered into the ground. I heard a woman I didn't know let out a gasp and a sob. My last thought for my father was, "Fuck You."

As I turned to begin my walk out of the cemetery to return to my apartment, Morgan approached me and called out my name. I turned as I saw him approaching, hunched over. It was obvious his back was ailing him.

"I am sorry for your loss, Patrick," he said, tugging at his bushy mustache. "I didn't know you were related to Mr. Fine. I heard it from Alderman Coughlin."

"We weren't that close," I said.

"It's a shame in our fine city that someone can just murder a man in an alley behind his place of work on Christmas Day and no one heard or saw a thing. Isn't that remarkable?"

The news that they had no leads made me feel a tad better. "I was going to ask how the investigation was shaping up."

Morgan looked over his shoulder, back to where they were planting father. "I've assigned the case to Riley and Loftus. They'll find the son of a bitch that did this."

"When they do, I hope they give him worse treatment than Kluge got."

Morgan eyes flared for a bit and then returned to his natural forlorn look. "They'll get him," he said. "Speaking of Kluge, I am a bit concerned."

I swallowed hard. "Sir?"

"The prostitute who was found murdered on Christmas Day, Eleanor Winter, you had ties with her?"

"I knew her from The Queens. "

"Yes, well, we've got a bit of a problem."

"A problem?"

"Patrick, this Winter woman was murdered in the same way that Kluge killed his victims. Coroner Hoffman stated that the type of cuts on the body were identical which can only mean that we have a very competent copier of Kluge's crimes or that we executed the wrong person."

A blast of anger went through me. "There is no doubt Kluge was involved. We had enough evidence to support that."

He waved his hand at me. "Of course. I know that, but it seems or looks like Kluge had an accomplice. So far, there's only been one murder, but if there's someone out there who was or is involved, this could be a very ugly situation."

"An understatement, sir."

"How are you feeling, both mentally and physically?

"Physically, better. Mentally, I'm not sure. I guess on my way to normal."

"We need you back and now, Patrick. With Krause still out and Langley dead, we are short two detectives. We have to find out what happened to the Harts and Mary Hastings from Sappho. Also Louie Pagano. Now I've got this Eleanor Winter murder and who knows what might spring from that."

"I thought Walker had the Harts, Hastings and Big Louie."

"Yes, but he has no partner. Nor do you. I want you to come back now and team up with Sam Walker. Do you think you can handle that?"

Although Sam Walker had pleaded innocent about knowing anything about Horace Langley's crooked dealings, I wasn't sure about him. I knew he was tough and competent, but thought he had as many doubts about me as I had for him.

"I need you, Patrick," Morgan said, deep concern etching his face.

"I'll be in tomorrow," I said.

•   •   •

The sun began to peek through some thin clouds as the day began to warm. I felt like I was sweating a bit under my heavy coat. I slowed my pace as a cool wind provided some relief and I heard someone call out my name. I turned and there was a short man approaching me. If I didn't know better I would have said it was my father; the figure approaching looked like a twin with the thin hair and dark, beady eyes. He stopped about five feet from me and appraised me, looking me up and down.

"Can I help you?" I asked.

"You look a bit like your mother, at least in the face and the eyes."

"Like my mother?"

"In the hair color, especially, and the eyes."

"Who the hell are you?"

He came closer and extended his hand which I shook meekly. "My name is Irving Fine. I was Jacob's brother."

For one thing, I didn't know Jacob, my father, had a brother. For another, I had no idea what he wanted to talk to me about. I had no idea of his relationship with my father. Would he still talk to me if he knew I was the one who had rid the world of Jacob? I thought for a second, felt a bit of compassion for his loss, and invited him for coffee.

The shop was quiet for a late morning, but I was hungry so I had a biscuit with my coffee. I didn't need the coffee. It made me feel warmer than I was. Irving Fine ordered tea and sipped it slowly as he sat across from me. He was thinner than my father had been, had a little more hair and looked several years younger, but there was a close resemblance.

"Well, Mr. Fine, you approached me in the cemetery, and I don't think it was just to tell me that I looked like my mother."

"I don't think you would feel comfortable calling me Uncle Irving, but Irving would be okay."

I laughed loudly. "No offense, Mr. Fine, but until about five minutes ago I didn't know you existed. Not only that but my father, who I despised, and my mother, who I've never met, put me up for adoption. I wouldn't say this was an ideal family situation so if you don't mind I'll stick with Mr. Fine."

Irving Fine nodded slowly, the whole time keeping his eyes on me. "I understand, Patrick. I also want you to understand that when Jacob and Rose put you up for adoption, it seemed to them to be their only choice. My brother, a Jew, getting involved with a Gentile prostitute was unheard of. He would have been drummed out of this town."

"This is supposed to make me feel better?"

His hands came up to calm me. "Please let me finish. Losing Rose and having to put you into Holy Trinity pained Jacob to no end. That is why he constantly made sure things were good at the orphanage, why he made sure you never wanted for anything. He also wanted to make sure you were never adopted, so he could watch over you."

"Why did he never intervene and take me into his own home?"

"Not a bad question. He told me he could never do that because you would remind him too much of Rose."

I looked out the window. The sun had gone back in and it had started to rain a bit. "You sound like you knew her."

"I saw her a few times with Jacob. She really was a lovely girl. Like I said it was a sad situation."

"So you came up to me to tell me that my father felt bad about everything that happened in the past and I'm supposed to cheer up? My father was a crook, a pimp and a white slaver. That's probably what got him killed."

His face blushed. He took a sip of his tea. "The reason I came to see you, Patrick, was to tell you this and I was only to tell you if Jacob was gone."

"I don't want any of his damn money."

He smiled. "No money, but I can tell you over the years that there was some correspondence from your mother, in New York, to Jacob here. She would ask what he knew of you and he would respond. The last letter was probably over three years ago. That's all that I know."

My stomach fluttered and jumped at the news. "My mother is alive?"

"As of three years ago, living on Manhattan Island, but I have no address, no place of employment, nothing more to tell you. Jacob would only tell me she was out there and I was to tell you upon his death. I wish I had more for you, but that is it."

I stood quickly over Irving Fine and saw a look of fear enter his eyes. I reached down with my hands and gently grabbed his face. "Mr. Fine, you have given me the best news I've had in years and what you have given me is enough to find her. After all, sir, I am a detective."

One

It was just after eight o'clock the next morning when I caught up with Sam Walker. He was in a small meeting room on the second floor of the precinct with a number of piles of papers around him. He looked immaculate in a navy suit, but had that ever present look of needing a shave.

"Good morning, Moses," he said. There wasn't much conviction is his voice.

I am sure that Sam had as many doubts about me as I had about him. I felt we were on a level field. "Sam, what have you got there?"

"This?" he said, waving his hand across the piles of paper. "I believe, Moses, that this is a conundrum, a true mystery."

I sat down across from him and could see the weariness on his face. "Morgan tells me he'd like us to work together for a bit."

Walker shrugged. "We're shorthanded."

"Look, Sam, I know we've had a few differences, but I'm willing to get past all of that and try to put to some of these cases to bed."

He looked at me for a moment, and I thought he was going to laugh. "For some reason, when I came on the force, I always felt like I had to compete with you. It was a very immature stance to take and it made no sense. We are both good detectives and good work will be needed to get some of these cases closed. I have no problem working with you."

I felt some tension leave my body. "That's good," I said. "Think you can call me Patrick?"

He smiled, but very weakly. "I may have to work on that."

I laughed. "Okay, so what have we got here?"

"On my right, here, these three piles, is everything that we have on the Harts, Mary Hastings and Louie Pagano."

None of the three stacks of notes was very thick. "Doesn't look like much."

"It's not. That's what's so perplexing. We can make the assumption that these four people were murdered because you and Krause were poking around in that "white slave" business while searching for Isabella Rossini."

"That seemed to spawn the whole killing spree," I admitted.

"It did, so these murders are connected. They are also similar in that we have exactly no clues as to who is involved, except for one. With Mary Hastings, no one saw her near that beach and certainly no one saw anyone with her. With Pagano, no one saw or heard anything out of line emanating from his apartment. It was like a ghost killed him."

"You said you had one clue."

"Maybe, not sure. Mike Hart was said to keep a lot of company with a big, blonde mute guy. One of the maids at the Marlboro saw this guy early on the morning that the Harts were murdered. He was kind of lurking in the lobby area. Langley and I tried to find the guy, but had absolutely no luck. I have a feeling he may be our ghost, but I can't find the son of a bitch."

I knew who the son of a bitch was and I also knew where we could find him. I had seen him not too long ago in the office of Big Jim Colosimo when Gunter and I had paid Colosimo a visit. "I think I know where to find him," I said.

"You do?" There was a look of surprise on Sam's face.

"He does some work for Colosimo. I think we can find him."

"Well, then let's get going."

"Hold on one second, Sam. We talked about three murders, three piles. What's the pile on your left?"

Sam glanced at the other pile of papers and I could see his shoulders slump. "I think you know, Patrick. This is the Eleanor Winter file."

"So you've not put them into the "white slaving" group?"

"I don't think they belong there."

"Where does Eleanor's murder belong?"

"I wanted to ask you that. I wanted to ask if you felt we should reopen the Simon Kluge case."

• • •

In the cab ride over to Colosimo's office, Sam turned to me. "How convinced were you that Kluge had acted on his own?"

I had to think for a second. With the bodies piling up around us, we were under a tremendous amount of pressure to break the case. We got our break when witnesses near two of the murder scenes luckily spotted Simon Kluge lurking around the premises. When Gunter and I visited Kluge at his State Street apartment we found several souvenirs from the crimes that linked him to the murders. I always remember asking Kluge one stupid question, "What do you have to say for yourself?" He just smiled at me and said, "These women, this vermin, needed to be extinguished." It was then that I grabbed Kluge, forced him to the floor and stuck my gun down his throat. If a young patrol officer, Jonathon Gilman, had not been present to stop me I'm quite convinced I would have emptied the chambers into the evil doctor.

"You with me, Patrick?" Sam said.

"Sorry," I said. "When we found out he might be involved and we arrested him we found quite a bit of evidence linking him to the crimes. We were sure it was him."

"And no idea that he might not be acting alone?"

"None."

"How about in your conversations with him?"

I laughed. "Dr. Kluge was a sick son of a bitch. When anyone asked him about the murders, including his own attorneys, he would only say that he was doing the work of God. Prostitution was a vile disease that was plaguing the city. It needed to be eradicated and that was his goal. Kluge thought he was doing the city a service by removing prostitutes from the street."

"One at a time?"

"Like I said, a sick man."

Sam sighed loudly. "So where do we go from here?"

"Same thing as with Kluge. We talk to anyone and everyone near a crime scene and see if they saw or heard anything."

"With Eleanor Winter, down by Bubbly Creek, there was no one who saw anything. That area is damn near deserted."

To hear her name mentioned as a murder victim sent a shard of pain into my side. "Then we may have to wait."

"Wait?"

"For another victim, Sam."

When we arrived at The Lucky Lady unannounced at ten-thirty in the morning, I wasn't sure that Colosimo was there or if he would see us, but we were quickly shown up the stairs to his office. Big Jim was sitting behind the mahogany desk, head down, seriously reading some papers. The blonde, mute man was nowhere in sight. For some reason I exhaled in relief.

"Come on in and sit down," Colosimo said, not taking his eyes off the papers.

Sam and I moved up to the two large leather chairs in front of the desk and sat down. I rested my arms in my lap waiting for our host to address us. Finally, his eyes came off the papers and he looked directly at me.

"Sorry about your father, Moses. He was a good businessman."

I smiled weakly. My father had been a good businessman. I wasn't sure he was much of anything else. "Thank you," I said.

"I hope your department has put all their resources into finding his killer. That makes a lot more sense than chasing around and accusing people of operating a "white slaving" ring."

I didn't comment, but kept my eyes fixed on Colosimo. He turned his head towards Sam.

"A new partner? I heard your other one got broken."

"He had an unfortunate encounter outside of the Bucket of Blood," I said. "This is Detective Sam Walker."

Colosimo ignored Sam and his gaze came back to me. He pointed a long index finger at me. There was a big diamond ring glistening on it. "That big fucking Kraut should have minded his own business. He seemed like the kind to stick his neck where it didn't belong."

"He was just searching for the missing Italian girl we

mentioned. Somebody, three or four men, jumped him and beat him with clubs."

Colosimo shrugged. "You're not here to ask me what I know about that, are you?"

"Do you know anything about that?"

"Not a thing," he smiled.

"What about your friend, the man who was here the last time, the mute with the blonde hair?"

Colosimo looked shocked. "You mean, Christian? He would never be involved in anything as petty as that and he would never use a club."

"What about a knife or a revolver at close range?" Sam asked. There was tension in his voice.

"I see your new friend has the same kind of fucking bad manners that your old partner had," Colosimo said.

"Mr. Colosimo, this man, Christian, he seems to get seen in a few bad places that indicate that he may be involved in some crimes. He was seen near a holding house for imprisoned prostitutes in Blue Island and was also seen near the Marlboro Hotel the morning Mike and Molly Hart were murdered."

Colosimo mockingly looked around the office. "So what has this got to do with me?"

I leaned forward in my chair. "I hope nothing, but since I saw him in your office, I thought you might be able to tell us his name and where we can find him."

He sighed. "His name is Christian Hanson. I haven't seen him in over a week. He was staying at the Abbott, but he may have moved on. That's about all I can tell you."

"But he did work for you?"

"He's a freelancer. He works for anyone that needs his type of specialty."

"What type of specialty is that?"

Colosimo smiled. "Christian is a problem solver. When people have a problem they hire him to get involved and solve it. It is very dangerous work."

"And what problems did you use Mr. Hanson for?"

"The biggest problem of all, debt collection. Getting people to pay what they owe is the biggest headache for the business owner today. Mr. Hanson cleared up a lot of those headaches."

• • •

We weren't far from the Abbott Hotel on Eighteenth so we walked in the gloom of the late December morning. We'd gone a block in silence when Sam spoke up.

"Do you buy that horseshit he was giving us?"

"No, but we weren't going to get much more than that. We did get a name and possible residence. Let's check it out and see what comes out of it."

What came out of it was nothing. Hanson still maintained a room at the hotel, but hadn't been seen in a week or so. No one knew where he was or where he had gone. We had to find him to move on the Harts, Mary Hastings and Louie Pagano. Without him, for now, we had nothing on those cases. With Eleanor's case, I thought we would need another body and a witness to help us. I was wrong here. Our next lead came from an unexpected source

Two

The night that I dispatched with my father was one of the best nights of sleep I'd had in a long time. The night after meeting with Sam Walker and then talking to Colosimo may have been one of the worst. The first thing I realized when I awoke was that it was New Year's Eve. The start of the New Year, 1906, was tomorrow. Maybe better things were waiting for me. I laughed at this thought. The second thing that occurred to me was how cold my flat was. I had been thinking about tracking down my landlord and find out where the heat I was paying for had gone. It certainly wasn't in my unit. Lastly, my back teeth ached and I figured I had clenched my jaws tightly during my attempt at sleep. I lay quietly on my back, blankets up to my neck, trying to loosen my jaw muscles and relieve the pain. I would have stayed there a bit longer had it not been for the slow rap on my door. I hesitantly got out of bed, grabbed my gun, and threw the door open.

The man who had knocked jumped about a foot in the air and when he landed and I saw who it was, I immediately pointed my gun at the chest that I knew contained no heart.

"Don't shoot, Moses," Gussie Black said. It hadn't been all that long since I'd seen Black, but the sight in my door was not the man I witnessed before. His eyes were bloodshot, his hair a mess, his face seemed to be covered in red welts that appeared to pulse and he looked like he was about to have a heart attack. On top of that, the suit of clothes he wore was completely rumpled.

"Tell me two things, Gussie. Why I shouldn't shoot you and what the hell are you doing here?"

He looked to either side of him nervously. It was eight in the morning. There was no one else around. "Can I come in?"

I had to give him credit for just showing up at my flat. That took a tremendous amount of courage. "Come in, but don't do or say anything to infuriate me or I will shoot you."

He came into the unit as I closed the door behind him. He sat in the chair by the desk; I stood a few feet away, my gun at my side. In the better light of the unit he looked worse.

"I had to see you," he said. "I had to see you so that I could clear a few things up and get back to my life."

"You look like hell."

He smiled weakly. "Feel like it as well. Since I gave you the note for the meeting on Congress, I knew you were coming for me. The Hustons said you knocked my door in. I had to get away. I had no doubt you would kill me on sight."

"You're perceptive, Gussie."

He waved a hand at me. "That fucking cop with the big teeth, Langley, he set me up. He gave me the note and told me to give it to you. When I heard it was a sham, and that Langley had been killed, I went into hiding. Then when I heard that Eleanor had been murdered, I knew I had to explain myself to you. I just didn't have the courage until now."

"What can you tell me about Langley?"

"A crooked cop. Ran a lot of drugs, arrested people who were in his employer's way, and liked to beat up prostitutes. Of course, this was after he had sex with them."

"Who did he work for?"

"I don't know. Honestly. Some of the things he did were so bad that I thought he was a problem for anybody. When I started to ask around about the Rossini girl he approached me and told me his people had her and that place on Congress was where she could be found. He gave me the note and told me to tell you. That's all I know."

"No idea it was a setup?"

"None. I was asking about this girl and Langley shows up and gives me the note. Of course, he told me to not tell you who gave it to him."

"Okay on Langley for a minute. What about Eleanor?"

"I didn't see her for at least a few days before she got killed."

"But you know something that you're not telling me?"

He looked straight up at me and his eyes narrowed. "Sometimes, Moses, I think you are one of the smartest people out there. Other times I believe you may be one of the dumbest."

"I never said I was smart."

"Maybe not and you aren't always. Eleanor was in love with you. She wanted nothing more for you to marry her and get her out of the Queen's. She wanted that to happen, but she knew it never would."

I felt my shoulders sag and had the feeling of a schoolboy being scolded. "I should have been a lot better to her."

"Well, she did love you, but she knew you could never get away from your past. She knew things were as good, or bad, as they were ever going to be."

I nodded. "What about you and her?"

"I liked her. She was beautiful and she was funny. I may have always wanted it to be more than it ever was, but she didn't. We were friends. We got together and we had fun, we laughed. Nothing more."

I noticed a change in Gussie's demeanor. "But you're not telling me something?"

He closed his eyes tightly and then reopened them as if to refocus. "She was seeing someone else privately. She had been for a couple of months. She was finally sure that nothing better was coming out of her relationship with you so she started seeing this guy."

"What guy?"

"I don't know. I never got a name, but I saw him once, from across Clark Street. He was tall and had a big mustache."

"That describes half the men in this city."

He shrugged. "That's all I've got."

"But she liked this guy?"

"I think she was falling in love with him, but that's not for certain. I didn't see her for a bit, gave you the note from Langley, and then I had to disappear. Then Eleanor was killed."

Maybe it was something, maybe nothing. "What's up for you now, Gussie?"

"I need some rest and then I need to get back to work. The Hustons need me." He smiled at this last remark.

I suddenly had an idea. I stepped closer to him and opened the desk drawer and took out the envelope from Field. I took out a hundred and handed it to Gussie.

"What's this?" he asked.

"I want you to do some work for me. We are looking for

some murderers and we are certain they are down here in the Levee."

"Murderers?" He looked like he might faint.

"Someone killed the Harts, Mary Hastings and Big Louie Pagano. We think that's one person. Somebody also killed Eleanor, another person. I want you to ask around, see what you can find. In particular, I am looking for a big, blonde mute guy. Goes by the name of Christian Hanson."

"Ask around?"

"You go to a lot of places, Gussie. A lot of people will talk to you that won't talk to me. See what you can find," I said. "I don't mind paying you for your services, Gussie, but I also don't mind coming for you if you cross me."

I saw him flinch a bit, but I knew, at least for now, that I had him.

• • •

For my New Years' Eve celebration I got two bottles of wine and I made a visit to see Gunter at Mercy Hospital. I had made a call earlier and he was still a resident. My only hope was that Margaret wouldn't be there when I showed up. After my last visit with her at the Palmer House, I was becoming convinced of her intentions and they made me uncomfortable.

The big German was sitting up in his bed, resting against some pillows and reading a book when I entered his room. He gave me a look and then he smiled.

"Is this an apparition?" he said.

"No, it's really me," I said. "Sorry I couldn't have gotten over here sooner."

"Busy, were you?"

"Gunter, look, it's been a tough week. I am sorry and I have no excuse for not visiting." I could see some of the tension leave his face.

"What's in the bag?"

I pulled out the first bottle of red wine, a Claret, and daftly removed the cork, using a small knife. I handed Gunter the bottle. "Sorry. No glasses."

He took a big pull from the bottle and his whole body seemed to exhale stress.

"Feel better?" I asked.

He took another swig and handed the bottle to me. "I know I have to be here, but I feel like a caged animal."

"Safer in here than out there." I pointed at the window.

"Patrick, I am sorry about what happened to Eleanor, and then I heard what happened to your father."

"Like, I said, a tough week." I took a drink of wine.

"Eleanor," he said, "I heard she was killed in the same manner that Kluge murdered his victims."

"Identical if I had one word to use."

"How can that be? We executed the son of a bitch."

"It wasn't Kluge, Gunter. He is gone."

"Then who?"

I shrugged and handed the bottle back to him. "He must have had an accomplice. We missed it. Anyway, the case has been reopened and Sam Walker and I are working together."

"Walker!" he boomed.

I put up both hands to calm him. "Only until you return. We are shorthanded."

He nodded, clearly not happy. "And your father?"

"I'm sure that there are quite a few people who didn't care

for my father. The investigation is proceeding. Riley O'Donnell and George Loftus have drawn the case."

"You are not a suspect, are you?" He smiled.

My stomach tightened. "Believe it or not, no."

He took a big drink from the bottle. "At least you found the Rossini girl. Margaret told me the story of what unfolded at the Palmer House."

"A brilliant piece of police work."

He laughed. "All of that talking to those prostitutes, The Ranch in Blue Island, and those murders and the little brat was just running around with her boyfriend."

"That's all it amounted to."

"So you and Walker are back on the Kluge case and all the "white slaving" related murders?"

"We are."

"I should be out soon. I hope not too much longer."

I took the bottle from him and took another drink. "There will be plenty of work for all of us when you return. The Levee has a way of keeping us busy."

Three

I awoke on New Year's Day amidst a feeling of calm. This was not due to any perceived notion that my future was going to be bright. Even with the tremendous amount of work that faced Sam and I, I felt good about things. We felt that the mute, blonde haired man was involved in the large number of "white slave" murders that we had. We just had to find him. I didn't think that would be that hard. The man, Christian Hanson, was tall, blonde and couldn't talk. Couldn't be that many out there like that, even in a city as large as Chicago.

With Eleanor's murder, the latest in the Kluge case, maybe Gussie had given us the lead we needed. Eleanor had been seeing a different man right before she died. Who was this man and could he have had anything to do with her murder? The only source I had to check this with was Kelsie Casey, Eleanor's friend from The Queen's House. I would check with her later in the day. I could tell that the sun was just beginning to rise from the faint light that came through my windows. I thought I might close my eyes and try and sleep a bit more. This thought was momentary at best as there was a persistent knock on my door.

Opening the door, blankets wrapped around me, I found a very young officer. He looked afraid, I'm not sure of what, and failed to speak at first.

"Yes, Officer," I said.

"It's Detective Walker, sir. He has sent me to find you."

This could not be good news, based on the last time Sam had sent for me. "Not to wish me a Happy New Year, I wouldn't think."

The officer looked perplexed, but recovered. "No, sir. He sent me to get you. There has been a murder."

My stomach tightened and I sighed. "Where is he at?"

"You might want to come along, sir. Detective Walker seemed highly agitated."

The young officer had commandeered a cab and as we made our way through freezing air and a new fallen snow, I could tell we were headed towards the Twenty Second Precinct. The precinct building itself is very nondescript. It is a two story brick structure offering no architectural wonders. In front of the building you will find a large statue of General Grant upon his horse, leading the troops into some battle. I don't know that Grant ever rode into battle, but it was an impressive statue. In the General's hand he held a sword, upraised and ready for the attack. The sword this morning was adorned with something that had never been there before. Perched on the tip of the sword, impaled, was a woman's head.

It was not yet seven-thirty and I'm pretty sure that this kept the number of onlookers to a minimum. It was also a holiday and it was freezing outside. There were a number of uniformed officers standing about and several detectives. One of these was Sam Walker. He seemed to be writing down some notes as I approached him.

"Good morning, Sam," I said.

"Not really, Patrick. At home for once with my wife and children, trying to enjoy a little peace, when I got called in."

"Sorry," I said, but why was I apologizing. I hadn't put the woman's head on the sword. "Any idea what is going on here?"

Walker pointed to the mounted head. "That is, or used to be, Bad Joanie, a prostitute from the Devil's Cellar."

"Any idea where the rest of her is?"

"None."

"How did you figure out who she was?"

Sam handed me a piece of paper that had a small hole punched into the top of it. This hole had a piece of ribbon looped through it. "This was tied to the horse's leg."

I took the paper and looked at it. I could see it was a poem.

Ode to New Year's

Well, All, take a look at that!
A New Year's gift for Detective Pat.
Look closely now, for it's no phony.
It's the head of the whore, Bad Joanie
~Kluge from Hell

"Oh, my God," I said, saying each word slowly.

"Not exactly what we were looking for on New Year's Day."

I looked up at the head." Anybody verify who she is?"

"One of the beat cops knew her from the District."

I stared at the poem and then up again at the head. I had no idea what to say.

"Someone is playing a game with you, Patrick."

"Not such a nice game," I said. "Nobody saw anything?"

"Not that I know of. It was so cold last night there weren't many people milling about outside the building. The head wasn't discovered until a shift change this morning."

"It's definitely somebody who used to work in concert with Kluge. There's no doubt now that he had an accomplice."

"You said we needed another body before we'd get any leads. Any bright ideas?"

I noticed a bit of sarcasm in Sam's voice. "The only thing I know for sure right now is that we need to get that head down or we're going to have the whole neighborhood gawking at it as if it were the lighting of the first Christmas tree."

• • •

The Devil's Cellar was a brothel located in an old warehouse on Wabash at the north end of the Levee. There wasn't much to the warehouse itself, a three story frame structure. We found the door to the brothel on the side of the building below an imposing bust of Beelzebub himself. It was still early and the woman who answered the door looked like she just woke up or hadn't yet made it to bed. She was still dressed in evening wear, but her dress was amiss and her hair was a mess.

"Help you?" she said stiffly.

Sam and I showed our badges, but this did little to add any warmth to her face. "We need to ask a few questions," Sam said.

"About what?"

"About one of the girls who worked here, Bad Joanie."

"Well, that whore didn't show for work last night so when you find her you can ask her your questions."

"We found her," I said. "She won't be answering many

questions."

"That's surprising. She always had such a big mouth, always cussing."

"Like I said. She won't be answering too many questions. Somebody cut her head off and stuck it on top of Grant's sword in front of the precinct building."

I could tell that that comment jolted her and she immediately let us into the brothel. The place was clean and neatly decorated. Our host, the place's madam, was named Wilma Batts. She showed us to a small parlor with a couple of chairs and couches. Sam and I sat on a couch; she took a seat across from us.

"When was the last time you saw Joanie?" Sam asked.

"Like I said, she didn't show yesterday. It would have been the day before New Year's Eve."

"Did you talk with her?"

"Of course. She worked for me and she was always talking, a real chatterbox."

"And the nickname, Bad Joanie?" I asked.

Wilma Batts laughed. "The only thing bad about Joanie was her language, rougher than the crudest soldier. Other than that, she was a sweet girl. I don't think she had or ever made an enemy. None that I knew of at least."

"She have any special friends here?" Sam said.

"She was friendly with everybody, nothing special."

I nodded. "What about men that she saw? Any special guests or arrangements?"

She smiled. "All of the girls have a few guests who liked to return to them. This was never unusual, but I would have to say I never saw anyone here who I thought would do any harm to Joanie."

"What about outside of here?" Sam asked. "She ever mention any friends or love interests outside of the Devil's Cellar?"

She shook her head. "Nothing I knew about. I can check with the other girls in the house and see if they knew anything, but that would have to be later. We just closed up a little while ago."

We agreed that Wilma Batts would meet with the other women in her employ and see if she could find anything unusual in what Bad Joanie did with her time once she left the walls of the Devil's Cellar. Sam told me he was going to return home for a bit. I decided to make my way over to The Queen's House to have a talk with Kelsie Casey, Eleanor's friend. I wanted to see if she knew anything about a man that Eleanor may have been seeing as Gussie Black suggested.

· · ·

I was greeted with far less than what I would call New Year's cheer by my old friend Miss Keesher at The Queen's House. The look she gave me was somewhere between a scowl and total disgust. She knew that Eleanor had become a victim similar to the killings of Dr. Kluge. What she didn't know was that the killer was somehow playing a game with me and Eleanor may have ended up being one of the game pieces.

"Detective Moses," she said politely. "I am a little surprised to see you back here."

"Why is that Miss Keesher?"

"I guess we would have expected to see you at the services for Eleanor. She was a friend of yours or so I thought."

"She was," I said. "I don't do very well with funerals. I guess all I can say is that I'm sorry."

Now she wore a smirk. "I don't suppose that you are here to tell me that you have captured Eleanor's murderer?"

"Not yet."

"Then what is the reason for your visit?"

"I would like to see Kelsie Casey. To talk with her."

Her eyes gave me a parental once over. "Just to talk? You have no other intentions with Kelsie?"

"Just to talk. I promise."

She sat me down in the front parlor and told me she would probably have to awaken Kelsie. The room, along with the other parts of the brothel I could see, showed the signs of a lively party the night before. As I sat in the parlor, I wondered if both Kluge and his accomplice had sat in this room as well, perhaps eyeing the girls and deciding on which ones would be their next prey. I wondered if one of them had stalked Eleanor from the very chair that I sat in or was she just chosen because of me. My contemplation was disturbed when I heard approaching footsteps and looked up to see pudgy, little Kelsie Casey enter the room.

She stopped just past the entrance to the parlor, looked at me and started to cry. I stood up and went to her and placed my arms around her. "It's going to be okay, Kelsie," I said dumbly.

She backed away and dabbed at her tears with a handkerchief. "It will never be okay, Patrick. He took my friend Eleanor and I will never see her, hear her or talk to her again. Things will never be okay."

I nodded. "I understand."

"I don't think you do, Patrick," she said loudly. I was a bit taken aback. "Eleanor loved you. She wanted so much for you to love her back and to maybe take her away from here, but you didn't."

"I did love her," I said weakly.

"Not enough. If you had she would probably still be here. Maybe she wouldn't have gotten so down that she needed to run around with Gussie Black. Maybe she wouldn't have ventured out…"She caught herself before she finished that last sentence.

"Ventured out with whom, Kelsie?"

I could see in the early day's light that she was blushing. "I probably shouldn't say."

"Gussie came by and saw me. He told me that Eleanor may have been seeing another man just before she was murdered, someone outside of The Queen's House."

She ducked her head. "I don't know."

"Kelsie, I know I wasn't always there for Eleanor. I know that I ruined our relationship. I also know that Gussie said she was unhappy about the way things were going with us. This led her to seek out another man."

Her eyes came up slowly. Fresh tears were brimming in them. Her cheeks were aflame. "Don't you ever think that Eleanor went seeking this other man on her own. For the longest time she waited for you. When nothing happened she started to accept some of these outside offers. She started to fall for this one man."

"What one man?"

"I don't know. I never saw him or got a name, but Eleanor told me he was a prominent attorney."

"An attorney," I muttered quietly. "Wait a minute, Kelsie. You said Eleanor started accepting some offers to do work outside of the Queen's. I am sure this was done without Miss

Keesher's knowledge, but who set these meetings up for Eleanor?"

She still wasn't happy with me. I could tell. "Eleanor's private meetings were set up by Maurice Von Bever."

. . .

With my newfound knowledge that Von Bever had set up some meetings for Eleanor with a lawyer I felt that maybe we were headed in the right direction. With the earlier murders of Dr. Kluge, the victims had been prostitutes of lesser known brothels. With the killings of Eleanor and now Bad Joanie, it seemed the killer had moved on to a better class of whore. Was I being discriminatory if I said these women might be smarter and that their friends might have some knowledge of who they were with when killed? I didn't think so. At least I hoped someone would know something about where they had been and this might lead us to the killer. I was hopeful that Wilma Batts, after talking with the remaining girls from the Devil's Cellar, might be able to tell us who Bad Joanie was fraternizing with.

With respect to the other four murders that Sam and I were working, our only clue was the big, blonde mute man, Christian Hanson. Colosimo had given us a name and an address for the man, but no one had seen him in over a week. I had asked Gussie Black to lend his eyes and ears to see if anyone knew anything about the murders or the man, but I wasn't sure what I'd get back, even though I'd paid Black for his services.

Back at the precinct, with another murder on our docket, I begin to daydream about the possibility of finding my mother in New York. If I had nothing else to do I might have been on the first train east to try and find her. As it was, I was suddenly very busy. Mother, if she was still alive, would have to wait a bit longer.

Sam returned to the precinct at just past noon. Even though he'd been able to spend a little time with his family on the holiday he didn't look very pleased. When I asked him how things were he had merely grunted at me. I went back to my contemplation of how to proceed on the cases, but this, too, was interrupted when Sam and I were summoned into a meeting in Captain Morgan's office.

I hadn't seen Morgan since my father's funeral and my first impression of him was that the New Year hadn't started well for him. He looked worn down and tired. Every line on his face appeared to be angling downward. His eyes showed gloom. His bushy mustache needed grooming. Perhaps the reason for this was the other person in his office, a visitor, my friend from the Isabella Rossini case, Lieutenant Shipley. For some reason, I felt there would be no congratulations given this time.

"Gentlemen," Morgan said, "Lieutenant Shipley from headquarters."

"Sam Walker," Walker said, shaking Shipley's hand.

I shook Shipley's hand, but he just gazed at me, a little like the way an owner looks at his dog who has shit on his carpet.

We sat again in the hard backed wooden chairs.

"The Department," Shipley started in his high pitched voice," is very alarmed at the new developments that our occurring down here in the Levee."

Sam hung his head. "What new developments would that be, Lieutenant?" I asked.

Shipley turned towards me. His cheeks showed red of anger.

His eyes appeared to want to burrow through my chest. "Not very funny, Detective Moses," he said. "We executed a man less than a month ago that we thought was responsible for the prostitute murders down here in the Levee. Now we find that a mistake has been made."

Morgan let out an audible groan. "The man we executed," I said, "Dr. Kluge, was at least partially responsible for those murders."

Shipley sniffed loudly. "Partially? What percentage and did that percent mean that we had to execute him?"

I felt anger rising in my chest, but held for a moment. "Kluge was responsible. The evidence that we found proved that. Where we erred was that Kluge either had an accomplice or he was the accomplice. Now, I have stated our mistake. I'm not making any excuses so what is the purpose of this meeting?"

Another groan from Morgan and shuffling of the feet and movement of his chair from Sam.

Shipley cleared his throat. "Fair enough, Moses. There is a purpose. I know that you and Walker our investigating the four murders that developed from the "white slaving" inquiries made about Ms. Rossini. That will go on, but you will make solving these prostitute murders your number one priority."

"And how do these "prostitute murders", as you call them, deserve the priority treatment?"

"The fact here, Moses, is that you and your partner, Krause, have embarrassed the department. Chief Collins lauded you two and acknowledged that Kluge was the killer and the crime had been solved. It is now apparent that this was not true and the Chief has a bit of egg on his face."

"So we are trying to clean up the Chief's face?"

"Again, not funny, but in a nutshell, yes. You will work

without leave until you find this killer. You will not leave any stone unturned. You must stop this murderer."

I nodded. "And the other four murders that Sam and I are working on? Where do they fall on the priority list?"

Shipley avoided this comment. "You will pursue those cases as well. I understand you are down two detectives."

"That is correct," Captain Morgan interjected.

"And now we hear, Moses, the killer has started to write riddles directly to you."

"There was a little poem tied to General Grant's horse under the head of Bad Joanie," I said.

"Which can only mean one thing," Shipley said. "The killer is turning up the flame by mocking you. I think he is now more out of control than he was. Things are going to start getting worse. You have got to find him and stop him."

I could see the look of intense concern on Shipley's face. Whether driven by politics or not, the decision to place the new murders at the top of the list was not to be taken lightly. A thought did come to me. "Less than a month ago you sat in this room and told us of a tremendous scourge in the city, the white slaving issue. Has that now abated?"

If it were possible, Shipley looked more forlorn. "I'm afraid not, Moses. That evil practice appears to be gaining momentum. We can't seem to get our arms around it."

With that the meeting ended, sending me into a deeper mood, realizing that this year would probably be no better than the one that had just ended.

• • •

Sam and I rode back to the Devil's Cellar in the late afternoon. The day had brightened, but it was still bitterly cold. I could tell that Sam's mood had not brightened. He seemed locked in a position of despair. "How old are your children?" I asked.

This managed to draw a smile. "Sam, Junior, is six and Marie is four."

"Fun ages," I said.

"Too young to realize all of the garbage that surrounds them," he said, looking out of his carriage window.

"There is still some good to be found."

He turned back to me and his look was more of a glare. "When you find it, Patrick, please be sure to point it out to me. I haven't seen anything that is good for a long while."

Wilma Batts looked a lot better the second time we visited her that day. She had freshened up, put on some new clothes and fixed her hair. The Devil's Cellar was still quiet for a brothel, but it appeared to have been cleaned up as well.

"I spoke to a number of the girls about Bad Joanie," she said. She appeared excited about what she was about to tell us.

"Not all of them?" Sam said abruptly.

"No, not yet," she said, taken aback. "Some have not arisen yet."

"It's three-thirty in the afternoon," Sam said.

"That's okay," I said. "What can you tell us now, Ms. Batts?"

Sam gave me another stern look and I wondered how long our new partnership would last.

"Two girls, Judith and Theresa, told me a very similar story. It appears that Joanie, on her nights off, would go into the Loop area and meet with a gentleman. This had been going on for the past couple of months."

This seemed to coincide with what Kelsie had told me about

Eleanor. I had not yet told Sam about those facts. "Do you know anything about this gentleman? Maybe a name or what he did?"

She shook her head from side to side. Sam emitted a bit of a grunt. "They never got a name, but Joanie mentioned that he was very handsome and appeared to be wealthy. There may have been some talk of Joanie and this man getting married."

"Joanie wanted to leave the brothel?"

Wilma Batts smiled. "I think all girls want to get out of the brothel."

"Nothing more to tell us?" Sam asked. "This man may have been handsome and may have been wealthy?"

"I'm sorry, Detectives. That's all that I have, but there is one more thing. Judith told me that Joanie said her suitor was a lawyer."

• • •

Sam slammed the door to the carriage that returned us to the precinct. "So now we are looking for a handsome lawyer here in Chicago. Think that will be an easy task."

"I spoke to a friend of Eleanor Winter's. She told me Eleanor also mentioned seeing a lawyer. I also met up with Gussie Black. He told me saw Eleanor with a tall man with a mustache."

Sam laughed. "Well, that's better. Now we are looking for a handsome lawyer with a mustache in Chicago. That should make it much easier."

Sam might be in a foul mood and might not think we had anything, but I didn't agree. I knew where my next visit would be, but it wouldn't be with Sam.

• • •

I didn't remember any knock on the door. I didn't remember getting out of bed to answer. I do remember only having a few drinks to end my New Year's Day and then returning to my flat where I fell into a sound sleep. What time it was when I answered the door I don't know, but the room was cold and it was completely dark. Was this a dream or a vision? When the door was opened there stood the most beautiful woman that I had ever seen. She wore a dress of lavender that hugged her body and did not miss showing any curves. Her coat, a brown wool thing was open and she wore no hat. Her long dark hair hung loosely about her shoulders. I said nothing as she pushed herself into my room. She stopped and removed her coat and then started to undo her dress. It quickly dropped to the floor. I could only watch as her undergarments came off much too easily, the perfect figure of a Goddess now present before me. She approached me and pushed me back onto the bed, her hands reaching for and removing my underclothes. She lowered herself to me and kissed me passionately on the mouth. Then she climbed atop me and the ultimate sin was soon complete.

"He will be released from Mercy very soon and I do not believe that I can go on living with him," she said.

The "he" she mentioned was my partner, Gunter Krause, now convalescing in Mercy Hospital.

"I am not ashamed for what I have done tonight. I have such strong feelings for you. I had to show you how I felt before he got back home." Margaret had told me that her two children were spending a few days with her mother. "He is a brutal man. He talks to the children and me as if we were like those pigs he used to slaughter in the Yards. I can't go on with him."

I knew Gunter had a temper. I also witnessed his tough attitude with Margaret and the children when I had visited their apartment before Christmas. I had no idea about the feelings she expressed for me other than a rushed kiss and a grope of my thigh under a table cloth.

"I know you must think I am not much better than those harlots you deal with all day long, but please hear me out, Patrick. I want to be loved by a man that knows how to treat me with respect. I do not want to live like a dog under the restrictive laws of his master. I want to be free and I want to be loved by you."

I heard all of this and yet I said nothing. She kissed me hurriedly and told me she wanted to see me again soon. She dressed quickly and made her way out of the apartment. The smell of her was in my unit for the longest time. I wasn't sure I wanted it to be gone.

When I awoke the following morning I wished that it had been a dream, that her figure in the door had been a vision, but it had all been real. What was I to do? My partner, Gunter Krause, the man who had saved my life in a deserted house on Congress was in the hospital, trying to get better. In his absence I had taken his wife, or had she taken me. It didn't matter. I knew better. I had committed an awful sin. Now the next question loomed. What was I going to do next?

Four

"I am looking for a lawyer," I said to my friend Stanley Kerjewski. Stanley had been an occupant of Holy Trinity's orphanage, but unlike me, he had been adopted at age nine. He went onto attend the University of Illinois and then graduated from their school of law. He had been prosperous, wore expensive suits and was getting a healthy paunch. He was also on the board of directors for the Chicago Bar Association.

"Have you killed someone, Patrick?" he said. We were sitting in a tavern called Calhoun's that sat in the heart of the financial district on La Salle Street.

"Of course not," I said, after first checking his eyes, "but I am looking for a lawyer who may have been engaged in a crime."

Now he rolled his eyes. "If you give me five minutes I may be able to give you a list of a hundred or so."

I pulled my chair closer to the table and leaned in towards him so as not to be heard by any of the other patrons. "Stanley, I am looking for a lawyer who may have murdered someone."

I could see he felt that I was serious. "A lawyer who may

have murdered someone?"

"That's right. Maybe quite a few people, women, more like prostitutes."

He took a sip of his wine, wiped his lips and cleared his throat. "Patrick, what in God's name are you talking about?"

Again I leaned closer. "Well, you remember the Kluge case that I was so wondrously honored for?"

"Of course. It was all over the papers?"

"It now appears that Dr. Kluge may have had an accomplice. This accomplice has committed at least two murders that we know of, both prostitutes, but these two women were from a better class of brothel than the previous sixteen that we had blamed Kluge for."

"What class of brothel were the first sixteen from?"

"The lowest class, many from Bedbug Row in the Levee."

He waved his hand at me. "I'll take your word for it."

"Anyway, the last two were girls who worked out of much better houses. It may or not be important?"

"I see," he said, "but for some reason you believe that a lawyer may be involved."

"I do. The last two murdered women were said to be cavorting with a wealthy lawyer prior to those murders."

"What makes you think he killed them?"

"Nothing really, but it's the only lead that we have."

"Not much says the former prosecutor."

"I know, but it is all we have."

"And what do you think I can do?"

"Look around, ask around. That's about all."

"So I should ask our membership if anyone is in the habit of murdering prostitutes?"

"Come on, Stanley. You know what I mean. The man is tall

with a mustache and supposedly wealthy. Kluge was forty-five so I would think his lawyer friend would be of a similar age."

He thought for a moment. "Occasionally I hear of some of the bizarre habits of some of our members. I hear of gambling, drinking, narcotics and sometimes that they wander into the arms of another woman. This man you seek likes the company of prostitutes and may like to get rough with them?"

"You could say that, Stanley. He cut the first one open from neck to crotch and then slit her throat. The second one's head ended up on top of Grant's sword in front of the precinct building. We haven't found the rest of her yet."

I saw Stanley's Adam's apple bob up and down a few times. "I will see what I can find out for you, Patrick."

• • •

I shouldn't have spoken so quickly about the missing remains of Bad Joanie. They were found soon enough. Someone, we could only assume the killer, placed them neatly into a cheap, pine box and laid them near the entrance of Graceland Cemetery on the city's north side. Once they were found the county's Coroner, Peter Hoffman, was contacted and he now had the body, or what was left of it, in the Cook County Morgue. That was where Sam and I went after being summoned by Hoffman.

The body of Bad Joanie lay fully clothed on a slab in the basement of the morgue. I was surprised with the head missing that there was a lack of blood on the last dress Joanie wore. It was green in color and didn't look like it fit her very well, but then Joanie had bloated since her last fitting.

"Whoever did this performed the dismemberment of the

head in a location where he could have Ms. Martin lying down with her head below the rest of the body. When he removed the head, the blood flowed downward and did not get onto her clothes very much. Whoever did this knew what they were doing."

"A doctor?" Sam asked.

"Maybe," Hoffman said. "At least someone who knew how to use a scalpel and saw. The head was very cleanly removed."

"Maybe a doctor or maybe someone who had witnessed a doctor perform amputations many times," I said.

Hoffman shrugged. "Perhaps."

"Can you tell us anything else?" Sam asked.

"Not tell you," Hoffman said. "I can show you."

With his left hand he pulled up the sleeve of Joanie's dress on her right arm. She was wearing a bracelet that looked like it had many silver coins as part of it.

"You see this bracelet?" Hoffman said.

I knew Hoffman didn't always think detectives were that smart. Now I guess he assumed we were blind.

"Look at this coin," he said after we didn't say anything. He took a small pliers in his right hand and snatched one of the coins with it. They weren't coins. They were flat pieces of round polished silver with no engraving or designs upon them. When he had grasped the piece of silver he wanted us to see he beckoned us to come closer.

"You see here," he said and we saw. "It is a clear thumb print. Sometime in moving Ms. Martin around the killer seems to have left a perfect thumb print on this piece of silver. Find someone who matches this print and you'll have your murderer."

Sam cleared his throat. "Joanie was a whore. How do we

know the print is from the killer?"

Again, Hoffman shrugged. "It is the only thing I can give you."

On the way back to the precinct, I heard Sam Walker laugh. "Something funny?" I asked.

"Just chuckling at all the clues we have. A tall lawyer with a mustache and now we might have his thumb print. We're really getting somewhere."

"Are you always so positive?"

He didn't answer and I wasn't sure I liked working with Sam, but he was right. We didn't have much on the prostitute murders and it would take a lot of luck to find the killer. With the other cases we were working on, the ones where we thought Christian Hanson was involved, we thought we knew who the killer was. We just couldn't find him.

•   •   •

We have a joke amongst the detectives in the precinct that if you don't like the case you are working on just wait a second and a new case will present itself. I'm sure this is true with all of the precincts in the city, but I was positive it was the situation down here in the Levee. We never had a shortage of cases, from the simple pickpocket to the worst murder. What we had at the present time was a lack of qualified detectives in the precinct to handle all of the cases. Gunter was supposed to come back shortly and Horace Langley was dead so we were down two. We weren't getting any help from anyone else so the cases began to mount up for all of the detectives.

Now Lieutenant Shipley had visited us just yesterday and

proclaimed that the prostitute murders were our new number one priority. Murders usually rank right up there with priorities whether it's a whore or not. I had no argument with that, but the case that came to Sam and me that afternoon jumped up the priority chart very quickly.

I had never heard the names Everett or Susan Hobbs before this day. I had also never heard the name of their twin daughters, Millicent and Holly. I might have gone my whole career without hearing any of their names if someone hadn't broken into the Hobbs' home and taken the two girls. What I learned very quickly was that priorities change and that Mr. Hobbs, the owner of several elevator patents, was very wealthy and a good friend of the mayor of our fine city.

"Where have you two been?" Captain Morgan bellowed as Sam and I entered the detective's room on the second floor. He approached us slowly, hunched over from back pain, stroking his mustache.

"At the morgue, looking at what was left of Bad Joanie," I said.

Morgan considered this for a second and handed me a sheet of paper. "Whatever it is that you were planning to do today put a hold on it and get right over to that address. It is the home of Everett Hobbs."

"Who the hell is Everett Hobbs?" I said smugly.

"Oh, Jesus," Morgan said.

"He invented the elevator, I think," Sam said.

"Close," Morgan said. "He is the patent owner on several elevators, an extremely wealthy and influential man. He is also friends with Mayor Dunne."

"Okay," I said dumbly.

"Someone broke into his house sometime between last night

and this morning and kidnapped his two daughters. You two were requested to handle the case because of Patrick's success in finding Isabella Rossini."

"We only dined in the same places."

"This case," Morgan said, ignoring me "will be your new priority."

"What about the prostitute murders? I asked.

"They are dead, Patrick," Morgan said. "These two girls are hopefully still alive and you are to put all of your energy into finding them."

I looked over at Sam and he only shrugged. "We weren't having much luck with those other cases. Might as well try another."

• • •

I hadn't been on Prairie Avenue since my last meeting with Albertine Field, Marshall, Jr's widow. I also wasn't surprised when I saw that the Hobbs family lived on the majestic avenue. Their house, smaller than Marshall's, was also a bit south of the Field residence. That did not mean that it lacked in stature. It was three stories tall, all brick and was surrounded by a white, wrought iron fence. It wasn't hard to pick out the house. There were three police vans parked in front and a number of cops on foot about the premises.

The carriage left us off on the curb and we sloshed through snow and slush to the front of the house. This home only had five steps but they led to a massive porch that lined the entire front of the building. Both the steps and the porch had been cleared of snow as we made our way up them. There was a large police officer at the front door and he pushed it open for us as we approached.

The house was beautiful as was to be expected. The furnishings and décor were top notch. We were told that the Hobbs were in the study awaiting us. When we entered we found two men and two women. One of the men, who was standing when we came into the room, approached us and extended a hand.

"Thomas Mallory," he said in a hurried voice. "I am Mr. Hobbs' attorney."

We shook hands with Mallory who then pointed to the man and the woman seated near a wide, stone fireplace. "This is Everett Hobbs and his wife, Susan."

The two people sitting in the chairs looked up at us. Everett Hobbs appeared to be in his mid-forties. He was about six feet tall and very skinny. He wore round glasses and had a thin mustache. He was not smiling, but he also did not look upset. He looked almost bored. The most telling thing about Everett Hobbs was that his shirt was pinching him tightly at the neck; the skin there had turned bright red.

His wife, Susan, was wearing a very plain blue dress. Her hair was somewhere between a blonde and a brunette, a kind of dirty color. She was about as plain looking a woman as you would see. She had also been crying a lot. Her eyes were bloodshot red and she held a withered, damp handkerchief in her hand.

"I am terribly sorry for what has happened to your family," I said. "I am Detective Patrick Moses and this is Detective Sam Walker. We are going to do everything in our power to find your daughters."

Susan let out a sob. Everett gave me a hard stare. "Do you

possess supernatural powers, Detective Moses?" he asked. I didn't like his voice. It sounded like each word was dragged out of his stomach.

"My guess is that my powers are about average for a police detective," I said.

"Then you will not find my girls or if you do they will be not be alive," Everett said. "I know this game. A demand for ransom will come, we will meet it, but we will never get the girls back alive."

This brought forth another sob from Susan, this one larger than the first. The other woman in the group stepped forward. She was a lovely creature, somewhere in her thirties, with red hair and piercing blue eyes. "Don't talk that way, Everett. The detectives are here to help. I'm sure that negative talk does them no good at all."

"None," said Sam Walker.

Everett looked somewhere off to his side. I don't think he said much more the entire time we were there.

"I am Alicia Stone," the woman said. "I am Everett's sister. I apologize for my brother's outburst. It has been a very stressful morning."

"I understand," I said, hoping for some normalcy to return to the discussion. "Is it alright if we begin our questioning now?" I took a notepad from the inside of my jacket.

"That would be perfectly acceptable," Thomas Mallory said.

Both Mallory and Alicia Stone had taken places behind the two sitting parents so the whole group was now in front of Sam and me. I wasn't sure who to ask what questions so I decided to just ask the group.

"At what time this morning was it discovered that the two girls were missing?" I asked.

"Millie and Holly," Susan Hobbs said feebly.

"I am sorry," I said.

"Can we please call the two girls by their names?" Mallory asked.

"Certainly," I said as I heard Sam groan behind me. "At what time this morning was it discovered that Millie and Holly were missing?"

This bit of questioning sent Susan into another crying jag. "That would have been around seven-thirty when the day nurse, Miss Balowski, went in to check on them," Alicia answered.

I turned to her. She really was lovely. "Who told you this, Ms. Stone?"

"It is Miss Stone, Detective, and I heard it from Miss Balowski myself. I am a guest here at my brother's house."

"I see. What happened when she found them missing? What did she do?"

"She went looking for Susan to see if the girls were with her."

"When she came to see me," Susan Hobbs said, trying to hold back tears, "I immediately went into shock. Someone had taken my girls."

Everett Hobbs made some kind of noise and wore an angry look.

"How could they have taken the children out of the house?" I asked.

"You need to see the girl's room," Mallory said.

The whole group then led us out of the study to a set of stairs that ran to the second floor. We followed the small group up the stairs and to a large room about midway down on the left. The colors in the room were easy pastels, a lot of pinks and yellows. There was a vast collection of stuffed animals and dolls. The room smelled of fresh flowers. It was also freezing cold. The window that sat between the two beds was wide open. The curtains that hung over it, soft frilly looking things, were blowing here and there. I walked over to the window, careful not to touch anything and peered out. Other than a vast gathering of foot prints in the dirty snow on the ground there was nothing more to see.

"Is there a guest bedroom on this floor as well?" Sam asked.

"It is right next door to this room," Alicia Stone said.

"Come with me, Patrick. Everyone else remain in this room."

I followed his command as he led me to the room next door. He seemed determined. When we opened the door to the guest room I could immediately tell one difference. It was very warm. This room had two windows covered by dull, blue curtains. Sam walked to the first and then the other pulling the curtains aside. The view through the windows was similar to the one from the twin's room.

"What are you looking for?" I asked.

"These are latched," he said. "See," he said pointing to the latch in the middle of the window. "The latch in the girl's room must have been unlocked."

"Maybe they did it to let a little air in," I said.

'Let's find out. If not, someone on the inside unlocked that window to let someone on the outside in."

Back in the twin's room you could see the look of expected questions on three of their faces. All but Everett Hobbs looked a bit nervous; he looked indifferent.

"The windows in the guest room," Sam started, "are all locked. What was the habit in the girl's room? Were their windows left unlocked and open or were they shut and locked?"

It was Susan Hobbs who spoke up. "I was very clear about this to the staff. I did not want the girls to catch cold. I was explicit that I wanted the windows closed during the winter months. You can see how dreadfully cold it gets in here."

"What about locked?" Sam asked.

"For security reasons, I instructed the Hobbs to keep their windows locked at night. We are not that far from that putrid Levee District. This house and its wealth could attract a certain criminal element," Mallory said.

"Can you tell us if you were in the practice of following Mr. Mallory's advice?" I asked.

"The staff," Everett said drolly, "was instructed to make sure all windows were closed and locked. They all knew that the penalty for not following these instructions was dismissal."

"Apparently, one of the staff, or one of you, failed in their duty and either left this window unlocked or open or both," Sam said.

"Detective Walker," Mallory said accusingly, "you can't really think that one of this group is involved in the kidnapping."

I hadn't really worked that much with Sam to get an opinion of the way he handled things. Right now he wore a grim look on his face.

"As of this minute," he said, "I don't have enough to accuse anyone or exclude anyone from the investigation."

I saw the looks of shock cover the faces of our hosts. "I think now would be a good time to speak with the staff that was on hand when it was discovered that the girls were missing," I said.

"That might be best," Mallory said.

The staff was made up of Rupert Conner, a chef, Amelia Johnson, a black maid, and Sarah Balowski, a petite, but attractive house nurse. She was the primary caretaker of the two girls. They were all seated around the kitchen table, drinking tea and munching on some cookies. None looked overly distraught or nervous.

"Miss Balowski," I said, "you went up to the girl's room about seven-thirty, is that correct?"

She looked at me for a moment, allowing me to see her pale gray blue eyes and thin, pink lips. She was a pretty lady. Her eyes were unusually engaging. "It was just past seven-thirty. That is the normal time that I check on the girls."

She had an accent, Eastern European, I thought. "And what did you find?"

She gave me kind of a curious look. "The girls, they were gone."

"What did you do?"

"I went looking for Mrs. Hobbs. When I found her I told her that the girls were gone."

"I see," I said. "What else can you tell us about the girl's room?"

"It was very cold because the window was open and the carpet on the floor was wet. I thought it was from the snow that someone had dragged in from the outside."

"About the window," Sam said. "It was our understanding that the window was to always be locked."

She seemed to think on this for a bit. "I haven't seen that window open for a couple of months. I don't know if it was locked or not. I can't recall the last time I locked it or unlocked it."

"You put the two girls to bed?" Sam asked.

"I did."

"It was locked then?"

"At least closed. I would have known if it was open."

"What was the last thing the girls were wearing when you saw them?" I asked.

"They were each wearing a pink sleeper, made from soft wool. Millie had on little yellow slippers; Holly's were pink like her sleeper."

I didn't think there was much else to ask Sarah Balowski. We asked a few questions of the chef and the maid but neither of them had much to say. We decided to make a trip to the spot outside of the girl's window. Once we got there we were disappointed. The spot on the ground below the window was a good fifteen feet from the bedroom. It was clear a ladder of some sort was used to get up to the window. After that nothing was clear. There were so many foot prints under the window it would be impossible to figure out who they belonged to. Once you got ten feet from the spot under the window the prints began to diminish in number and in quality. The snow and the wind were covering everything.

"Goddamn weather," Sam said.

I walked back over to the spot just under the window and looked up. I hadn't seen it when I looked out of the window from the girl's bedroom, but now I saw it clearly. There was a piece of cloth snagged in the outside trim of the window and it was blowing from the wind. It looked like a little flag calling to us.

Sam had laughed at me when I retreated to the bedroom and secured the piece of cloth from the inside of the room. He made fun of the fact that I thought we could find the kidnapper from this piece of his coat or shirt, but I wasn't deterred. Like the print that Coroner Hoffman found on Bad Joanie's jewelry, this cloth could possibly tell us what direction to go in. If we ever had a suspect and he owned such a coat then you would have some evidence to support his, or her, arrest. I thought it was interesting; Sam thought it was a joke.

• • •

The precinct had hired a man, Harold Pinter, a layman, whose specialization was the new study called Forensic Science. I heard him speak to the detectives once and he spoke of the wonders being conducted from finding miniscule pieces of evidence such as hairs, blood or finger prints. I hadn't heard him mention cloth, but I wondered what he would say when I presented it to him in his office/lab in the basement of the building. Sam decided to start building a list of interviews for all three of our cases. He stayed at his desk.

Harold Pinter was a small man. It would surprise me if he was over five feet tall. He had receding hair and wore thicker glasses, making him look like a school professor

"You found this where?" he said. He was looking at the piece of cloth under a magnifying glass.

"It was stuck outside of the window of the twin's bedroom. We think the kidnapper escaped by a ladder from the room and his coat or garment snagged on the wooden window frame."

"Well," he said, flipping the cloth over with a tweezers and looking at the other side. "It is common enough, maybe denim, and old. It is not from a new garment. It might be hard to figure out where it came from except for this." He held the magnifying glass over the cloth and I was able to make out a little spot.

"What is it?"

"Don't know for sure," he said, "but finding out who wears simple denim could be in the thousands. If this spot is traceable to the owner's occupation perhaps it will lead us to him."

"How the hell are you going to find out what one little spot is?" I asked.

Pinter swiveled on his seat. "Science, Detective Moses. Science."

I had no idea what he was talking about, but I wasn't smart enough or arrogant enough to question his methods. I left the little lab and started making my way back up to the detective's room on the second floor. I was only to the first floor when a uniformed cop called my name. I turned to see a young patrolman, maybe twenty- two years of age.

"Detective Moses," he said. He sounded like he was out of breath.

"Yes," I said. What could have possibly happened now?

"The captain was looking for you and sent me to find you. He's in the lockup area."

I smiled. "Who do they have locked up?"

"Some man they caught over near Freiburg's Dance Hall. He was poking around in the alley where your father was shot. They picked him up and he admitted to killing your father."

• • •

The man they had arrested for "murdering" my father looked more like the baker he was than a killer. His name was Frank Pelicanos, a Greek, who owned a bakery on Twenty-Fifth Street. He was of medium height, with a big belly and long gray hair only on the sides of his head. The top was completely bald. He also had deep, dark grooves under his eyes indicating little, if any, sleep.

They had him housed in the biggest cell where they kept special prisoners. He was sitting on a wooden chair in the middle of the cell. Surrounding him were George Loftus, Riley O'Donnell and Captain Morgan. Pelicanos didn't appear nervous or scared. In fact, he looked confident. His eyes did widen a bit when he looked up and saw me enter the cell.

"This is Frank Pelicanos," Morgan said. "He claims to be the man who shot your father on Christmas Day."

I knelt down and looked right into the man's face. I stared at the liar for a good moment or two without saying anything. "Well, Mr. Pelicanos, what do you have to say for yourself?" I asked.

"I am sorry, Detective," he said loudly. "That bastard Fine. He cheated me and he wouldn't let me into the dance hall. He deserved to die."

I couldn't argue with Jacob Fine being a bastard, but I was curious. "How did he cheat you?"

"I was at my location for fifteen years. I always pay my fee when they come to collect. Then Fine's friend, he opens a bakery about two blocks away. Fine and his people tell me my fee goes up. I can't afford it. I couldn't pay. He also tells me I'm no longer welcome in the dance hall."

"I thought he was a baker," I said to the room.

"He runs a dice game in the back," Loftus said. "Small time."

"It helped me pay the bills," Pelicanos said. "Then Fine kicked my fee up and I can't afford to pay it."

"So you killed him?" I said.

"I did. I went to see him Christmas Day and we argued. We went out into the alley behind the hall and I shot him."

"And you decided to admit to it today?" I asked.

"We caught him hanging around in back of the dance hall," Riley said. "He looked suspicious so we picked him up. When we brought him in he started talking like crazy."

I grabbed Pelicanos by both arms, startling him. "Where is the gun you used to kill my father?"

His eyes moved around all of us in the cell. "I threw it in the garbage behind the dance hall that night. It is probably long gone by now. That bastard Fine, he deserved to die. I have no regrets."

I removed my hands from his arms, but continued to look at him. He looked back at me with cold, dark eyes. "This should be easy for the court," I said. "Let him swing."

•   •   •

Later in the day Sam and I returned to the scene of the Hobbs' kidnapping. From underneath the girl's windows we walked west, following the supposed path the kidnappers had taken to make their escape. The snow and the wind had not abated much that day so it was hard to make out anything, especially footprints. The back yard was sizeable and led only to the neighbor's yard on the western end of the property. This yard was large as well and it was a while before we trudged through it and reached Indiana Avenue. This was the street just west of Prairie. We found nothing physical to point us in the direction of the kidnappers.

"They had to come this way," Sam said. "They wouldn't just

park an automobile or a carriage on Prairie and then traipse around in back to carry out the girls."

That made sense to me as well. It was also our conclusion that we were dealing with at least two kidnappers. Somebody had to carry the ladder as well as the two little girls, not an easy task. "Maybe someone in one of the houses along Indiana saw or heard something," I said.

Sam looked both ways up the street. There were at least ten homes in the vicinity that might have been able to see something. "We can request some two man teams to visit these homes and see if anyone noticed or heard anything out of order."

I looked back across the trek we had just made from the Hobbs' home. There were lights on in the house, but I knew only darkness reigned in that dwelling this day. "Until then?"

Sam lit a cigarette. The wind and snow were biting cold. "Hobbs is right. Until the kidnappers speak to them about a ransom or until somebody spots something we have very little. We'll have to wait and see if they seek money and also if the two man teams come up with anything. Once we find someone," he smiled at me, "maybe we can match your missing swatch of cloth to them."

• • •

As we ended the day and started the usual waiting period for something to develop, I made my way over to Freiburg's Dance Hall. I didn't know Solly Freiburg very much at all, but he had been my father's partner for many years. I found him in the office adjacent to the one I had met my father in on Christmas

Day. He was smoking a cigar and reviewing a pile of invoices. The dance hall was quiet at this time, waiting for the nightly activities to begin. Solly stared at me for a minute as I stood in his doorway. He smiled weakly and blew smoke in my direction.

"Detective Moses," he said in the way of a greeting.

"Solly," I said. "I was wondering if I could have a word with you."

Solly was a tall thin man with very little hair on his head. Spots of skin on his scalp showed red, irritated blotches. His face was a pale color, eyes almost gray. His nose was long and there was a black mole in the middle of it. "You want to talk about your father?"

"No," I said, perhaps too quickly. "They have arrested a man, Frank Pelicanos, a baker, who says he was the one who shot my father. He was running a small dice game at his location and he said Jacob Fine helped someone else open a competing bakery and then raised his weekly fee for his dice game. He despised my father and says he shot him."

"I guess that's a plus for the police department."

"You know Pelicanos?"

He shrugged. "A very small fish, little trouble, but always complaining about his fees to Jacob. I know Jacob gave him some leeway on his payment several times."

"Do you think he could have shot my father?"

He blew out more smoke and rolled his head to relieve tension. "Could have, yes, but did he, no. This guy was all talk, just a complainer. He was not the kind of man to be able to shoot another man in the head. I don't believe he did it."

I wonder what kind of man Solly thought could do that. "Why would he confess?"

"If Jacob was mad at Frank Pelicanos for anything it was because he kept coming in here and wanted the girls to service him. Jacob told him to stay out. This was to be permanent."

"Why?"

"Frank Pelicanos was not okay. He was beginning to unravel."

"From what?"

Solly exhaled again. "Our guess was syphilis."

• • •

After the long day, I wanted to spend my time quietly. I liked Cooper's, the little pub near my home. It was a quiet place for the locals with good food. It also boasted a roaring fireplace which helped purge the cold from my bones. I found a spot near the hearth and ordered chicken with a glass of whiskey.

It hit me as soon as I sat down that I was leading a pretty lonely existence. With Luigi and Eleanor both gone I was down two people that I used to talk with on a regular basis, two people that I could share my concerns and fears with. I could talk with Gunter, but it wasn't the same thing. We lacked closeness. Now with the new twist of having Margaret pursue me that closeness would probably never be there. The fireplace's warmth snapped me out of my thoughts as I shivered.

I decided to stop feeling sorry for myself. No one else would so it was doing me little good. I tried to focus on the multiple cases that were before us. Sam and I both felt that the mute man, Christian Hanson, was at least partly responsible for the deaths of Big Louie, the Harts and Mary Hastings. What we didn't know was where the son of a bitch was. I thought my best hope was to get a lead from Gussie Black. Black dealt with the underbelly of the city and he would have the best shot at finding out something about the mute. Other than that, we were relying on luck.

With the prostitute murders we weren't much further along. I hated to label them that way because of Eleanor being included on the list of victims, but that was what they were. I still felt it hard to believe she was gone and my nagging sense of guilt did nothing for my mood. I quickly bolted my first whiskey and ordered a second. I wanted to believe we were getting somewhere with the potential leads about a lawyer being involved, but I wasn't sure. A tall lawyer with a mustache. Not much as Sam and my friend, Stanley Kerjewski, had said. Maybe Stanley could find a lead on an attorney who liked to associate with whores and even get rough with them. Maybe Maurice Von Bever could shed some light as he supposedly arranged some dates for Eleanor. He would be next on our list of visits. Other than a few trinkets left on my doorstep and an amateurish poem, we had very little. I hoped there wasn't a new victim very soon.

Our newest case, and now our top assignment, was the kidnapping of the Hobbs' twins. Someone had placed a ladder under the girl's bedroom, gone through an unlocked window and snatched two eighteen month old girls. Their retreat, after the theft, appears to have gone west of the house to some sort of waiting conveyance. The two man teams assigned to interview all the residents of the houses on Indiana Avenue had turned up nothing so far. All we had was a swatch of cloth, snagged on the windowsill. Again, not much. Perhaps Sam was right. Maybe we needed the kidnappers to contact us. The unlocked window had me thinking someone we had talked to knew something.

They would all have to be interviewed again. Something was not right. There was also something amiss about the behavior of Everett Hobbs, the twin's father. He didn't seem upset at the kidnapping. He seemed annoyed, like the crime was taking up his valuable time. His attitude irritated me. If my kids had been kidnapped I would have been beside myself. He was not acting right.

As my dinner was served, I saw a woman enter Cooper's and immediately go into one of the other rooms. I only saw the side of her face and her dark, raven colored hair. For a moment I thought it was Margaret, but then I knew it wasn't. I was spooked. I was also out of line. My behavior with her repelled me. I needed confession and penance. I needed to see Father Seamus McCoy.

It was while I was having these thoughts about my immorality that the changes in my vision occurred. I began to see some wavy and blurry lines and it was hard to focus and to read things. I blinked to try and clear the lines, but that was no use. I felt very tense at once and irritated. My head began to throb at the left temple, a stabbing pain. I had never experienced this before. I fumbled for my wallet and tossed several bills on the table. I rose and left Coopers without eating. As soon as I was outside, the cold air helped me feel a little better, but my head was pounding. I threw up whiskey in the street. I thought I was getting a bad case of influenza. I needed to calm myself. The only place I could think of was the den in the basement of Soon Lee's. I had nowhere or no one else to turn to.

Five

I wasn't as fresh as I would have liked, but I managed to make it to the precinct in time to meet Sam. He had called ahead and we had a ten o'clock meeting with Maurice Von Bever at The Palace. I hadn't seen Von Bever since Gunter and I had questioned him about Clara Hunter's allegations of white slaving that were taking place at Paris, the other well known Von Bever brothel. As he had that day, he wore a very subtle, bored look. He was dressed in a dark black suit with very thin pinstripes running vertically on it. I could see that his cufflinks were solid gold as was the watch chain that hung across his chest. Never let it be said that he didn't look good regardless of what a scum I thought he was.

"More talk of white slaving, Detective Moses?" We were sitting in his office across from his beautiful oak desk.

I smiled. "Nothing like that, Mr. Von Bever. This time something a little more serious."

I saw him glance at Sam and then his eyes came back to me. "More serious, you say?"

"This time our questions involve murder."

He laughed and it wasn't a little chuckle. "The first time you come in my office you suggest I am keeping sex slaves. Now you come in here and want to question me about a murder. What person do you think I killed?"

"Mr. Von Bever," Sam said, "we are not here to jest with you. We are only here because your name came up in a murder investigation."

Von Bever's Adam's apple bobbed convulsively. "A murder investigation?"

"Two as a matter of fact," I said.

"Two," he sputtered.

"Two prostitutes, Eleanor Winter from The Queen's House, and Bad Joanie from The Devil's Cellar. Both were killed in a gruesome manner."

"Wait a minute," Von Bever said, veins bulging on his forehead. "You have somehow connected me to a woman who was slashed to pieces and another who was beheaded."

"Not the murders," Sam said.

"Then what?"

"When we were talking to girls at The Queen's House we were told that you might have arranged some private dates for Eleanor Winter," I said.

"Ms. Winter was a client of mine."

"I would like to see a list of the men who you set Ms. Winter up with. Is that possible?"

"Most of the men who come and see me are wealthy types. Discretion is the reason they use my services. I don't believe I can divulge to you the names of the men who have hired me."

"God damn it!" Sam said loudly, standing and hovering over Von Bever's desk. "We think that one of your so called clients, wealthy or not, may be a murderer. We are trying to stop him from killing again. I would suggest you find the list and find it soon."

Von Bever understood this clearly and used a small key to unlock a drawer on the lower portion of the desk. He removed from it a leather, bound notebook that had its pages divided by tabs. "This book contains a log of all of my clients. The tab that is marked referral will contain the list of men that contact me to secure private dates for them."

"How many do you have under that tab?" I asked.

He flipped the book open and checked under the requested tab. "One hundred and sixty-eight."

"Can you narrow it down to those who met with Eleanor Winter and those that met with Bad Joanie?"

"I can," he said, and he began to go through the names and write down notes for us to use.

• • •

When I returned to the precinct I was told that I had a visitor waiting for me in one of the holding rooms on the first floor. I wasn't surprised who the visitor was, but I was surprised he was back to see me so soon.

"Black," I said. Gussie was seated at a table, looking better than he had, but still forlorn. He was dressed in a better suit and was smoking a cigarette. From the look of the tray in front of him it was not his first.

"I think I met him," he said, staring at me through a haze of smoke.

"Who?" I asked.

"The blonde, mute man. I met him at The Golden Goose."

The Golden Goose was a brothel that was owned by Big Jim Colosimo. It was on the southern edge of the Levee on Wabash. "So what happened?"

"I was making a delivery to the brothel. These two men greeted me in the lobby. One was a tough looking Italian named Romano; the other was the mute guy."

"You're sure?"

"Well, the guy didn't talk or anything, but it had to be him. I transacted all of the business with Romano while this big dummy stood behind him with his arms folded across each other."

"Describe him."

"Big, thick in the arms and shoulders, blonde hair, parted down the middle."

That was our guy. "Who was the delivery for?"

Gussie laughed. "I never know that really. The Hustons told me to make the delivery to The Golden Goose and that this guy Romano would meet me there. That's all I know."

As much as I wanted to not believe Gussie, I had no choice. He had made a delivery and the mute guy was just there. "Keep looking and listening, Gussie. I need to find out where I can find this guy."

He nodded. "Anything on the bastard who killed Eleanor?"

I could see the hurt on his little ferret face, and I still hated to have him ask about her. "Nothing yet."

"Think you'll ever catch him, Moses? It seems you missed him the first time."

No one wanted to believe that Kluge was involved in the original batch of killings. "We'll catch him," I said quietly, but I had no idea when.

I was walking out of the room after my short meeting with

Gussie, a meeting that left me with clenched teeth, when I saw Sam Walker at the foot of the stairs that led to the second floor. He was waving his arms at me.

"You seem awfully excited," I said.

"Mr. Mallory and Miss Stone are upstairs. It seems they have heard from the kidnappers."

"Not Mr. or Mrs. Hobbs?"

"Mrs. Hobbs is still too upset to be out and about. Mr. Hobbs …" Sam shrugged.

"Where is he?"

"His sister said he was in his downtown office if we really needed him."

I thought of his casual approach to everything in our first meeting. "My God," I said.

Mallory and Alicia Stone were in a meeting room on the second floor. Mallory still wore his heavy wool coat and he sat in one of the wooden backed chairs. Miss Stone wore a dark blue dress, her red hair piled high on her head. "We have heard from the kidnappers," Mallory said. He tossed a piece of folded paper in my direction. I opened it.

We have the girls and will not harm them if our demands are met. Place a lit candle in the front window of the house on Prairie tomorrow night if you understand this request. If the candle is there we will get you further instructions. If the lit candle is not there one of the girls will die.

"It could be a bluff," Sam said. "The papers have carried so much about the kidnapping that anyone could decide to try and recover some cash."

I knew Sam was right. The Chicago papers had almost never ending coverage on the kidnappings, but at the moment I had no comment.

"If we don't light the candle and they go ahead with this threat what would we say about that?" Mallory asked.

"We can't let them harm those little girls," Alicia Stone said, and there were tears glistening in her eyes.

"They gave us no way to communicate with them," Sam said. "No way to tell if it is a genuine demand."

"I agree with you all," I said finally. "It could be a false note. Today it's hard to tell. We obviously don't want to gamble and let harm come to the girls. I would not be able to live with myself if I were to make that decision and it were wrong."

"Then we light the candle?" Sam asked.

I nodded. "It is only the next step. We are not giving up anything yet. Until we get a different demand we should play along. It can't hurt to light the candle. We don't have to do anything definitive until we get their further instructions."

I got three nods from the others in the room. "Light the candle in the front window as soon as dusk appears. Make sure it burns until daylight. We'll see what happens after that."

"Any other leads?" Mallory asked.

"None at this point," I said. "Our physical search turned up nothing and none of the neighbors saw or heard anything." I didn't mention the piece of cloth that we'd recovered.

"Okay," said Mallory. The man looked exhausted.

As they were about to leave the room I knew I had to ask a question. "Miss Stone, if I could have a private word with you."

Alicia Stone looked surprised at my request. Sam gave me an odd look as well, but left the room. When it was just Miss Stone and me I spoke. "I can understand Mrs. Hobbs not making it here today for this discussion, but what about Mr. Hobbs?"

She raised her eyes to mine; there were still tears there. "I thought we had told Detective Walker. Everett has gone to his office to work today."

"This situation with his two daughters does not take precedence over his work?"

She gave a short laugh. "I shouldn't laugh, but you don't know my brother. His work, regardless of wife, children, family, will always be number one in Everett's life. I believe he made that clear to Susan when he married her. I know that may seem a little odd, but that's the way he is."

I nodded. I didn't agree or care for Mr. Hobbs' approach to things. "When we met at the house he seemed a bit callous and uncaring."

"Oh, he cares, Detective. He cares a lot. He's just not good at showing it. I think that will become clearer once you get to know him better."

She was right. I would get to know Hobbs and all of them better. Someone had to have a tie to the kidnappers. Someone unlocked that bedroom window. "We'll be revisiting the staff again tomorrow," I said. "We talked to them all together. Now we will talk to them separately. We have to try and break them down to see what they truly know."

She smiled and reached out and touched my hand. Hers was warm. My stomach fluttered. "We were told you were the best. We will support whatever you decide to do."

· · ·

We were no sooner done with the delegation from the Hobbs' home then we found ourselves in a slow moving coach on the way to The Lucky Lady, Colosimo's base. The day was clear, not a cloud in the sky. The sun was glaring off all of the snow of the past two days. I found my eyes to be sensitive to the light, something I had never experienced before. There was a tightening at my temples. I had felt better since Cooper's where my symptoms had led me to the opium den at Soon Lee's, but I still didn't feel right. I wondered if a discussion with Doc Watson about my episode would help. I hoped it was just a temporary ailment, but it was new, frightening. I hadn't liked the way it made me feel or left me.

"Dreaming of Miss Stone?" Sam asked.

His voice drew me out of my haze. "Not exactly."

"Are you going to fill me in on the private discussion that the two of you shared or was it just that, private?" His tone suggested anger, but leaned a little toward jealously.

"I'm sorry if my handling of the situation offended you. I wanted Mallory out of the room while I asked Miss Stone some questions."

"Questions about what?"

"Her brother mostly. Doesn't it seem odd to you that Mr. Hobbs has gone to work not more than a couple of days after his two daughters have been kidnapped?"

"Not only odd, but a bit outrageous. If it were my kids I'd be pulling my hair out. I can't imagine losing your children."

I know I made a little sound at the comment, and I must have looked like I'd seen a ghost. I felt Sam's hand on my arm.

"I'm sorry, Patrick. I forgot for a moment who was I was talking to. I didn't mean to be insensitive."

I nodded, but averted my eyes from him. It had only been slightly more than two years since the fire at the Iroquois Theatre had consumed my wife and two children, but Sam was right. If my kids had been kidnapped I would have been so crazed that work would not have been possible. My brain would have been too addled.

• • •

We found Colosimo at work in his second floor office. The office was impeccable and smelled of linseed oil. Colosimo was dressed in one of his trademark white suits. His broad, bushy mustache looked professionally trimmed. All the fingers on each hand, besides the thumbs, had a ring on them. He looked very good, handsome, but he was not glad to see us.

"I thought we were done on this topic the other day. I gave you the man's name and his address. I also told you that I have no idea where he is."

Sam had simply asked him if he knew where Christian Hanson was.

"We have a source that spotted Mr. Hanson in The Golden Goose yesterday," I said.

"So now you think I know where he is because he went into a brothel that I own looking for a woman's companionship?" This was about as mad as I'd seen Colosimo.

"The person who gave us the tip was making a delivery. He said that Mr. Hanson was in the company of another man named Romano," Sam said.

I wish that Sam hadn't stated it that way, but it was out of his mouth. I saw Colosimo's eyes flicker in recognition and I was instantly worried about Gussie Black. "Why don't you ask Romano where he is then?"

"Romano works for you?" I asked.

"He is in distribution."

"Where can we find him?"

Colosimo smiled. "He moves around, but he has an apartment on Taylor Street. I can get you the address."

"No idea why Hanson was with him?" Sam asked.

Colosimo's hard stare flared. "Romano hires who he needs for his pickups and deliveries."

"So if Romano works for you and he is able to find Hanson how come you can't locate him?" I asked.

His eyes swiveled toward me. Hot anger showed. "You are very much out of line, Detective Moses. Do I need to talk with your superiors?"

I wasn't sure who he meant, but I had an idea. "If we find that you are harboring Mr. Hanson in any way, Mr. Colosimo, we will be back for you."

He laughed. "You two gentlemen have a good day and be careful out there. With cops getting beat up and shot it seems the world is a bit crazy these days."

I felt the anger rush up my back and over the top of my scalp, but I held myself in check. Sam must have seen something. He grabbed my arm and we were soon on our way back to the precinct.

• • •

Later in the day, after we had tried unsuccessfully to track down Carmine Romano, I found myself alone at my desk. I thought about the man they had locked up in the basement, the man who "confessed" to murdering my father, Frank Pelicanos. It made sense that he was upset if my father and the two aldermen had raised his fee for running a gambling operation in the ward.

He was probably even more upset if the story was true that my father had aided someone else to open a bakery not far from where Pelicanos had his. There wasn't much that made sense about him confessing to a crime he hadn't committed except the fact that Solly Friedman told me Pelicanos was sick.

I found out where he lived, a small house on Thirtieth Street and took a slow, horse drawn carriage to have a look. I wasn't sure what I was looking for and wasn't sure I'd see anything, but I had the carriage driver drop me off across from the house and there I sat hoping to see some of the other occupants. The house was very small with white dirty paint and a broken screen on one of the windows. I thought the place might be deserted. For some reason I didn't have the courage to go up to the house and bang on the door. If there was someone there they had probably seen enough cops for a lifetime. I decided to stay where I was across the street. Fortunately, the weather had warmed and the sun was out. It wasn't a bad day to watch the house.

I had been there for almost a half an hour when I saw the front door open and a small toddler, a boy, not more than two or three, came out of it. He was followed by an older girl, maybe five or six, and then a woman, not older than twenty-five. She was a small woman and it looked like she had taken the kids out to play in the melting snow. I saw them begin to form a small snowman in the front yard. They looked to be having fun, especially the children. They were all laughs and smiles. After a bit the woman strode away from the children and sat on the steps. For a moment, I thought she looked over at me, but she was only staring off into space. I could see her face pretty well. I could see she was as sad as her kids were happy. It was then that she burst into tears and buried her head in her hands. The two children didn't see this as they played in the snow. Eventually she stopped crying, wiped her eyes with her coat sleeve and returned to the children. I don't think she ever saw me.

The reason for her tears, at least what I could figure, was her missing husband. He might be a little crazy and maybe she had picked up the disease herself, but he was a missing part in her family. If he was gone who would provide for her and the children? I didn't know much about their little family but the prospects looked grim. As crazy as Frank Pelicanos might be he didn't kill my father. My father had done enough damage and paid for it. I didn't want the Pelicanos' family to be another victim.

• • •

When I returned to the precinct, I found George Loftus sitting at his desk writing a report and puffing madly on a cigarette. I hadn't talked to him alone since our discussion about Marshall Field, Jr.

"Is this your monthly trip to my neck of the woods?" he said. His voice was laced with sarcasm.

"Just been a little busy, George," I said.

"You can say that again. What's up today? More questions about the Field case?"

I laughed. "Not that, but a concern about Frank Pelicanos."

Loftus sat back in his chair and looked at me for a bit without speaking. "What concern is that, Moses?"

I cleared my throat. "I don't think he killed my father."

"What? The guy gets arrested hanging out by Freiburg's and

confesses to the whole thing and now you say you don't think he did it. Want to fill me in?"

"I understand he had a lot of reasons to be mad at my father, but this guy is just a little baker, a baker with a perversion for prostitutes. I found out he might be suffering from syphilis. I think it might be impairing his brain."

"Yeah. Who's your source for this?"

"Solly Friedman."

Now Loftus was quiet and the look on his face softened. "You think he might be just a bit off?"

'I'm not sure, but all the makings are there. I just think you guys ought to try and break him. Get him to tell another story. I'd hate to see the guy get strung up for something he didn't do."

Loftus nodded. "He did seem a little in a hurry to spill the beans on the case."

"I think he just feels better thinking he's the one who killed my father," I said. "Can you take one more crack at him? He's got a wife and two small kids."

Loftus nodded again. "I'll talk to him again and we'll see if he changes his tune."

· · ·

Captain Morgan caught up with Sam and me before we left for the day. He looked harassed and tired. His hair was uncombed and he was walking a little more stooped over then I'd ever seen. He wanted updates on our progress.

"What case, Captain? It's hard to keep them straight."

"Enough bullshit!" Morgan snapped. "That's all I get from

the detectives around here, how overworked they are. I know that. I don't need to be reminded. I just want a status update."

I looked over at Sam. He rolled his eyes. "The Hobbs have been contacted by someone claiming to be the kidnapper," I said. "They want a candle burning in the front window tonight to indicate that a connection has been made. If they see the candle in the window they will forward more instructions."

"Any reason to doubt that the note came from the kidnappers?" Morgan asked.

"Not really," I said. "It could be a hoax, but other than that we have very little."

"What do you mean very little?"

"Clues, Captain. None of the neighbors heard or saw anything. We had every house in the nearby vicinity canvassed. The house staff knows nothing. We did find a piece of cloth from a coat that was snagged on the window outside of the girl's bedroom. I took it to the new crime lab and hope to get some results soon."

Morgan waved a hand at this. "Your next move?"

"See if the kidnappers contact the family and run a second batch of interviews on the staff. This will start tomorrow."

Morgan nodded. "How about the Harts, Mary Hastings and Louie Pagano?"

Sam spoke up this time. These had originally been his cases. "We think we know who did it, a blonde, mute guy. We know he's done work for Jim Colosimo. We just can't find the son of a bitch."

"I got a call from Bathhouse John," Morgan said after a minute. Bathhouse John was Alderman John Coughlin. "He got a call from Colosimo complaining that you guys were leaning on him too much about this."

"He knows this bastard, Captain!" I said. "I think he's protecting him."

Morgan gave me a stern look. "Just lay off Colosimo for a little bit."

There was a silence in the room. Sam had been yelled at and I was chastised for trying to find a killer. Not a great mood setter.

"What about the prostitute murders?" Morgan finally asked.

Sam nodded towards me. "We talked to people at the houses where Bad Joanie and Eleanor Winter worked. It appears both had been doing some outside work for Maurice Von Bever. Both girls were said to be getting involved in a relationship with a lawyer."

"A lawyer. You think a lawyer might be the one slashing and killing these whores?" Morgan blurted.

"Kluge was a surgeon," I said. "If he was in concert with someone he might have shown them how to use a knife properly."

"I don't think it's a lawyer," Morgan said. "It doesn't seem to fit."

Again Sam and I looked at each other, but neither of us spoke. Morgan's last comment didn't seem to merit much of a response.

• • •

She came to my apartment again that night. It was just past nine o'clock when the knock came. I let her in and watched as she removed her heavy overcoat and her hat. She laid these items across the chair in front of my desk. She stood there a moment dressed in a light blue dress and let me admire her. Her beauty was overwhelming; I was transfixed and was unable to say anything. She began to undo her dress.

"Stop," I said. I'd had nothing to drink or to smoke. I was one hundred percent in control of myself. I had no excuses.

"You didn't enjoy my last visit?" she asked. She wore a wicked smile and then licked her lips. "I think you did."

I wanted to say the right things. I wanted to do what was right. "I enjoyed it," I admitted, "but it was wrong."

"Wrong?" she said. "When two people make love and they both enjoy it how can it be wrong?"

I cleared my throat. Just having her there in my room was arousing me. "It is wrong because you are married to my partner and my friend. As much as I want to do this, I can't. I can't do this to Gunter."

She took a step closer to me. I could smell her. Dots of perspiration appeared on my forehead. "He won't always be around," she said. "Don't pass up an opportunity."

"What do you mean he won't always be around?"

She laughed and I didn't like the way she was laughing. "Bad things are happening to cops every day in this town. Listen to what Big Jim told you."

"Colosimo? How the hell do you know Colosimo?"

"I know a lot of people," she said and then she was right in my face laughing. I thought she was laughing at me. I swung at her.

And then my head jumped off my pillow. The pain at my temples was flaring. Even though it was dark in my room I saw flashing lights in my eyes. I stumbled for the light in my room and turned it on. I had a tough time focusing my vision, but one thing was clear. Margaret Krause was not in my room. She had not returned, but the terrible headache had.

Six

I rode with Sam to the Hobbs' house on Prairie the next morning. My headache had calmed and I was able to get some sleep, but I was very tired. Sam wasn't in a good mood. He barely said a word to me until we were in the coach and the horse was dragging us slowly through icy, slushy streets.

"You okay, Sam?"

"We've got to start with the staff interviews, see if we missed anything, see if the kidnappers have made further connections, and then try and catch up with Carmine Romano."

This all sounded logical and well thought out. "I'm in agreement with all of that, but I asked you if you were okay."

He looked at me for a minute. "I heard when you got close to Colosimo when you were looking for that Italian girl that he called Coughlin and Kenna and the two aldermen came down on Morgan who came down on you and Krause."

"That sounds about how it all happened."

"So the aldermen tell the police how to handle the crimes down in this district, depending upon who you're looking at? "

"Again, that sounds about right."

"That sounds like absolute horseshit?"

"Oh, it is. You have to watch where you step and back off if we feel we're pressing to hard."

"And if we find that Colosimo is anyway involved in these murders?"

"Then we press him as hard as we can. If they tell me to stop they can have my fucking badge."

"I have a family, Patrick," he said. "Losing this job would not be a very wise thing to do."

"I respect that," I said, "but I want you to know that I always do whatever I think needs to be done to get to the bottom of a case. I don't always think first."

Sam was looking out the carriage window as I said this. He turned back to me. "I will do my best to support you."

The news that we received when we arrived at the Hobbs' house was that they had burned a candle all night long in the front window. They had heard nothing from the kidnappers. The second piece of news we got, not surprisingly, was that Everett Hobbs was not present in his house. We were told he was in his Loop office.

The interviews of the three staff members took place in the kitchen. The first person that we talked to was Rupert Conner, a fifty-three year old, plump, balding chef. He did all of the cooking for the Hobbs' family except for Mondays, his day off.

"I had very little contact with the twins," Conner said. "If they were awake, I might see them at the dining table, but that was about it. They never came into the kitchen or the serving area."

"When was the last time that you had any contact with the girls?' Walker asked.

"I thought about this and it was probably three or four days before they were taken."

He seemed calm, truthful. "And the last time that you were on the second floor?" I asked.

He looked at me and our eyes met. "I have never been on the second floor, Detective."

We took all of Conner's information, where he lived, and who he lived with. We would follow up with a visit to his home, but we both discounted his involvement in the crime.

The black maid, Amelia Johnson, wasn't calm. In fact she was a nervous wreck and tearfully cried through the entire interview. She'd come apart since we'd first met her. "I can't believe those two little angels are gone," she said. "I can't believe that someone would take those little girls."

"How often did you see them?" Sam asked.

She wiped away tears and blew her nose into a handkerchief. "I saw them every day."

"And you had access to their bedroom?" Sam asked.

"I did, sir. I can get into every room in the house except for Mr. Hobbs' office. No one is allowed in there except for him."

I was taking down notes when she spoke up again. "You're gonna find Millie and Holly, aren't you?"

"We are going to do our best to find them," I said.

"I can't sleep since it happened. I won't be able to sleep until they are found. If you don't find them, I may never be able to sleep another night."

As upset as Amelia Johnson seemed at the kidnapping, it would have been very easy to dismiss her possible involvement, but Sam and I had both seen this scenario before in other cases. The person who seems the most upset or sorry that a crime has been committed is often the person who is most involved in the crime. Just like Rupert Conner, she gave us her personal information and would get a further looking into.

The most intriguing of the three employees was Sarah Balowski, the twin's nurse. She is the one employee that had the most access to the twins. It went beyond daily; it was almost hourly.

"I have a room on the lower level so that I am available at all times to take care of the girl's needs," she said. "The only day I am not here is Tuesday, my day off." She was a plainly attractive woman of Polish descent. She had blonde hair and haunting blue gray eyes. They were very unique. Her smile, when she did smile, was very weak, never broad. She seemed very serious.

"When was the last time that you were in the girl's bedroom?" I asked.

"The night before they were taken, probably around eight o'clock."

"The windows in the room, especially the center window, were closed when you were in the room?"

"When I was in the room, I recalled that it was very warm and I had no reason to check the windows. I believed they were totally closed."

"What about the locks?" Sam asked. "When was the last time that you checked the locks on the windows?"

Her eyes drifted over to Sam. There was little expression on her face. "Mrs. Hobbs didn't want the room to be too cold. I would doubt that those windows have been opened after Halloween when the weather started to turn."

"And you had no need to check the locks?" Sam persisted.

"None," she said calmly. "The room was warm and the windows were closed. I had no reason to ever look at them."

She seemed so calm it was unnerving. "What kind of people are the Hobbs? Are they good people to work for?" I asked.

That impassive look never left her face. "They are good people, fair people."

"Do they ever fight or argue?"

Now she showed the weak smile. "What married couple do you know, Detective, that never fights or argues?"

Sam laughed, but I continued to look at her face. There was something there. I wouldn't call it the trace of a lie, but there was a tell showing. Right now all I could do was lump it under mysterious. We took her personal information and then let her return to her duties. As expected, other than my uneasiness with Miss Balowski, our discussions with the staff turned up little to aid us in the investigation.

•   •   •

After the seemingly useless interviews with the staff at the Hobbs' home, we caught a carriage and had it take us to the apartment building that Carmine Romano lived in on Taylor Street. Our first visit there had yielded nothing. It was still early enough in the day that we figured we might catch him at home. The day was going to be another warm one for January. Ice and snow were melting everywhere and the streets were becoming a trail of slop. I thought about the snowman that the wife of Frank Pelicanos and his children had made and the thought of it melting away made me feel awful.

Carmine Romano lived on the second floor of a three story brownstone that housed six units. We weren't sure what kind of reception we would receive when we pounded on the door so we drew our guns and Sam gave the door three good, closed fisted knocks. There was no sound from inside so Sam pounded again after several moments.

"Hold the fuck on," said a voice from inside. "What's all the commotion?"

The door was opened by a big man, well-muscled, with a dark complexion and dark hair. He was dressed only in his underclothes and was staring at us from barely open, hangover glazed eyes.

Sam stuck his badge in Romano's face. "Police, Carmine. We want to ask you some questions."

This seemed to get Carmine's attention, that plus the drawn revolvers. "Sure, Officers," he said. "Come right in." He opened the door and we were led into his small apartment. There was a main room, a bedroom to our left, a bathroom and a small kitchen area. "Sorry but the cleaning woman has the day off."

The place had not been picked up in a while. There were a number of bottles and papers strewn about a table in the main room. An overflowing ashtray was spilling its contents onto the table top. "Anybody in the bedroom, Carmine?" I asked.

"Just Vicky," he said smiling.

"Who's Vicky?"

"Have a look."

I walked over to the door to the bedroom and pushed it open. The light in the room was good enough to see. There was a woman, a blonde, a big girl, big breasted, lying naked on the bed. I didn't see her moving, but as I got closer I could see her large chest rising and falling. With all the noise we made, she still didn't seem close to waking up. I moved back into the living room.

"She's nice, huh?" Carmine asked. He was awake now and had a wide smile on his face.

"Yeah, she's real nice," I said, "but we're not here to talk about your love life. We want to know where we can find Christian Hanson."

Carmine tilted his head to one side, giving my inquiry some thought. "I don't know anyone named Christian Hanson."

"You sure?" I asked.

He smiled and spread his arms wide. "One hundred percent."

With this, Sam backhanded Carmine with the butt of his gun, knocking him to the floor. Sam then knelt down and shoved the barrel of the gun under Carmine's chin and into his throat. Carmine now stared up at Sam, eyes wide. There was a trickle of blood under his nose. Sam definitely had his attention.

"Detective Moses and I are getting tired of all of the bullshit your boss, Colosimo, and now you are giving us. Big Jim has his protection in the ward, but you are just a little fuck. Tell us what you know right now or Vicky is going to be looking for a new boyfriend."

"I don't know that much about him," Carmine stammered, never taking his eyes off the gun. "We meet each other to make sure deliveries go well and then I distribute the product wherever it's supposed to go."

"Are you talking cocaine?" I said.

"Cocaine, heroin, opium, all of that."

"What does Christian do?"

"He's just muscle. That's all. He's a big scary looking bastard."

"We've met him," I said. "What else do you know about him?"

"Not much. The son of a bitch can't talk."

"But you can reach him to help with the deliveries?" I asked.

"Not true. The people shipping the drugs contact us each

separately and we meet up at the site."

Sam jammed the gun a little harder into Carmine's throat. Carmine gasped. "You must know where Hanson hangs out. He seems to have vacated his hotel room," Sam said.

"All I can tell you is what I heard. I hear Hanson likes things a little rough. I thought it was so bizarre when I heard it that I didn't believe it."

Sam pulled the revolver from Carmine's neck. "What the hell are you talking about?"

"It's true. Hanson like things a little rough. He likes to be whipped by women who dress up in costumes, including scary masks. I heard it from a whore that that's the only way he can get off."

Sam and I both looked at each other. I think we were each a little shocked. "Where does he go for this special treatment?" I asked.

Carmine smiled at me. "You have to ask?" he said. "He goes to Palace de Sade."

·   ·   ·

I knew where the Palace de Sade was, but I had no idea what went on behind its walls. The brothel was a nondescript, three story brownstone located in the middle of Bed Bug Row, the seediest part of the Levee. Most of these places offered a variety of services from the women they employed and many of these ladies were paid less than a dollar for their services. It was no secret that these women were of the lowest form, many sick and diseased, a lot mentally dysfunctional. Before we made our visit to the Palace de Sade, we were told that the prices there were not cheap, the women not used up and that the services provided were unique.

The inside of the brothel was tastefully decorated, but the lighting gave the appearance of a hazy, cloudy experience. The woman, known as Madam Claire, who greeted us was anything but cloudy. She was a shapely woman, mid-forties, full figured and wearing a severe black dress, closed tightly at the neck and as tight as it could be. A simple strand of pearls hung around her neck. Her hair, makeup and eyes all projected darkness. Her face, although beautiful, scared me.

"This gentleman that you seek, what name does he go by?" Madam Claire asked. Her accent was unmistakably French.

"His name is Christian Hanson," I said. "He is tall, thick through the shoulders and has blonde hair that he parts down the middle. He also doesn't speak."

"He doesn't speak?" she asked. She sounded surprised.

"He is a mute," I said.

"He does not sound familiar to me at all. Your description was fairly detailed. I would think I would remember him from that. The fact that he is a mute makes it simpler. I would have remembered such a man."

"This man, Madam Claire," Sam said, "is a suspect in several murder cases. He is a very dangerous individual. We know you like to maintain confidentiality for your clients. We understand that, but this is a special situation. We also don't care what goes on here at the Palace de Sade. We are only trying to find Mr. Hanson."

She thought for a moment, tugging at her ear with two fingers that showed black polish. "Murder, you say?"

"At least four that we know of," I said.

"Give me one moment," she said and she left the parlor.

After a few minutes she returned and motioned for us to follow her. She said nothing as she led us to the back of the brothel to a small room that had only a few soft chairs in it along with a sofa that had a red throw covering it. The room contained a strong smell of old perfume and cigarette smoke. On the sofa sat a large girl, not fat, who wore nothing but a short robe and her underclothes. Her ample features were easily seen. She was smoking a cigarette in a gold holder. Her hair, which was mussed, was flaming red. She smiled as we entered the room.

"Colette Vitriol, this is Detective Moses and Detective Walker," Madam Claire said. "They would like to ask you some questions about Mr. Swede."

"Mr. Swede?" Walker said loudly.

"That is the name he goes by when he visits," Colette said. "I've never heard the name Hanson."

"How often does he visit?" Sam asked.

She exhaled a large plume of smoke. "I would say a couple of times a month for the past year or so."

"Any idea what he does for a living?" I asked.

"We don't talk," she said quickly. "He can't talk."

"How do you communicate?"

She laughed. "He wrote me a note, just once. That's all I ever needed."

"What did the note say?" Sam asked.

She looked coolly at Sam. "It said he liked to be whipped by a woman who dressed in costumes and wore a mask. His favorite costume was the devil. I have this one dress all black and red and a devil's mask."

"And you whip him?" I asked. I was no prude, but I was stunned.

She exhaled again. "He gets totally naked, lies on the bed on his stomach and I whip his back and his buttocks with a leather strap. I'm not sure, but I believe this is the only way he can reach a climax."

"What happens when you're done?" Sam asked.

"He puts his clothes back on and he leaves. Sometimes I see tears running from his eyes."

"So no conversation, no other notes, no idea what he does and probably no idea where he lives?"

She pointed the cigarette holder at me. "Correct on all counts, Detective."

"He ever touch you?" I asked.

"Just once," she said quietly. "He got up from the bed, took a couple of steps towards me and slapped me. Then he put his clothes on and left."

"Any idea why he slapped you this one time?" Sam asked.

She shrugged casually. "He was upset with me. I checked the sheets and they were clean."

Other than gaining some insights into Mr. Hanson/ Swede's perversions, we were no closer to locating him than we were before our visit to the brothel. We again advised both Madam Claire and Collette Vitriol that Hanson was a dangerous man and they should be careful. We also told Madam Claire to call us the next time Hanson was on her premises.

• • •

Sam said he had to check something on an old robbery case so he headed off toward the south. I caught a cab for a ride into the financial district after placing a call to Stanley Kerjewski. He said he'd had time to review the list of men we had received from Maurice Von Bever's client log.

I met with Stanley Kerjewski at a nice place on LaSalle called The Chicago Room. Most of the business types that I saw milling about or dining were dressed better than I was. They were almost all men and they all appeared very serious, talking their business deals in hushed tones. I was led to a small table in the rear of the place where Stanley was seated; he had a glass of red wine in front of him. He smiled when he saw me and pointed to the chair across from him.

"Glass of wine, Patrick?" he asked.

I laughed. "I am on duty, Stanley."

"So be it," he said and took a sip of his wine.

"You were able to review the list of names that I sent over to your office?" Von Bever had given us a list of thirteen men who had private dates with either Eleanor or Bad Joanie. I had sent the list via courier to Stanley's office.

"I was and I found a couple of interesting tidbits of information." He paused, it seemed for theatrical effect.

"Are you going to tell me?"

"Of course," he said. "You gave me a list of thirteen men. Von Bever indicated to you that five of these men were listed as attorneys in Chicago. I was able to verify this for three of the men. One of these men is named Harold Braxton. Harold Braxton has a reputation as a drinker and a womanizer. It was suspected once that he had beaten his wife Sophie although no charges were ever filed. He has been known to gamble and to cavort with prostitutes. Drug use has been suspected. Of the three that I verified, this is the only one that stood out as a little quirky."

"But the others did use the dating services provided by Von

Bever which meant they saw prostitutes."

"True, but their other character references are impeccable."

"Okay, so we have Braxton. What about the two men you couldn't verify?"

"Really only one."

"One?"

"You listed Calvin Rymer. I was able to find him as a past Chicago Bar member."

"Past?"

"He died December first of nineteen-hundred- five, before either murder. I think you can rule him out." Stanley smiled broadly.

"I'll be the detective here. What about the other man?"

"Leonard Fillmore. I looked everywhere I could and I placed a number of calls. I couldn't find Mr. Fillmore listed anywhere as a practicing attorney in Chicago."

I rubbed at my chin as Stanley sipped his wine. "So what if he's not an attorney?"

"I went one step further, Patrick. I tried to locate an address for Mr. Fillmore in Chicago. I couldn't find anything in any records. I think Mr. Fillmore is not a real person or at least is not using his real name."

• • •

So we had Harold Braxton, who might be a consideration based on his past history, and Leonard Fillmore, a customer of Von Bever, but someone using an alias. Using a fake name, especially when visiting gambling houses or brothels, was not unusual. It was also not illegal. Some people didn't want their real names out there when going to these various entertainment venues. Our other mysterious friend, Christian Hanson, was also using an alias, Mr. Swede, when he visited Collette Vitriol at Palace de Sade. So, in each case, we had a little bit more to work on, very little I conceded, but I guess it was something. We would pay a visit to Harold Braxton to see what he thought about slashing prostitutes, and we hoped that the ladies of Palace de Sade would call us when Hanson aka Swede made his next visit.

• • •

As soon as I got out of the carriage in front of the precinct building I saw George Loftus. He was standing outside, in the still pleasant weather, smoking a cigarette. It had gotten so warm that Loftus wasn't even wearing his overcoat. He smiled and waved at me as I walked towards him.

"I was looking for you, Moses," he said. "No one was sure when you'd be in."

"Just loose ends. That's all we seem to chase some times, huh George?"

"You can say that again." He took a large drag off his smoke and exhaled. "Anyway, I wanted to tell you that I had a nice visit with our friend, Frank Pelicanos."

I took a breath, picturing the poor wife and the two children playing in the snow. "And what did our new friend say?"

Another drag, another exhale of smoke. "Same thing, really. Told me that Jacob Fine had it in for him, raised his fees for the little dice game, and helped set up a bakery not far from Pelicanos' store. Then he refused to let Frank visit Freiburg's Dance Hall. All of this caused a tremendous amount of anger to build up in him. It got so bad that he saw no choice but to kill Fine. He saw an opportunity to do so on Christmas Day and he did it. At least that's the story he gave us."

I nodded. "What did he say about the gun that he used to commit the crime? Could he identify it?"

"He said he got the gun from someone a couple of years ago for a few dollars. It came with some ammunition. He didn't know guns very well, but knew how to load it and fire it. Said he wasn't even sure what brand it was."

"Nothing in his confession seemed a bit odd."

Loftus, head cocked, cigarette dangling from his lips, gave me a wary look. "The guy admitted to killing your father, Moses. Why are you so adamant that maybe he didn't?"

"I told you. I have it from a good source that he might be a little crazy, maybe suffering from the effects of syphilis."

"There's no doubt that he's a little nuts, but he tells a pretty good story. When I told him I wanted to talk to him, man to man, he didn't hesitate."

"So what was said?"

"I told him he's due in Judge Kirk's courtroom tomorrow for arraignment. The judge will hear his initial plea. I told him if he pleads guilty to murdering Jacob Fine there will be no need for a trial and the judge could skip right to sentencing. I told him that based on the nature of the crime, and who Jacob Fine was, there was no doubt in my mind that Kirk would sentence him to die by the rope and the carrying out of justice would be swift."

"What did Pelicanos say to that?"

"He looked at me, beaming like he was kind of proud, and told me that he had little to live for, Fine had ruined him in this city, that he was glad that he had killed Fine and was ready for whatever the courts threw at him."

My temples tightened a bit. I saw the little flashing lights for a second. I felt nauseous.

"You okay, Moses. You went a little pale on me," I heard Loftus say.

I took a deep breath and some of my anxiety cleared. "Thanks for looking into it and talking to him, George. I guess there's not much that can be done." I left Loftus and entered the building. I started up the stairs to the second floor, but had to stop as I felt dizzy for a moment. My head ached. I made it up the stairs and to my desk. I sat, trying to clear my head. The pain prevailed, but lightened. I had to do something, not for Frank Pelicanos, but for his wife and two children.

•   •   •

It was late in the afternoon on a day that seemed to move along as slow as the Chicago River flowed in a deep freeze. I talked with Sam briefly, but he was tied up with his burglary case. There wasn't that much going on with our three cases that couldn't wait. I tried to go through the case files for notes that showed that something might have been missed, but this was useless. I felt stupid and somewhat useless myself. The vice that had loosened on my temples returned and for a moment I thought I might be sick, but I got through it okay and returned to the files. My only serious thought was the opium den at Soon Lee's, but this would have to wait as well. Captain Morgan called Sam and me into his office at four-fifteen. The Hobbs had heard from the kidnappers and a demand had been made. Sam and I made a hasty exit for the Hobbs' residence on Prairie.

They were all in the small library that we had met in the first time. Mr. and Mrs. Hobbs were seated by the fireplace that was quiet on this warm afternoon. I noticed right away that Mrs. Hobbs had been crying again and was clutching a well-used, damp handkerchief. Mr. Hobbs wore his usual look of disinterest. I was starting to not like him very much. Alicia Stone was near her brother, dressed in a dark green dress with a black necklace. She would always look pretty, but today that look was definitely saddened. Thomas Mallory, the family lawyer, wore a fine, wool suit but his look was anything, but pleasant. He, too, looked distressed.

There were very simple, hollow greetings exchanged, except from Everett Hobbs. He didn't need to greet the detectives assigned to find his daughters. At least that was the way I took it.

"You have heard from the kidnappers?" Sam asked, breaking a hanging tension in the room.

"We have," Mallory said. "In the form of a letter sent to my office this afternoon. Shall I read it?"

Sam exhaled loudly. "Please do."

"The price for the two girls to be returned unharmed is one hundred thousand dollars. This cash, all in non-concurrent bills, will be placed in a large, brown satchel and placed in car number five on the number eleven El train as it leaves the Wells Street Station at six- forty- five in the morning the day after tomorrow. If anyone riding the train remains on the train through the entire Loop ride, the satchel will not be picked up and the girls will not be safe. A candle should be placed in the window tomorrow night from six o'clock PM until ten PM to indicate that you have understood the directions. Once the cash has been picked up with no hindrance the girls will be returned."

There was a bit of silence once Mallory was done with the reading. This was interrupted by Susan Hobbs who let out a loud sob and began crying again. Everett Hobbs only looked at her with a glare of annoyance.

"What do you make of this?" Mallory asked.

Sam considered this question only briefly. "I think at this time we must assume that the letter is from the kidnappers," he said.

"How can you make that assumption?" Everett Hobbs said loudly. "The papers have endless news about the kidnappings. This letter could have come from some crazy person."

"At this point," I said, "we have nothing else. We have heard from no one else. The demand sounds rather ominous if we avoid it. "

"Can you raise the necessary funds, Everett?" Mallory asked.

"Of course I can," Hobbs boomed, "but what if this is a ploy by someone other than the kidnappers? What if we do place the money on the El car only to see it disappear into the hands of the wrong party? It is a hundred thousand dollars, not a paltry sum. "

"This is true," Sam interjected. "Detective Moses and I are only thinking of the safety of your daughters, sir."

"I think we are being played," Hobbs said defiantly. "I would like to see more proof that they have my daughters."

I was certain that Sam and I were stunned by this little development. We knew Hobbs had the money as did everyone else in that room. I thought he was trying to play a dangerous game. "What do you suggest?" I said.

He looked at me smugly. "We wait them out. We don't burn the candle. They don't even know for sure if we saw the note, do they? We'll see what happens next. They are only looking for money. My guess is they don't want to hurt the girls. They might not like it, but they'll try something different."

"You feel good about this?" I asked.

"I do, Detective Moses."

I shrugged. "I just want to make sure."

"I am sure."

"I would hate to see something bad happen to the girls. It is a difficult thing to have to deal with."

"You are an authority on this, Detective Moses?" Hobbs asked.

In the proper setting I might have bashed in Hobbs' face with my gun, but we were in his home and there were ladies present. I took a deep breath. "I lost my wife and two children in the Iroquois Theatre fire. I have not yet recovered. I don't think I ever will."

I saw all of their looks, including Hobbs'. There was horror there. I could see it. Mrs. Hobbs was crying loudly. I felt Sam's hand on my shoulder. He stepped slightly in front of me.

"This is your call, Mr. Hobbs," he said. "Don't burn the candle tomorrow night and we'll see what happens. For the record, since your attorney is present, Detective Moses and I concur. We think you should place the money on the El car and hopefully we'll see the girls returned. Once the kidnappers start to spend the money, we will find them."

"And if it's not the kidnappers?" Hobbs persisted.

Neither Sam nor I had a response for the fool. We left the residence quickly after giving them more instructions should the kidnappers contact them.

· · ·

On the porch, outside of the house, Sam grabbed my arm, turning me towards him. It was hard for me to imagine he could not see the anger I felt. "You okay?" he asked.

"Now, not entirely. I will recover."

"That man is an idiot. He just doesn't know…"

I looked Sam in the eyes. "What you mean is he doesn't know what it's like to lose your children or your entire family. This is true. If he did he wouldn't have made those ridiculous comments."

He nodded solemnly. "Let's just hope the decision that he has made regarding the ransom doesn't lead to more loss."

"He seems awfully confident that we are not dealing with the kidnappers."

"We can only hope, for the twin's sake, that he is right."

I was thinking of the Hobbs' twins and suddenly I was thinking of the little boy and girl I saw playing with their mother in the snow in front of Frank Pelicanos' house. "Is there anything else that we're needed for at the precinct?" I said.

"Not from me," Sam said. "I'm going to go straight home."

"Fine," I said. "I have a little errand I need to run."

• • •

For some reason, I felt my heart beat quicken as I began to knock on the door at Frank Pelicanos' house. I didn't know why I was nervous, but maybe it had something to do with an innocent man confessing to a crime I had committed, a confession that could lead to him being hanged. I was mulling over this absurdity when the door was opened by the wife, a small, petite woman, dark haired and looking as scared as I felt nervous.

"Yes," she said.

I showed her my badge and told her my name. She didn't look any less scared. "May I come in for a moment?"

She led me into a small living room and I took a seat on a worn sofa. She sat across from me on a bench in front of a window that looked out onto the snow covered yard. I could see the remnants of the snowman, almost melted. "My name is Sylvia," she said. "You have news about Frank?"

"He is well," I lied. "I saw him the other day."

She smiled and for the first time I saw the bruise that circled a good part of her left eye. "Do you think he will be coming home soon?"

My stomach flinched at this question. I wondered how much she knew. "Your husband has confessed to a serious crime," I said. "This crime took place on Christmas Day late in the afternoon."

"Yes. I have heard all of this before, but there is no way that Frank killed that man. It is impossible."

I let out a deep breath. Maybe this would be easier than I thought. "Do you mean to say that Frank was here with you and the children all day on Christmas?"

She shook her head vigorously. "I don't mean that at all. He left the house somewhere around four and he did not return until after midnight."

I felt my insides sink. "You have no idea where he was or what he was doing?"

"None."

"Then why did you say that there was no way that Frank killed that man?"

"I know my Frank. He is not the kind of person that could

kill a man in cold blood. There is no way he could have done this."

I nodded. "How did you get that bruise around your eye?"

She blushed. "I stumbled and fell into a dresser. Frank is always telling me how clumsy I am."

Just then the little girl, the one who was about six, walked into the room. She was a mirror image of her mother, but her hair was a bunch of tight curls compared to her mother's straight locks. She had a picture in her hand that she quickly showed to her mother. When she saw me, she looked surprised.

"This is Detective Moses," Sylvia said. "He is a police officer. This is Stephanie."

"Hello, Stephanie," I said.

Stephanie looked me over for a bit and then walked over closer to me. She wore a serious look the whole time. "Are you going to be able to bring my daddy home soon?"

The wide brown eyes were haunting. With all the garbage I dealt with everyday, it was sometimes hard to keep our thoughts straight. All that Stephanie wanted was to get her father home. I did something that I was becoming better at. I lied. "I hope to have your father home to you very soon."

As soon as it was out of my mouth, I wished that I hadn't said it. I also wished that I hadn't seen the smile on little Stephanie's face.

•   •   •

I noticed that the more frustrating that my life became, the more I would turn to opium. There was definitely frustration with finding the blonde, mute, Christian Hanson. We knew who he was. We knew he was possibly responsible for several murders. We didn't have direct proof, but he was our only lead, a lead we couldn't find. Other people had contact with him or had seen him, but we had nothing.

With the prostitute murders and with the Hobbs' kidnapping case, these were different types of frustration. We had no idea who had committed these crimes. No one had seen or heard anything. In both of these cases we were locked in a battle of wits as we waited for something to happen, something that would inch us closer to finding the crooks. The frustration here was that something might happen that wouldn't be good. We could only wait and see.

My last, and newest, bits of frustration came from the ridiculous discussion we'd had with Everett Hobbs and the talk I'd had with Sylvia and Stephanie Pelicanos. Hobbs clearly had the money to pay for the ransom for his daughters. That seemed like a logical step to try and secure his daughter's safe release. Why would he play the game of bluffing with the kidnappers? It made no sense to me and had riled me up terribly. His last insensitive remark about being a parent who had lost his children had nearly put me over the edge. I was glad Sam had intervened and gotten me out of the house with no damage occurring.

With Frank Pelicanos, I was unsure of what I should do. He was going to be arraigned tomorrow for a crime he didn't commit. If he persisted in claiming he was guilty he would hang and it would be soon. What could I do to free him? I couldn't give myself up or I would certainly swing. I had seen the bruise around Sylvia's eye and had heard about Frank from Solly Friedman. He was not a mentally healthy man, was potentially dangerous for his wife and family, and didn't seem close to changing his tune. Maybe everyone involved, including me, would be better off with him dead. That last thought made my temples tighten and drove me to a visit to Soon Lee's.

I told myself to maintain control and I did. I smoked for a bit and I felt good, but I did not fall asleep. Why was it that the only time I felt any peace was when I had smoked opium? I felt relaxed and my head didn't ache at all. I caught a carriage in front of Soon Lee's at just past midnight. The mild weather was ending. A cold front had arrived and there were snowflakes plummeting from the sky. I would have been content to just get home and climb into bed. Tomorrow was not promising to be an easy day. This seemed like a good plan until I arrived at my building. When I got out of the coach I immediately noticed that the lights were on in my first floor apartment. I don't always lock my door, a scary thing in the city, but I always turned the lights out. I withdrew my gun from its holster and mounted the stairs. I could see my door through the glass of the main door and nothing appeared amiss. I entered the building and stopped outside of my unit. My heart was pounding wildly as I reached for the knob and turned it.

I pushed the door open with my left hand, gun extended in my right. There was only one light on in the unit, a small lamp that sat on my desk. In the chair in front of the desk sat Margaret Krause. She wore a hat and a heavy coat, but even in the marginal light that the lamp afforded, I could tell she had been crying. She peered up at me as I re-holstered my gun and entered the unit. She stood and gave me a firm embrace.

"Margaret," I said, slowly letting out the breath I had been holding. "What in God's name are you doing in my apartment?"

It wasn't a wicked smile or anything seductive, but it was a smile. If she hadn't been crying, I would have assumed she was happy. "I came to see you."

"That's evident."

"I knocked and when there was no answer I tried the door and it opened. I thought I'd wait for you for a bit. I was actually just getting ready to leave."

I nodded. "I had business in the loop and it ran on a bit longer than I thought." I suddenly felt foolish that I had to give her any excuse at all. "What did you want to see me about?"

"It's Gunter," she said and I was instantly alarmed.

"Is he okay?"

"He's fine. He is being released tomorrow from the hospital."

I pointed at the tears. "You don't seem too happy to have your husband returning to your home."

"Patrick, please," she said as more tears ran from her eyes. "Do you think I would have visited you the other night if I were happy in our relationship?"

I lowered my head. "I can only think that you are not. I have noticed a bit of tension between the two of you before, but I had no idea how bad things might be."

"They are not good. He drinks too much, spends little time with me, is very gruff with the children and when he gets mad he gets physical."

"Not with you, I hope?"

"He has never hit me or the kids, but the fear is there. He is a very frightening man."

This was also my partner, the man who had saved my life. "I am ashamed of the way I acted with you the other night when you visited me. I should have stopped it all. It was a mistake."

She took my hand. "But you enjoyed it, didn't you?"

This was not the position I wanted to be in. "The physical

part of it, yes. The emotional part, no. I couldn't consciously do anything that would hurt Gunter, especially with his wife."

Her hand went to her hips. She stared at me through tear soaked eyes. "And if I were no longer his wife?"

Even with the teary eyes, she was so beautiful. "That might actually be worse," I said. "I would always have to think about Gunter."

"I see," she said. "If I walk out that door, I think it's probably best if we do not see each other for a while. I don't know if I could look you in the eyes if Gunter were around."

"That's probably best," I said.

And with that, she left the apartment without another word. The bestial man in me wanted to chase after her, to take her again in my apartment. The man that Father Luigi raised to be a good person began to remove his clothes for what he hoped would be a peaceful night's rest.

Seven

When I arrived at the precinct the following morning, I was surprised at the mood I was in which was a good one. Nothing had happened in any of our three cases to bring about this good mood. I was certain from my little meeting with Margaret, and my rebuttal of her advances, that I had made the right decision, at least for my conscience and that was the reason I felt better.

I felt even a little better when Murphy, the big desk sergeant, told me that Harold Pinter, my little friend from the Forensics Department had climbed out of his covey in the basement to try and find me. Murphy said the little man was either agitated or very excited, but he wanted to see me as soon as I arrived.

Pinter was sitting behind his desk, peering at something on a slide through a microscope. I stood in the doorway of his little lab, not wanting to upset him. I cleared my throat. He didn't hear me so I tried again, this time louder.

"Ah, Moses," he said, standing quickly. "I went by your desk, but no one in the detective unit could tell me where you were or when you would be in."

"I guess I don't necessarily have fixed hours," I said,

stepping into his little space.

"Yes, I guess not," he said. He didn't look very happy with me.

"You've found something with the fragment of cloth?"

"The two Hobbs' twins that were kidnapped. How is that going?"

"Slowly," I said, becoming annoyed. "The piece of cloth?"

He came around his small desk and moved to a smaller table. On it, I could see that that piece of cloth I had originally given to him had been sliced into six even strips, maybe an inch and half long by a quarter of an inch. Each strip was fastened to a piece of white paper and there were notes on each.

"It was actually a bit harder to identify the stain," Pinter said, "than I thought it might be. We tested it as well as we could and came up with very little. It did not come from a fluid that was easily recognized or identifiable. It's amazing how the source was detected."

"Mr. Pinter, I appreciate all of the background information, but I am trying to find these two girls and quickly."

"Yes, quite right," he said. "There's a young chap, Byrnes is his name, at Calimer Labs where I take things like this for testing. He had been quite unlucky with all methods of testing, but something was bothering him about the cloth."

"Bothering him?"

He waved at me. "Not in a way that would cause anxiety. What bothered Byrnes was the smell. He knew it and then he tested for it. The piece of cloth was stained by liquid that contained yeast and barley which are, as you probably know, readily found in beer."

I wasn't sure I liked the way he said this. "So we are looking for a beer drinker? In this town that gets narrowed down to ninety percent of the men."

"Detective Moses, you really need to show more patience and understanding. Jumping to conclusions without evidence will only lead you in the wrong direction and get you into trouble."

I thought of Kluge and his accomplice. "I am sorry, but I am pressed. How do we find this one beer drinker?"

"You didn't let me finish. The concentration of yeast and barley in the stain could not have come from a refined glass of beer. Both were way too high. The person you are looking for works in a brewery somewhere in production before the beer is ready to be put into barrels."

• • •

I was coming out of the lower level of the building in search of Sam when Murphy told me I had a visitor in one of the first floor meeting rooms, a lady. I didn't know what lady would visit me here at the precinct. My fear level ran to Margaret while common sense told me it was probably one of the madams or prostitutes who might have information for us. I was totally wrong. When I opened the door to the little conference room I was surprised to see the lovely face of Alicia Stone smiling at me.

"Good Morning, Detective Moses," she said. Her tone was quiet and polite.

"Good day, Miss. Stone. I'm surprised to see you here. Has there been a change in plans regarding the ransom?"

She shook her head slowly; I could see the pain on her face. "I wanted to come and see you to apologize."

I was perplexed. "Why do you need to apologize?" I asked.

"Not me," she said. "I am here to apologize for my brother."

I noticed that she was still wearing a heavy, dark blue coat and her hat and gloves. "Are you comfortable?" I asked. "Can I get you anything?"

"No. That's fine. I didn't mean for this to be a social visit. After the way that things ended yesterday, I just felt it was necessary to come and say I'm sorry for the way that Everett acted and for that cold remark he made about you being an expert when it comes to losing your children. I am quite sure he was not aware that you had lost your wife and children in the Iroquois fire."

"I can forgive him for that comment. What I don't understand is the way that he has acted throughout the entire ordeal."

"He is very upset over the kidnapping," she said quickly.

"He has an odd way of showing it. He seems like he is mad at us. It's like he's only concerned that the kidnapping is cutting into his time at the office."

She nodded. "His work is a high priority."

"And what of his wife and family?"

She looked surprised. "He loves Susan very much. He told me once that she was the first distraction he allowed to take him away from his work."

"What about Millie and Holly?"

"You have to understand, Detective Moses. Susan was not supposed to be able to have children. This fact was told to her by several doctors. When she became pregnant it was a total shock. When it was known that she was carrying twins all of the doctors were shaking their heads."

I was confused. "What am I supposed to understand from

this?"

She smiled. She really was pretty. "Everett was more than ready to give up some of his time for Susan. What he was not ready for was the obligation, responsibility and time that go into being a father."

"He didn't want to be a father?"

"I don't think so. I think he loves the two girls very much, but I don't think he wants to spend all of the time being a father. I think he finds it overwhelming. As much as the birth of the two girls sent him reeling a bit, I think the kidnapping is even worse. I don't think he can cope with either one. I think that's why you see the attitude that says he is put off by the whole ordeal."

I was trying to understand this logic when something hit me. "What of his refusal to pay the ransom?"

Her look saddened. "I don't agree with him on that stance, but he is clear on it. First, he doesn't really think we will get the girls back alive. Secondly, he thinks we are dealing with pretenders, not the actual kidnappers. He thinks he has worked too hard to get bamboozled out of his money. He thinks if we don't pay nothing will happen to the girls."

I nodded. "I can only hope that he is right."

· · ·

Sam was at his desk when I returned from my talk with Alicia Stone. His mood was becoming easier to read just by looking at his face. Today didn't look good. He wore a deep scowl.

"I have been looking for you," Sam said.

"Anything new?"

"That's just it. There is nothing new and this leads me to little sleep which leads me to get here earlier than I want to find that you are not here yet."

"Sorry," I said. I didn't recall being told to report to Sam Walker. "I was actually in the building, talking to a couple of people."

"Anything new?" he asked. I thought he might be mocking me.

"The first meeting was with Harold Pinter, the forensic science investigator in the basement."

I saw Sam's face darken. "This ought to be good."

"I think it is. The piece of cloth we got from the Hobbs' home was soaked with a large concentration of barley and yeast."

"Meaning what?"

"Pinter thinks the person that was wearing this jacket or coat works for a brewery."

Sam shrugged. "Okay, but what can we do from here? There are several breweries in the city. We can't canvass all the employees and ask them who stole the two Hobbs' girls."

"No, but it is something."

Sam smiled at me. "And the second meeting?"

"Alicia Stone stopped by, first to apologize for her brother's behavior. Second to tell me that he never wanted to be a father and that it is a major distraction for him. It takes him away from his work too much."

"He shouldn't have had children."

"That's just it. Susan wasn't supposed to be able to have any kids and then all of a sudden there are two. Kind of threw a wrench into Hobbs' overall plan."

He scratched his chin. "I'm not sure this information does a whole lot for us on the case."

"I was thinking," I said slowly. "What would you do if you had something in your life that you found to be an annoyance?"

"You're not saying?"

"Maybe," I interjected. "He's so odd about things and he seems firm in his belief that the real kidnappers have not demanded the ransom."

"That's too farfetched, Patrick. Give me something real."

"Phillip Braxton," I said.

"Who is Phillip Braxton?"

"My good friend Stanley Kerjewski is on the board of the Chicago Bar Association. I asked him to check around, amongst their membership, for leads on anyone that might have some odd habits, including getting physical with women. I gave him the list of Eleanor and Bad Joanie's clients that we got from Von Bever. He gave me Braxton."

Sam pointed a finger at me. "That, Patrick, sounds like something real."

• • •

Phillip Braxton and Associates had their offices in a five story building on State Street just to the north of the river. The door to the office was unlocked so we walked in. There was a small reception area with a desk and a few chairs, but these were all empty. To the left was another door that led to a big office. It was there that we found Phillip Braxton, sleeping, with his head on his desk in the middle of a bunch of papers. The office itself was large and it was a mess. There were files, notices, briefs and newspapers covering every inch of space we could see. On the desk, to the side of Braxton's head was a finished bottle of

Kentucky bourbon, the all too obvious reason for Braxton's early morning nap. Sam looked at me, a disgusted look covering his face, and reared back and kicked the base of the desk as hard a he could.

Braxton's head shot off the desk like it had been fired. I'd like to repeat what he said, but it came out of his mouth so quickly I can't remember. I do know that his first words were laced with profanity. Some of the combination of words I had never heard before nor could I imagine. He sputtered and swore and looked for his glasses and finally, after finding them, was erect in his chair and looking at us.

"Who the hell are you two?" he stammered. He was a big man with a full head of gray hair. His suit was expensive, even though slept in, and his face was flushed red. His eyes had more red in them then white.

Sam slapped his badge on the desk rudely with no further introduction. "Always sleep in your office, counselor?"

Braxton looked at the badge and then back at us. "Only when my God damn wife locks me out. What do you want? Is it that fucking whore, Ruthie?"

"Who's Ruthie?" I asked.

He took his glasses off and wiped his sweaty brow with his sleeve. "A girl I see over at Heaven's End. A little too mouthy for my liking."

"So why would Ruthie call the police?" Sam asked. I could hear his temper rising in just those few words.

"She gets a little mad at me now and then and I have to put her in her place. After all, she's just a whore."

Now I felt my blood rising. "So you hit her?" I asked.

Apparently Braxton could tell by looking at us that he had hit some kind of nerve. He suddenly looked a little nervous.

"We got into a bit of a row. I can't remember. I may have hit her. I was drinking quite a bit."

"Do you always go to Heaven's End?" Sam asked.

"I move around," Braxton said. "What is this about?"

"How often do you get girls sent to you by Maurice Von Bever?" I asked.

"Von Bever? He told you that? He owes me money, that bastard."

"Answer the fucking question," Sam said.

"I don't know. I don't keep track. Maybe once, twice a month."

During this short discussion I looked Braxton over. He was obviously a drunk. Maybe if he hadn't slept in his clothes and had an opportunity to bathe he might have been decent looking. I didn't know Bad Joanie, but I knew Eleanor. This was not her type.

"Are you two going to tell me what this is about or are you going to just stand there looking at me?"

"Did you know Eleanor Winter from The Queen's House or Bad Joanie from The Devil's Cellar?" I asked.

He thought for a minute. "I'm not sure I know either of those ladies."

"Where were you New Year's Eve?"

"That's easy. I was at my brother's home in Hinsdale. We spent most of the day before and almost all of New Year's there."

"It's not him," I said.

Sam looked at me and understood. As much as a pig and detestable as Braxton was, he was not a murderer.

"Not him, meaning what?" Braxton asked.

Sam stepped around the desk, wading carefully over piles of

files and papers. Braxton looked up nervously at him. Sam reared back and slapped Braxton so hard his neck snapped ninety degrees to the left and his glasses flew off. Braxton let out a girlish sound and reached up with his hand to his flaming red cheek. "Listen, maggot," Sam said. "I don't give a shit what you do with your free time, but if I ever hear that you touched a woman down in the Levee again, or that you have hit your wife, I am going to come for you. Do you understand me?"

All Braxton could manage was a weak nod of his head.

As we exited Braxton's building, I couldn't resist. "Do you think he got your message?"

"Fucking degenerate," Sam mumbled.

I decided to leave the matter alone.

•   •   •

We used a call box at State and Grand to check in with the precinct. I watched as the look on Sam's face changed. It went from complacent to looking unraveled. I wondered what news he had. I wanted to talk to him about our next move, whatever that might be. I suddenly had the fear that something bad had happened to the Hobbs' girls. My stomach clenched, but then I realized the money drop wasn't supposed to occur until tomorrow. Unless we had been dealing with a false kidnapper. Sam hung the phone up and came out of the booth.

"Something wrong?" I said.

I could see Sam's hands were trembling as he tried to light a smoke. "We have to get back to the Levee, to the Westgate Apartments."

The Westgate was a flophouse on Clark near Twentieth.

"What's going on there?"

"He's struck again, and this time there is a note for me."

I didn't have to be told who he was. We caught the first cab we could and headed back across the river towards the Levee.

The Westgate was a large, U- shaped, three story brick building. The rooms you could get there included a bed, a toilet and a sink. They could be rented for as little as one day or for as long as you liked. For this reason, most decent, law abiding types avoided the place. The apartments were generally used by low, down on their luck folks, bums and prostitutes. We were used to the large group of cops that were milling about one of the building's six entrances. Since it was getting later in the day there was also a large number of onlookers grouped around trying to see or hear something about what had happened. There was a big sergeant standing by the door and he told us to go up to the second floor. He told us Loftus and Riley were already in the apartment.

Once inside the building you were immediately hit by the smells of urine, sweat and just plain old. What I could see of the walls showed old, chipped, light blue paint. What heat there was in the building was struggling to do its job.

We found a patrolman outside of one of the second floor units and he pushed the door open for us. Loftus and Riley were both there to the side of a bed that faced the windows. They were both smoking. Loftus nodded at us; Riley looked like he'd seen a ghost.

"We got the call," George said. "We knew it was yours." He pointed towards the bed.

We stepped into the little unit and the first smell that hit me was human blood. We both walked around to the side of the bed and the first thing I thought of was how much blood there was. The woman who was in the bed was partially fully clothed. What I mean by this is that she had all of her clothes on but they had been ripped in such a manner that you could see most of her body. Clothed or not, the figure in the bed was drenched in her own blood. It was clear that her throat had been cut, deeply, from ear to ear. I thought I could see bone inside of her throat. It was also clear that she had cheaply colored blonde hair. Why you noticed her hair color was because she wore a rather nice looking bowler. A little gift from the killer.

"What the fuck!" Sam said loudly. "What the holy fuck!"

I looked from the dead woman to Sam. He wore a look of stunned horror. I wondered if he had recognized her. "Know her?" I said.

He shook his head silently and pointed a shaking finger. "That is my hat."

I looked again. "Your hat?"

"I lost it a couple of weeks ago. Simply couldn't remember where I'd left it."

"Jesus!" I said.

"There's more," George Loftus said. We turned and he gave us a little piece of paper. Sam read it out loud.

"*Why hello there, Detective Sam. Any idea who you think I am? You need to be quick, I think you'll see. Before I visit your family.*"

It was then that we heard Riley O'Donnell lurch and whatever he had for eaten for the day came up in the corner of that room. Riley had a wife and five kids and the thought of this killer going after his own family must have gotten to him.

"I've got to get right home," Sam said. "I've got to make sure they are all right."

"You go," I said. "Take one of those patrolmen with you. I will stay here and figure out what I can."

I watched Sam bolt from the room and, less quickly, saw Loftus help Riley regain his strength and make their exit. I asked the patrolman outside the door to call the precinct and request that Harold Pinter, the Forensics man, get over here as quickly as possible. While he went to place the call I wished I had a drink or that I smoked. I couldn't wait in the death room so I stood outside the unit in the hall. For the first time in a while, I felt rattled. I felt the intense crushing of my temples, start to act up. Not now, I thought. Not now.

• • •

It felt like it took an eternity for Harold Pinter to get back to the crime scene, but in reality it had taken less than half an hour. I remembered him telling me something about being able to examine the victim at the scene of the crime as soon after the act had been committed to gain the most from the investigation. A vagrant by the name of Dancing Walter had found the body at just before eleven o'clock. It hadn't taken Loftus and Riley long to get there or to track us down. In my estimation, the woman on the bed hadn't been there past twelve hours. I didn't know if that timing would fit Pinter's description for perfection, but it was all we had.

"It's a tad gruesome," I told Pinter as he was about to enter the apartment, his bag of instruments under his arm.

He eyed me warily. "I worked in a field hospital during the incursion with Spain," he said evenly. "I have seen men with missing body parts and also men with not enough body parts to figure out who they were. I appreciate your concern, Patrick, but I have been a partner with gruesome for some time now."

I followed Pinter into the room and watched closely as he rounded the bed for his first glimpse of the victim. He made some sort of sound, like a groan, and removed a handkerchief from his pocket. He placed it over his nose and mouth.

"You okay, Harold?" It was the first time I had used his first name and I felt sorry for the old guy.

"This is not like the war," he said. "Man doesn't kill this way. Only an animal could do this. Were they all like this?"

I assumed he meant all of the Kluge victims. "The cuts were similar. The throat and then from the neck down to the crotch, but here, with her, there's a lot more blood."

He nodded and put the handkerchief back in his pocket. He stepped close enough to stoop down closely to the victim. "Any idea who she is?"

"Probably a prostitute, but no name yet if that is what you mean."

"The cuts here are deep," he said, getting his head within inches of the slashed throat. "What was the weapon used in all of the other cases?"

"The coroner told us that as well, and as neat as the cuts were it indicated the use of a scalpel by someone who knew how to use it well."

He stood up, removed his glasses and again took the handkerchief out of his pocket to wipe his eyes. "No scalpel here. My guess would be something from the military order of knives, probably a bayonet. The wounds I can see are deep, viscous, rough and jagged. He has almost cut this poor woman's head off."

"What does it mean?"

He laughed. "He's getting meaner."

"And the hat and the note?"

He shrugged. "Like the poor woman whose head got stuck on Grant's sword and the note left there for you, this is all part of the game."

"Game! You think this is a fucking game?"

"Not me, Patrick. The killer. And I think he is just starting to have fun."

• • •

Other than the body, the hat and the note there wasn't anything else in the little room that Pinter could find to help him or us with the investigation. The coroner's people were called and the body was wrapped and taken to the morgue. Pinter would call ahead and ask to be present when Hoffman or his designee did the autopsy. Pinter promised to get to me as soon as possible with any findings. He also took the hat for "further analysis" whatever that meant. When the body and Pinter were gone, I wanted to have a word with Dancing Walter, the vagrant.

They were holding Dancing Walter down the hall next to an old, clanking radiator. The vagrant was very small, not touching five feet, and his clothes were old and tattered. The pants that he wore were a dirt encrusted, red and white check. I could see under his rumpled hat that he had gray hair and it was not clean. His face was lined with several scars. One of his eyes didn't seem to focus properly and moved about uncontrollably. I was also certain he hadn't taken a bath in a long time. He stunk.

"You're Walter?" I asked.

He was resting against a window sill with a patrolman to

guard him against disappearing. He looked at me with his one good eye, the other looking off to the left. "That's me, Captain."

"I'm not a Captain," I said. "Just a lowly detective."

"Yes, sir," he said. "What happened to that woman in there?"

"Why don't you tell me what you saw?"

"I don't know what time it was," he said. "I don't have a time piece, but I heard a noise. It sounded like a woman's scream. From where I was sitting, I was able to get a pretty good look at the apartment that she was in. I could see right down the hall."

I looked back over my shoulder and I could see what Walter was saying. "Go ahead."

"I heard this noise and then I thought I heard another. I looked down the hall and I saw this man come out of that apartment, a big man, a little hunched over. He was wearing an overcoat and a large brimmed hat. That much I saw clearly. When he turned to leave I could see a little of his face; he had a big mustache. There's a light right across from that apartment. It lit it up pretty good. Anyway, I saw that he had a mustache and then he was gone down the stairs. I didn't think too much about it and I went back to sleep."

"No idea what time it was?"

"No. I said I don't have a watch. It was still pretty dark."

"Okay. Then what?"

"I woke up this morning and I was going to leave to try and find something to eat and maybe a cup of coffee. I walked down the hall and that apartment door was more than half open. I looked inside, and as my eyes adjusted, I saw the woman's arm dangling over the side of the bed. I also saw the blood on the floor. I went in to take a closer look and, well, I wish I hadn't.

Worse thing I'd ever seen.

"I almost got sick so I left the apartment and went downstairs. I was going a bit crazy, not knowing what to do, when I stumbled out into the air and walked almost right into that big cop that I told. He came and took a look and then he called your precinct."

I nodded. "A big man, a little hunched over with a mustache?"

"That's as good as I could see him."

"That's pretty good," I said. "Look, if we need to find you where's the best place?"

Dancing Walter laughed. "Wherever I can find food or a place to sleep in the Levee. Don't got a home."

"Okay. I'm sure we can find you," I said. "Tell me, why do they call you Dancing Walter?"

He smiled. "Used to work with Ringling. I'd dance around in the ring with a live bear. Guess it was funny."

I smiled and felt sorry for him. I wondered where his life had taken the bad turn that led him here.

As I started to walk away, he reached out and grabbed my arm. I looked down at him. "He won't know about this, will he?"

"Who?" I asked.

"The man that did that."

"Don't worry. The papers won't know that you tipped us off."

I could see the relief on his face. "The devil did that, sir. If I have to meet him I would prefer that it happens when I'm gone, if you know what I mean."

Unfortunately, I did. "Don't worry, Walter. No one will know you spoke to us and gave us information."

. . .

I could see that it was getting dark outside when Sam Walker finally returned to the precinct. I've said this before. Sam was a tough guy, but he looked anything but tough right now. In fact, he looked scared. Morgan told me to grab Sam when he returned so that he could be brought up to date on the facts of the case. Sam nodded when I told him this. We walked in silence to Morgan's office.

Morgan looked more alert than usual. Normally he gave me the impression of someone who wanted to just get through the day. Today there was something there that made him look different.

"Everything okay on the home front, Sam?" he said.

Sam nodded. "Kids are all home from school and everyone is tucked in nice and neat. I appreciate you allowing a patrolman to guard my house."

"That's the least we can do," Morgan said. "Tell me what you know."

"Not too much really," I said. "The victim, unnamed as of now, was slashed in a similar fashion as all of the other victims, but this time, according to Harold Pinter, the knife seemed larger. Pinter suggested the cuts were made rather violently."

"Pinter?" Morgan said.

"You know, Captain. Our new forensic science man."

"Yes, of course," Morgan said, but I could see he was still trying to place the person.

"Anyway, the cuts were similar, but deeper. There was a tremendous amount of blood at the site. Other than the hat and the note that were left at the scene, there's not a lot to report."

Morgan nodded and shifted his gaze to Sam. "The note was addressed to you, Sam, and the hat was yours?"

"That's true," Sam said. He was ringing his hands together, maybe trying to free the tension in them.

"Anything pertinent in the note?"

"Nothing," Sam said, "except that he threatened my family.

"That's new," Morgan said, "and the hat?"

Sam's eyes finally came up to face Morgan. "I lost it about ten days ago, maybe more. I thought I had worn it to the precinct, but really can't remember exactly when I'd worn it."

Morgan looked to me. "Patrick?"

"Pinter is going to attend this woman's autopsy with Hoffman's people to see if they find anything. This may not help us find the killer, but may help identify him once he's caught."

Morgan shrugged. "Nothing else?"

"Just the witness, Dancing Walter?"

"Dancing who?"

"Walter," I said. "He's a little bum called Dancing Walter. He's pretty sure he saw the assailant leaving the apartment after the murder. Said he was a tall man, wide brimmed hat, with a bushy mustache. He didn't have a very close look so that's what we have."

"That describes a lot of men in this town. We'll need more than that."

Both Sam and I nodded. The killer had been seen, but not that well. So far, as Captain Morgan had mentioned, we had the description of many men who walked around Chicago. When I considered that I realized we didn't have much.

• • •

I went looking for Harold Pinter in his basement lab, but there was no sign of him. I checked the door and found it locked. Probably a good practice. Things like evidence had been known to disappear from the precinct. I'd hoped to find that he had found something after examining the latest victim, but I'd have to wait. I checked my watch and it said six-thirty. A long day had gone on too long. I needed to get away.

I walked back up the one flight of stairs and was about to exit the building when the door swung open. In came a big draft, cold snow and George Loftus. His overcoat and hat were wet and covered with flakes.

"Blizzard, Moses," he said. "Can't see a fuckin thing."

"It is winter," I said. "Not totally unexpected."

He took his hat off and shook it. "Still don't care for it."

I nodded. "Sorry you had to catch that one this morning. How's Riley?"

"Riley's a tough egg. You know, though, we just don't always get used to the stuff we see. Any news?"

"That vagrant, Dancing Walter, he saw the killer. At least he thinks he did. Big guy, large brimmed hat, mustache. Anybody you know?"

"Sounds like half the people walking the street."

"That is the problem. How did the arraignment for Pelicanos go?"

"We got there just when it started. I was watching him when the bailiff asked him to rise and the charges were read. Pelicanos looked very calm. He was then asked by Judge Kirk what his plea was and just as calmly he answered, "Guilty". No hesitation at all."

My stomach didn't feel right. I hoped it was hunger. "Sentencing?"

"One week from today at ten in the morning. Still think he didn't do it?"

"Yes," I said.

"Look, Moses, I don't know what it is about that guy, but he hasn't wavered one bit that he killed your father. His story makes some sense and he has no alibi for Christmas night. The only thing I can tell you is if you're convinced he didn't do it you'd better find some evidence to support those thoughts. Otherwise, Kirk is going to sentence him to be hanged and justice will be swift."

. . .

I spent a quiet dinner at Cooper's eating food and drinking beer that I didn't taste. I'm sure my personality was far from stellar, but I was somewhere else. My head was trying hard to understand the life of sins that I was surrounded by. Was there nothing to be faced with but depravity and death? What was I becoming when the viewing of a woman who had been virtually chopped up has little effect on me? What was even more troubling was the question of whether or not I could let another man, a family man, pay for a sin I had committed. On one hand when Pelicanos swung from the gallows there would be no more questions about who killed my father. Good for me or was it? Could I honestly let him be hung for a murder I had committed and not feel anything? Could I let Sylvia's husband and Stephanie's father be taken from them? I pondered this with no answer coming forth and my temples tightened. Suddenly any appetite that I had was gone and I had to be outside. The air was frigid and the coach I caught to Holy Trinity not much warmer. I had to talk with someone.

An old priest, Father Conner, let me in thru the kitchen door. There was usually someone near the kitchen and he had been there by himself drinking tea. He told me to have a seat while he went and found Father Seamus Mc Coy.

I was sitting at the kitchen table, after removing my hat, coat and gloves when Father Seamus came into the kitchen. "I wasn't sure that you would ever return here," he said. I noticed the sarcasm and saw the look on the face of the old boxer.

"Father Seamus," I said. "I just needed someone to talk with for a bit."

I saw his look soften and he took a seat across from me. He was dressed in lay slacks and shirt. His face had stiff, gray stubble on it. If I didn't know he was a priest I would presume he was just another street tough. "I'm sorry I barked at you. I guess I thought you would have stopped by here before tonight."

"You're right," I said. "I have no excuse."

"I was sorry to hear about your friend, Eleanor, and your father. That's an awful lot of stress to be put on someone."

I considered this for a moment. The headaches came to mind. "I hadn't thought about it from that perspective."

"I am glad that you have come here tonight to talk, Patrick, but you don't have to go anywhere to talk with God."

I nodded. "I understand that," I said.

"Unless you have removed God from your life. It that it, Patrick?"

I wanted to think this over before answering. If I'd ever

answered yes to this question around Luigi he would have cuffed me in the head. Seamus, as tough as he was, always seemed a little more tolerant. "I have a question?"

"One moment," Seamus said. He got up from his chair and went to a cabinet where he retrieved a bottle of whiskey and two glasses. He quickly sat back down and poured an even amount of the brown liquid into the two glasses. "A bit of Irish warmth," he said.

He took the glass and downed most of it in one gulp. I sipped at the whiskey and it gave me a warm glow.

"What question do you have for me, Patrick?"

"I have to ask you how God can allow all of these bad things to happen. How can there be murder and kidnappings and prostitution and God just lets it all happen? Things never seem to get any better, maybe even worse, but where is God?"

Seamus poured us each more whiskey even though I'd barely had any of mine. He sipped his this time. "God can expect man to be good and probably hopes they are, but this is not always the case. I suspect that he hopes good will prevail in the end, that some of this lawlessness will get better. In the end it is God who will have the final say when we all come to our judgment day."

I understood what he said, but my doubts were there as to whether or not I believed it. "And how do you think that God would judge a man that lets another suffer for his sins?"

Seamus laughed. "That is a complex question. Give me an example."

I shrugged. "Let's say one man commits a crime and the law arrests another man. They go through all the proceedings and the innocent man is punished while the guilty man does nothing. How would God treat this man?"

It didn't take him long to answer. "I can only see God treating the one who committed the crime as if he had committed two crimes which he did. The man committed the original crime and then let someone else pay for it. I do not think God's judgment would be light in this case."

I had known the answer, but I needed to hear it again. We sat for a while sipping whiskey and talking of things of less importance. It was late when I finally decided to leave. It didn't matter how I treated the Pelicanos issue while on the Earth; God would reckon with me when I left the planet. This didn't make me feel any better.

To top things off, I had the carriage swing by the Hobbs' residence before returning to my apartment. I noticed there was no candle burning in the front windows. They were making it clear they were not following the kidnappers' instructions. This, as Sam and I stated, seemed a dangerous tactic. I only hoped it didn't lead to a catastrophe. I wasn't optimistic.

Eight

I was hoping to carry some of my conversation with Father Seamus into the next day, but I was no sooner at my desk then the tasks at hand took my attention from all other matters. I noticed that Sam was very quiet. I assume this was due to the amount of stress we were both under along with his family being directly threatened by a murderer. I wasn't going to say anything to him until he got up from his chair and I saw that his shoe was untied.

"Sam, your shoe," I said, pointing.

"Oh," he said absently. "Thanks." He put his untied shoe on the chair and pulled his pant leg up before retying. I noticed a knife scabbard strung to his lower leg.

"What's with the knife?" I asked.

For a moment he looked like I had caught him doing something wrong. "You know, Patrick, this guy has me thinking more than I want. It's spooking me a bit. I decided to take a little extra precaution in the event I'm not armed. At least, I'll always have the knife with me."

I knew who "this guy" was, but I couldn't figure out when

you'd be unarmed. I don't sleep with my gun, but it's never too far from me. I only smiled and nodded as Sam finished lacing up his shoe.

I had really wanted to go over the cases with Sam, but saw the diminutive figure of Harold Pinter approaching our desks. The little scientist looked excited. "Ah, just the two detectives I was looking for," he said.

I saw Sam give a reproachable look. I knew he didn't agree with Pinter's methods. I found Harold interesting and always thought a fresh approach might help. "Find anything, Harold?"

"A few things. You can judge their interest level. Have you a moment?"

"Sure," I said before Sam could speak.

"First, the autopsy was conducted by Coroner Hoffman himself. Quite a self-assured fellow and not too friendly, but when I told him I was assisting you with the case he didn't seem to mind very much."

"We're old friends," I said.

Harold smiled weakly. "Anyway, we concurred that the young woman, still unidentified, was killed with a much larger knife, as I had said, something on the lines of a military issue. The wounds were deeper, thicker and had some jagged cutting to them suggesting that the blade may be serrated near the tip.

Sam rolled his eyes a bit. "We knew most of that. Anything else?" I said.

"I have the piece of metal that the finger print was left on from Bad Joanie's slaying. Coroner Hoffman gave me that bracelet to keep for further testing."

So far I didn't see much to help us proceed.

"Lastly, we have this." He held a small glass case. I had to get close to him to take a look. Sam did likewise.

"What the hell is that?" Sam asked.

Harold smiled. "These are two small fragments of skin taken from under the right thumb and forefinger from the victim."

"Meaning what?" I asked.

"Meaning the killer has a pretty good gash on him somewhere, probably one of his arms, but that is not all." Harold removed a little vile from his suit pocket and showed us it. Inside were two hairs, each about a half inch long. Both were clearly red. "Our killer has red hair on the area that our unknown prostitute friend scratched."

"Wouldn't the hair on his head be red?" Sam asked, fully engaged.

"Not necessarily," Harold said, "but most likely a shade of brown or darker blonde."

"Sum this up, Harold," I said.

He thought for a second. "Our killer is a tall man, probably brown hair and mustache, but always wears a wide brimmed hat. He may have had some surgical training, because of the proficiency of some of the knife wounds. He lacks much conscience and doesn't care for prostitutes. Right now he has some pretty deep finger scratches on him, probably on one of his arms. That's about all I can give you."

Sam and I looked at each other. That was a lot more than we'd had before the morning started.

. . .

I was expecting that we would hear something soon from the Hobbs' girl's kidnappers. It had been more than full day since their demand letter had been delivered to Mallory's office.

Obviously, no money had been placed in a valise on a morning El train. No move had been made by the Hobbs. It seemed to be the next move would come from the kidnappers. This did not make me feel well as the morning eased along. I had asked Sam what he had thought earlier.

"Awfully dumb decision by Everett Hobbs," he said in disgust. I gathered that he didn't think good things were going to come out of it.

I settled in at my desk, waiting, I didn't know what for. I didn't expect what happened next. We were told we had a visitor at the front desk. I was surprised when I went downstairs to find Maurice Von Bever waiting for us. He didn't look well, kind of pale, and a bit nervous. I doubted that a police precinct station made him comfortable.

I took him upstairs to one of the meeting rooms. He quietly removed his coat, hat and gloves and took a seat. It was only a short time before Sam joined us, closing the door behind him.

"Mr. Von Bever," I said. "You wanted to speak to us about something."

He nodded, still very quiet. "The woman that was murdered the other day, at the Westgate Apartments. I believe her name was Pearl Radd."

"How did you figure this out?" I asked.

He looked at me for a moment and looked like he might cry. "I sent her there, Detective Moses. I sent Pearl Radd to her death at the Westgate Apartments." He took out a handkerchief and wiped at his brow which appeared moist.

"Tell us about this," Sam said.

"Actually, I got the call for the date from a pimp named Andre' Dubois. He told me his client was looking for a girl who would come to him at the Westgate Apartments. I had been contacted earlier that day by Pearl. She was off that night and she was looking for an outside date. I got a hold of Dubois and told him I had a girl. He told me she was to meet the date at the Westgate, apartment two-twelve, at ten o'clock. I didn't put a lot of this together until I saw that the poor woman had been murdered in the *Tribune*."

"So," I said, "Dubois called you and you found the girl to fill his client's needs?"

"That's how it worked on a lot of occasions. A lot of the time the dates were arranged by me."

"Did Dubois tell you the name of the client?"

"He did not."

I looked down at my notes. "What can you tell me about a client of yours named Leonard Fillmore?"

Von Bever thought for a moment. "An attorney, I believe. Hasn't called for a bit."

"His name was on the list of men you'd set up with Eleanor Winter and Bad Joanie."

I saw that strong look of condemnation return to Von Bever's eyes. "I know that."

I suddenly felt angry. "Did you set up Fillmore with those women for the nights that they were murdered?"

He shook his head. "I checked those dates. I hadn't placed either Eleanor or Bad Joanie with a date on either of those nights."

"Which means what?" Sam blurted out.

"Which means," I said, "the killer set up those dates with the girls on his own"

Von Bever, if possible, looked sadder. He only nodded at my comment.

Before he left, Von Bever gave us the address and phone

number for Andre' Dubois, the pimp. We tried to call him several times from the precinct, but there was no answer. We were on our way out the door to go and visit him when we were stopped. The Hobbs had heard from the kidnappers. We were wanted there as soon as possible.

• • •

The temperature outside had gotten warmer, probably in the low thirties. Sometimes, in Chicago in January, this is reason alone for a celebration, but this day that hovered slightly above freezing was accompanied by a steady cold drizzle and persistent fog. By the time we were able to get near the Hobbs' home we were both drenched. This did nothing to improve our mood, especially Sam's. His had been ruined the day before.

"We are absolutely nowhere on these three cases," Sam said. He was looking out of the carriage window away from me.

"I disagree. We are gathering bits of information in all three of the cases. Soon enough this information will help us close these down."

He turned towards me. "An optimist, I see. We have one case where we are pretty certain we know who the killer is; we just can't find him. In another, the killer walks around town murdering women and leaving the detectives handling the case poorly written poems. Lastly, we have two kidnapped girls who are probably scared out of their minds. One of the kidnappers works at a brewery, we think. The father of the girls doesn't seem to care one way or the other about the outcome. That pretty much sums up the three investigations. Tell me, my optimistic friend, how close are we to closing a case?"

141

I turned away from him. "Maybe today will bring us more clues," I said defensively.

We made the rest of our short trip in silence.

• • •

The group that we faced at the Hobbs' was now too familiar. Susan Hobbs was present, as was her sister-in-law, Alicia Stone. Lastly, the always present figure of Thomas Mallory stood behind Susan who was crying uncontrollably. Missing, still surprising to me, was Everett Hobbs.

"Mr. Hobbs will not be joining us?" I asked.

Mallory spoke, somewhat quietly. "Mr. Hobbs is in the Loop at his office. We have attempted to reach him, but have so far been unsuccessful."

I am certain that Sam Walker's grunt was heard by everyone in the small study. "You have heard something from the kidnappers?" I asked.

Mallory bent down and lifted a rather plain brown box. "This was delivered by currier less than an hour ago."

Sam was standing closest to Mallory and took the box. He peered into it and then reached his hand inside. From within he extracted a piece of children's clothing, mostly pink, and stained red in several spots.

"The girls were wearing these pajamas the night they were taken from us," Mallory said.

Susan Hobbs let out a loud sob; Alicia Stone knelt by her, taking her hand and trying to reassure her.

"That's all that was in the box?" I asked. "No note or anything else."

"That is it," Mallory said.

"Which currier?" Sam asked.

"Advanced Chicago Curriers. I have a copy of the receipt that was signed for by Miss Johnson, the house maid."

"We'll need that," I said. "I will go immediately to their offices and learn what I can about the person who ordered this delivery. Sam, if you don't mind, bring the pajamas to Harold Pinter for testing."

"And what do we do, Detective?" The voice came out strained and damaged. It came from Susan Hobbs.

"Mrs. Hobbs, we are at the point in the case that something is about to break. The kidnappers made their first demand that we rebuffed. I am sure there will be another demand. I don't think they took your girls to hurt them. It is money that they want."

"What of that blood on the pajamas? How can you say they have not hurt them?" she blurted.

I nodded. "We do not know where or what that blood came from. I know it is difficult, but please try to not let this upset you until we can get some confirmation. I hate to sound cold, but I think this is a bluff, a fear tactic."

My answer sent Susan Hobbs into a crying fit. While Mallory and Alicia tended to her, Sam and I reasoned it was time for us to proceed with our plans and leave the house.

As we waited for the carriages that were called, the rain falling around us, Sam turned to me. "You really believe this is a kidnapper's bluff?"

"I am praying to God right now that I am right."

• • •

The address that I was given for Advanced Chicago Curriers was for a storefront location on Clark Street several blocks south of the river. The name of the company was displayed in big red letters across the windows. Upon entering the business I could see that they were quite busy. There was a large counter that faced the customers and the street. Behind it were a number of workers, all busy trying to wrap or enclose items in different types of packaging. Standing directly behind the counter was a dark haired man, big nose, chomping on an unlit cigar. I took him to be a Jew and the owner of the business. I stepped closer to the counter, but failed to garner much attention. The man was looking down intently on a copy of the *Transocean.*

"You in charge?" I asked.

"I am," he said, still looking at the newspaper. I wondered if he handled his clients in this manner.

I placed my badge on the top of his newspaper and he looked up suddenly. "Oh, sorry Officer. I didn't mean to be rude."

"It's Detective and you were rude."

He had a ruddy face, bad complexion and unusually thin lips. He smiled. "I'm sorry, Detective. I am Howard Roth. How can I help you this fine day?"

I placed the copy of the delivery receipt for the package that had been sent to the Hobbs' in front of him. "This package was sent by your business to this address on Prairie."

"I can see that. What do you want to know?"

"Did you handle this transaction?"

"Yes. The HW on the bottom of the form indicates that I handled this."

"What can you remember about the person who came in to arrange for the delivery?"

"That's too easy, Detective." He smiled broadly. "This woman comes in early this morning, maybe eight-fifteen. Good looking woman, light brown hair, big bosom, you know the type. The dress she had on fit her very well. You know, not a lot to the imagination. Anyway, the box was all taped and wrapped with an address on it, no name. All we had to do was deliver it."

"Didn't you record the name?"

"No need to. She paid for the delivery in cash. She said she was one hundred percent certain someone would be at the home where the package was going. She had utmost confidence we could make the delivery."

"So, a good looking woman with large breasts and no name."

He laughed. "You got it. She also had some sort of Eastern European accent."

"You an expert on these things?"

"No, but my grandfather and grandmother emigrated from Eastern Europe. Her English sounded a lot like theirs."

I nodded. "Not bad, Mr. Roth. Anything else you can tell me?"

"Yeah. The oddest thing about this woman, the thing that stands out the most, she was very nervous during our whole discussion."

I thanked Roth and stepped back out onto Clark into a now sunny day. I put my hand up to block the sun's glare and noticed a two story, block building across the street. The lettering that was on top of the building read Hobbs Elevator Company.

• • •

The reception area for the Hobbs Elevator Company was very nice, decorated with tasteful furnishings and artwork. The carpet that I stood on looked new and I felt bad that my shoes were dripping dirty slush onto it. The young woman who was behind the desk was also very pleasant and not an insult to the eyes. She saw my badge, heard my name, and told me she would go tell Mr. Hobbs that I was in the lobby and wanted to see him. When she left me she had appeared cheerful. When she returned I could see that her demeanor had been tampered.

"I am sorry, Detective Moses, but I did not realize that Mr. Hobbs was tied up in a meeting and is unavailable to see you at this time. Maybe if you leave a number where he could reach you." As she relayed this message, I thought she might cry. Her lower lip quivered.

I smiled. "Perhaps you can relay a different message."

Now she looked like she might faint. "What would that be, sir?"

"Please go back there and tell Mr. Hobbs that the police are here and that they would like to question him right now. Tell him if he says no again, I will come back there myself."

Fear was the only look on her face. I didn't know if she was afraid of me or her boss or both. "I don't know if I can do that."

"That's okay," I said. "I will find him."

I pushed through a half door that they had separating the lobby from the remainder of the offices. Soon I was in a walled off section where I saw a number of serious looking men going over blueprints and plans. No one seemed to mind that I was there. Further into this section, I spotted some private offices and, being the good detective that I am, I looked for the one that was the biggest. In that one I found Everett Hobbs staring intently at some plans spread out on a table in his office. He was dressed in a nice suit sans the jacket. Whatever meeting he was in was apparently over because he was undoubtedly alone.

"Mr. Hobbs," I said, stepping into the office.

"Yes," he said, looking up and realizing it was me. "You! How did you get past the reception area?"

"Don't blame the poor woman, Hobbs. She told me you were busy and couldn't see me. I just had to see for myself."

"Detective Moses, this is highly unreasonable and I am extremely busy."

I slammed his door behind me and approached him. My hands flew to his vest and I grabbed his suit tightly and pulled him close to me. "Listen to me you pompous son of a bitch. Your daughters are involved in a serious situation at the present and your poor wife is going through hell as we speak. Are you aware that the kidnappers have contacted your family?"

"I don't know," he said. His face was flushing red.

"You don't know because you are not paying attention. These are your children whether you wanted them or not. Your family is in a crisis and you should be there." I shoved him, but he caught his balance before he fell. I knew I was in trouble.

"Your behavior, sir," he stammered. "I am close friends with Mayor Dunne."

I took another step closer to him. He backed away. "I don't give a shit," I said. "Tell the fucking mayor I said that. You make me sick."

Somehow I had accomplished nothing, but getting myself into a lot of trouble, but I felt better. I left the Hobbs' building and found myself at a tavern on the opposite side of the street. I called the precinct, but there was no news and Sam was out. I had one whiskey and then I had another. Soon it was four or five. I watched Hobbs' office. No one ever exited the building. I was about to leave when a fine carriage pulled up in front of the building, a private livery. I expected Hobbs to leave the building and enter this cab. Instead the driver got down and opened the door on his side. A young lady stepped down; she wore a dark blue coat and hat. She stopped for a moment and looked up the street in my direction. My view was clear. It was Sarah Balowski, the Hobbs' house nurse.

· · ·

I can't explain how I acted over the next couple of hours. Something came over me and I became transfixed with the entry of Sarah Balowski to Hobbs' office. What was the attractive house nurse doing there? Perhaps it had something to do with her duties, but heavy doubt was weighing on my mind. There was also something about her that bothered me. I think it was her detached attitude. On top of that she was of Eastern European descent. My head began to spin with theories, some reeking of conspiracy. Could she be involved in the kidnappings? Was Hobbs, the twin's reluctant father, connected to the case in a more evil fashion?

I had to shake myself from these thoughts and I did so by stepping outside into the cold air. I knew I was in trouble for the altercation with Hobbs and now for not returning to the precinct, but I felt I could deal with all of that. I felt something bad was happening across the street. I began to feel tense and had to take several deep breaths to calm myself. I returned to the warmth of the bar and felt lightheaded. I never took my eyes off the entrance to the office building across the street. An hour passed and then another half hour. I saw the nice coach return and then I saw the front door to the office open. Sarah Balowski came out of the building and was quickly helped up into the cab. Soon the carriage was off in a direction away from me. It was dark. The day was over. My temples were tight with pain. I was drunk. I was also confused and disillusioned.

I wanted to be far away from the Levee. If I could get on a train or a boat and disappear I would have, but that wasn't about to happen. I soon found myself in the lower level of Soon Lee's and the pipe was at my mouth. I remember momentarily that I felt like I was floating. That was my last thought as the opium hit my system and then I rested.

I recalled awakening in a hurry, too quickly, and wanting to be home. I was ashamed at how I acted. I knew to some extent I was unraveling. I had an intense headache and I couldn't tell how much of it was due to the whiskey I had drunk. I made it home to my chilly apartment, removed my clothes, and climbed under the covers. My entire head throbbed and I was shivering. I needed sleep.

What I got was a tormented dream. In it I was spinning, like on a carousel, but not very fast. As I rotated I saw every dead person I had come in contact with in the past month. They were all there. I saw Marshall Field, Jr, Mary Hastings, Mike and Molly Hart. These people all appeared sad and said nothing. Louie Pagano was there and he was yelling at me, but I couldn't hear him. Next was my father and he only mouthed one word, "Why?" Then I saw Horace Langley with a massive hole in his forehead next to Simon Kluge with the hangmen's noose around his neck. These two were very angry, swearing and pointing fingers at me. Next was only the head of Bad Joanie. She wanted to know where the rest of her body was.

In the dream, my body became saturated by sweat. I felt like I had a fever. Next I saw Father Luigi. He said nothing, but had the most questioning look on his face I had ever seen. Eleanor was next, looking as she had before she was murdered. She clutched the heart shaped locket I had given her. She was crying. I wanted to stop spinning, but couldn't. I tried to say something to Eleanor, but no words came out. Then I stopped spinning. I was able to walk forward. There was someone in the distance, a small person, walking funny. I got closer. Everyone else in the dream had been dead. This person was alive. I got closer. The small figure was Dancing Walter.

I awoke with a start and sat up in my bed. I was covered with sweat. I got up and got a drink of water. My head was better, but only physically. What had the dream meant? I checked my watch. One-fifteen. There was a lot left to this night. I wondered how, and if, I was going to get through it

Nine

"Tough night?" Sam was standing by my desk looking down at me. I hadn't slept much, hadn't eaten and only had a cup of coffee. My head felt strange, leaning towards dizziness. My stomach rumbled, not from hunger, but from bouts of near nausea.

"It wasn't great," I said. "Yourself?"

"This prostitute killer seems to like to taunt the detectives on this case. First he sends you some trinkets, then he kills your girlfriend, leaves a poem for you and now he has written a poem for me and stolen my hat."

I wasn't ready or prepared for this type of dialogue. "Where are you going with this, Sam? He likes to have a little fun with us. He's a sick bastard. What surprises you?"

"That's just it, Patrick. It doesn't surprise me that someone so deranged could poke fun at us. What does get me is that he seems to know a lot about us. What really bugs me is how he got his hand on my hat."

Now he had my attention. "What do you think this all means?"

He cautiously looked about the floor, looking for interlopers. "I think he knows us. I think he might be here."

"Suggestions were that he was a lawyer."

"And now you believe everything you hear?"

•　•　•

It wasn't long after this short discussion, one that left me with more daunting questions, that I was called into Captain Morgan's office. He wore a scowl on his face, one that normally wasn't happy anyway. He told me to close the door and have a seat. I sat in a hard backed wooden chair and noticed its legs were uneven and it leaned to my left.

"I received a couple of disturbing phone calls this morning, Patrick. One from Chief Collins' office; the other from the mayor's office. It seems Mr. Hobbs has filed a complaint against you." He stopped and looked up at me.

"A complaint?" I said. I thought there was a chance I might vomit right there.

"It says you visited his place of business without invitation or reason, barged into his office, questioned his concerns about his daughter's kidnappings and then grabbed him and shoved him. True or not true?"

I thought on how to respond. "I would say mostly true."

He nodded and then stood to stretch his poor back. He was a very tall man, a bit stooped due to his pain. "I told them that our detectives had been under a lot of stress due to case load and also the large amount of serious crimes. I told them our work was unnerving. They seemed to hear this and understand this, but they, especially the Chief, advised that nothing like this had better happen again. I'm sure they have taken your past record into consideration when making this decision."

I nodded, still not feeling well. "I appreciate that."

"You will call Mr. Hobbs' office and make an appointment to go in and apologize personally. There will be no other punishment, but this must be taken care of very soon."

I wanted to tell Morgan what I had seen with Sarah Balowski and what I'd heard from Roth about a woman with Eastern European ties, but I held off. I would run that by Sam first.

"Are you okay, Patrick?" Morgan said. He wore the look of a concerned father.

"I am fine, sir. Perhaps a little tired."

"Get more rest," he said, "and stay away from Soon Lee's. Krause will be back shortly, but until then I need everyone rested and ready to go."

How he knew about my visits to the opium den, I didn't know. What concerned me more was seeing Gunter the first time since I'd had relations with his wife. That thought chilled me.

"You are good to go, Patrick."

I did indeed want to vomit. "Thank you, sir."

•   •   •

I went immediately to the lavatory where I was sick to my stomach. All of the good whiskey I had taken in the night before disappeared into the bowl. My ribs ached and my brow was covered with sweat when I was done. I don't know if I felt better, but I was alive. I proceeded back to my desk, perhaps a bit humbler than when I had started at Morgan's office.

"You look like dog shit," Sam said, handing me a small flask that he had removed from his inside pocket.

I took a swig of the whiskey which was more medicinal than anything. I instantly felt the Irish glow come over me. I felt righted. "Thanks," I said handing the small bottle back to Sam.

"You need to take better care of yourself."

I waved at him in acknowledgement of his advice.

"You should come for dinner," he said. "My wife would like to meet you."

I don't know how long I stared at him, but I did for a bit. A not too distant memory brought back the feeling of Margaret grabbing my leg under the table at the dinner before Christmas. That encounter had led to bad things and had not ended well. "We'll see," I said.

"Word is that you punched our friend, Mr. Hobbs, in the face."

"Untrue. I merely gave the bastard a light shove."

"You don't care for him?"

"Do you?"

"He's an odd sort, probably extremely smart in scientific matters, but lacking in normal things, such as dealing with human life and its many pitfalls."

"Yes," I said, wishing for another drink of the whiskey, but not asking for one. "Let me ask you, Sam, do you think Hobbs could somehow be involved in the kidnapping?"

The look he got on his face said I had approached being ludicrous. "You can't be serious?"

"I'm not sure, but I may be. When I saw this man, Roth, who owns the currier service the kidnappers used, he told me that the woman who dropped off the package had light colored hair and spoke with an Eastern European accent. If you will recall, the Hobbs employ a day nurse, Sarah Balowski who also has an Eastern European accent."

"Like many other immigrants in this city."

"True, but not many of these immigrants visit their employer's office late in the day and stay there for almost two hours. She is, if I forgot to say, an attractive young lady."

Sam shrugged. "Maybe she performs some functions for Mr. Hobbs."

I smiled. "What functions?"

He knew where I was going. "You know what I mean."

"Then we have Miss Stone telling us about Hobbs' despair when he learned he was going to be a father, his inability to understand the commitment. Maybe he wants to be away from Susan, away from the two girls."

"Why not just divorce her? He has the funds to pay her off and still live quite handsomely."

"True, but I was thinking that if the girls were gone permanently Mrs. Hobbs looked as if she might go insane. I have not seen her when she is not a complete mess. Not getting them back would push her over the edge, maybe to an asylum, away from Hobbs. Enter Miss Balowski."

"You, Patrick, seem closer to that edge, now that I hear that."

"We should look further into Miss Balowski."

Sam was going to say something, but we were interrupted when Harold Pinter approached the two of us. He was holding the blood soiled pajamas.

"You are supposed to be testing those, Harold, not walking around the precinct with them," I said.

"Please, Detective Moses. My good friends and I were intrigued by the task and stayed up all night to complete the testing."

Nothing was said for a moment as Sam and I awaited the results, if any. "Well?" I said.

"Pig's blood," Harold said. "Your kidnappers, so far, are trying to trick you into believing the girls have been hurt. I would venture to say the two girls are probably fine."

Sam looked at me. "We'd better get over to the Hobbs' house."

"Yes," I said. "I need to apologize to Mr. Hobbs anyway."

"Maybe we can peek up Miss Balowski's dress to make sure she's not a spy disguised as a woman."

"Maybe I will," I said, rising from my desk, feeling much better.

• • •

We called Thomas Mallory, the Hobbs' family lawyer, and told him we wanted to speak to the entire family as soon as was possible. He called back shortly to advise us that the family, including Mr. Hobbs, were all present at the Prairie Avenue residence. Sam and I caught the first coach we could and headed in the direction of the house. Sam said our mission was to tell them the news about the pajamas, and since we had no other strong leads, to tell them to get to us as soon as they heard further from the kidnappers. Sam said he knew this was going to happen since the blood on the pajamas was a ruse.

I didn't disagree with him, but I wanted to talk with Alicia Stone privately. I would keep my thoughts to myself about Everett Hobbs being potentially involved in the kidnappings, but I wanted to ask her if she heard or knew anything about any possible relationship between Hobbs and Sarah Balowski. It couldn't hurt to ask.

It occurred to me as the coach sloshed through weather plagued streets, that I'd made two promises to myself that morning before leaving my apartment. I had taken two hundred dollars of the Field fee money and had promised to stop by the Pelicanos' house and give it to Sylvia Pelicanos. It was a lot of money, but it would help them out for some time.

Secondly, I vowed to get into see Judge Kirk to ask him about the case and try and convince him that they had the wrong person locked up for a crime he hadn't committed. How I was going to achieve this with a judge, one known for his toughness, was beyond me, but I had to start somewhere. As stupid, and perhaps as sick as Pelicanos was, I had to do something for that family. Seeing him swing from the gallows would probably destroy four lives, not just one.

• • •

The Hobbs' ensemble was once again gathered in the small library and they had all taken their familiar sitting or standing spots. There was no noise coming from the room as we were led into it by the black maid. As they say, you could hear a pin drop. The looks on their faces told of their apprehension and fear. This ordeal was tearing at them mentally and physically. I noticed that Everett Hobbs was present. At first he wore his same look of disinterest, but when he saw me it turned to disdain. I guess he figured, after he had reported me, that I would be drawn and quartered or at least whipped. That I was still on the case probably shocked him.

"You have discovered something about the pajamas?" It was

the lawyer, Thomas Mallory, who broke the silence in the room.

Suddenly all of the eyes were locked on Sam and me. I noticed that Alicia Stone had tears glistening in her eyes; she clearly expected the worst of news.

"The good news," Sam said slowly, "is that the blood on the pajamas is from a pig, not a human."

There was a collective sigh of relief from the group. Mrs. Hobbs then broke down to tears, overcome with knowledge that the blood had been a lark. Miss Stone dabbed her tears away. Everett Hobbs tense face appeared the same.

"The bad news, Detective?" Mallory said.

"I wouldn't necessarily call it bad news," Sam said. "More like no news. We have continued to have junior grade detectives and beat patrolmen in the neighborhood asking questions. There have been no leads. No one seems to know what happened to the girls. It's almost as if they…"

"Vanished," Everett Hobbs finished the sentence for Sam. "Millicent and Holly have vanished and we are not going to get them back."

This bold statement brought forth another stream of sobs from Susan Hobbs and Alicia knelt by her to offer comfort.

"How can you be so confident, Mr. Hobbs?" I said firmly. "Do you know something we do not?" My earlier thoughts of an apology were now replaced by wanting to choke the man.

"Because Detective Moses. It is my thought that the girls will never be found. It is also my thought that the police department doesn't have the capabilities of finding them. This coupled with the detectives in the case being inept has led me to this conclusion."

Sam and I both stood silently for a moment. I knew if I reacted harshly to Hobbs' comments I was asking for a suspension. I bit my tongue so hard I tasted blood.

"What do you propose?" Mallory said, again saving the day.

"At this point," Sam said, "we must wait to hear from the kidnappers. They will make contact again. This time, if we want to get the girls back, we must cooperate with them or else, as Mr. Hobbs said, we may not get them back."

Mallory nodded. I seethed. The rest of the group looked exhausted.

"We will cooperate the next time," Susan Hobbs said weakly. "We will stop this game playing and do what we need to do to get Holly and Millie back. I want my daughters back." She started to sob again and was actually comforted by her husband.

• • •

I told Sam I had two stops to make before returning to the precinct. He reminded me we needed to update Morgan about what Von Bever had said. We also needed to look up Andre Dubois, the pimp that Von Bever had mentioned. I agreed and Sam left me to take the next carriage that came along. I was waiting on the porch for a second cab to take me on my rounds when Alicia Stone came out on the porch. She had put on a hat and coat and gloves. Regardless of all the bad weather wear, she was very pretty.

She eyed me for a bit and I said nothing. She had obviously come onto the porch to speak to me. "I heard about your altercation with my brother," she said finally.

"It was more of a dispute, an argument. Again, we disagreed on aspects of the case."

"His personality leads to more arguments than not. Under

all of the gruff and seriousness is a good person."

"But you told me his aloofness towards the kidnappings came from his belief that his wife was barren, that there would be no kids."

"That is probably true."

"He didn't want children and when they came along it may have derailed his thinking altogether?"

She thought for a moment, the cold air coloring her cheeks. "I would say that is true. I don't think he wanted children and I do believe that when they came along he felt they were a bit of a nuisance."

"Do you also think that they have caused his wife to spend more time with the girls, taking time away from that spent with Everett?"

Again, she considered this. "I am sure that is natural and for someone, like Everett, who didn't want children, this effect would cause some problems."

I decided now was a good a time as ever to switch topics. "Tell me what you know about Miss Balowski, the day nurse."

Her eyes narrowed. "What about her?"

"Nothing particular. Background, where she came from, that sort of thing."

"From what I recall her family emigrated from Poland some years back when she was a little girl. They had lived in Milwaukee, but moved to Chicago several years ago. She is an excellent nurse and helps Susan, Mrs. Hobbs, with the two girls immensely. She is a very reliable employee."

"Does she perform any duties for your brother?"

"Where are you going with this, Detective?"

"Just a curiosity. As we said, everyone is a suspect until the crime is solved."

"She shouldn't be," she said sharply, "but to answer your questions, her only employment functions are helping with the girls."

"She does live here at the house?"

"Yes. She is on call for six days. She has one full day off a week."

"What day would that be?"

"She was just off yesterday."

Yesterday, the day I had seen her enter Hobbs' office. "Would you say that your brother's relationship with his wife has gotten better, worse or stayed the same since the girls were born?"

She smiled. "Now I see where you are headed with this and frankly I am ashamed that you would even consider such a thing. I can only see now that you are overexposed to all of that rubbish that the Levee provides and you feel everyone is susceptible to weakness. I have most recently begun to campaign with Mr. Ernest Bell and his reformers. I think there are many out there that need to make a change. I strongly think that you might want to consider attending a meeting. Perhaps you are in need of a change." With that she spun quickly on her heels and returned to the warmth of the house. I was left alone with my thoughts awaiting a carriage. One of those thoughts was listening to what Ernest Bell had to say. Maybe I could be reformed. Maybe I needed it.

• • •

I found Sylvia Pelicanos and her two children where I had first encountered them, trying to build a snowman in their small front yard. The wind and cold had abated a bit and there was a bit of warmth in the air. There's something about the wind in Chicago. It makes everything feel ten to twenty degrees colder. With no wind the air was pleasant and the slight break in the chill caused the snow to become easy to mold. The mother and two children were well on their way to erecting a good looking snowman when I stepped from the carriage in front of their house.

When Sylvia saw me emerge from the cab she immediately left the two kids and came over to me. I could tell from the look on her face that she was worried. Maybe she thought I was bringing bad news. I saw that the coloring around the once blackened eye had returned to near normal.

"Detective Moses," she said slowly, "do you have any news about Frank?"

Then I felt bad. I should have gone to see the prisoner before coming to see his wife. Maybe there would have been a message, any message, to pass onto her or his children. "I don't really have any news," I said.

Her face scrunched up as if she wasn't sure what to say. She looked pained. "You know nothing of his case?"

"Well," I said slowly, "I do know that he has pleaded guilty and that he is due for sentencing very shortly."

She stood up straight and was about to address me when her son yelled to her to look. He had found an old branch that had three or four twigs sticking out from it, like fingers. He had stuck it on one side of the snowman and now it had one arm. "That's very good," she said. "Stephanie, help Timothy look around for another stick to use for an arm."

"Look, Sylvia," I said, "this is not a good situation that Frank has put himself in. Pleading guilty to a capital crime could lead to harsh punishment. We have to find an alibi that shows that

Frank could not have committed this murder."

She looked around for a bit, at her kids, her small house and up and down the street. She seemed to be thinking that it could all fall apart very shortly. "Will they hang him?"

I took a deep breath. "Frank has admitted to murder. The punishment in this case is death. I'm afraid that's what's going to happen if we don't find something that tells us he didn't do it. Can you tell me anything about Christmas and Frank's whereabouts?"

"I told you," she said quickly. "He wasn't home."

"No idea where he was?"

She laughed. "Frank is his own man," she said. "Asking him a lot of questions is not such a smart thing to do."

I nodded. I reached into my pocket for the two hundred dollars, four fifty dollar bills and handed it to her. She pocketed it without looking at how much it was.

"This will help you for a bit," I said. "Keep thinking. Maybe ask some of Frank's friends. Where or who he was with that afternoon that can confirm he couldn't have killed Jacob Fine."

A tear appeared in her right eye and ran down onto her cheek. "I will check. Please give me a day or so. In the meantime, if you see Frank, would you please tell him that we love him and we want him to come home? Maybe if he hears that he will just tell the judge the truth and will not get into any trouble."

I reached out and touched her arm, but she turned and went quickly back to her children. Little Stephanie looked at me and gave a short wave. I turned and got back into the waiting carriage.

. . .

My arrival at Judge Kirk's chambers in the Cook County Courthouse coincided with the end of the lunch break. I was told by the judge's secretary, a short, severe looking woman, that the judge was completing his lunch and normally did not like to be interrupted. She said the judge considered this his quiet time, the period that he could reflect and think about the cases before him.

"It is an absolute emergency that I see him," I said.

She looked bored. I was sure that everyone who came to see the judge claimed some sort of emergency. "Your name again, Detective."

"Moses, Patrick Moses."

She pointed a short, stubby finger in my direction. "Don't come and see me soon with another problem." She got up from her desk and disappeared behind the door that led to the chambers.

It wasn't long, not more than a couple of minutes, before she returned. She wore a thin smile. "Judge Kirk will see you now, but he is very busy, so please keep your visit short and concise."

I thanked the woman, never getting her name, and walked into the judge's office. Judge Henry Kirk was almost as short as his secretary, but this wasn't his most noticeable feature. The judge had to weigh close to three hundred pounds. As fat as he was in his body, his girth showed on his face with enormous jowls and a flappy throat. He was wearing a gray vest over his shirt and this was covered with stains from some of his last meals. He gave me a warm smile. "Ah, Detective Moses. I don't believe I've had the pleasure." He didn't stand, but he extended his small hand which I shook. "Mrs. Avery tells me you have a situation that is an emergency."

"I do, your honor," I said. "This is about a man named Frank Pelicanos who appeared in your courtroom earlier this week and pled guilty to murdering my father, Jacob Fine."

"Yes," Judge Kirk said. "A terrible incident and on Christmas day. How is your family handling it?"

Since I was my family, I had to be careful how I selected my words. Telling the judge that I was happy about the murder didn't seem to be the thing to do. "We're handling it as well as can be expected."

"That's good to hear. Now, what is it about this man Pelicanos?"

"First of all, I believe Pelicanos to be a sick man, perhaps suffering from the effects of syphilis. Secondly, I do not believe Pelicanos was the one who killed my father."

This comment seemed to cause Kirk to begin coughing, a hard dry cough. When he was done his eyes were watering and his face was bright red. I hoped he wouldn't have a heart attack. "You don't think Pelicanos killed your father?"

"I don't believe so, sir."

"But the man admitted it to me in open court."

"I understand that, your honor, but as I said, the man is sick. I also have a witness," I lied, "who can verify that Mr. Pelicanos was with them at the time of the murder."

The judge stared at me for a moment. "You seem very sure of this, Detective Moses. The man did admit to killing *your* father."

"I am sure of it," I said. I knew I was way out there on a limb.

The judge leaned back in his chair and I hoped his bulk

wouldn't collapse it. "The sentencing is in a few days. You have to accomplish two things before then. I want to hear from this witness and, I want a doctor to examine Pelicanos and find out if he has the affliction that you say he does."

Why, I'm not quite sure, I felt relief. "I will do just that, your honor."

"Understand one thing, Detective." His look now was very serious. "I have a man who has admitted to committing a capital crime. If you can't prove he didn't do it or that he is not sick, I am likely to sentence him to die by hanging."

. . .

It wasn't until later in the day that we were able to get in to see Captain Morgan. When we did he didn't seem as indifferent as he normally appeared. In fact, he appeared agitated. "Fill me in on the Hobbs first," he said bluntly.

"Well," Sam said, "with the aid of Harold Pinter we were able to determine that the blood on the pajamas delivered to the house was from a pig."

Morgan laughed. "Meaning what?"

"Probably that the girls are unharmed and the kidnappers are contemplating their next move. That's about all we have out of it."

"Nothing? No clues?"

"The package that was sent to the Hobbs was left at the curriers by a woman with an Eastern European accent," I said.

"And?" Morgan said.

"That's all we have," I said. "Those two girls seemed to have disappeared. No one in the area of the house reported seeing or hearing anything."

"That seems improbable," Morgan said to no one in particular.

"It does," Sam said, "but not untrue. We are waiting to hear from the kidnappers with further instructions."

I didn't mention what we had learned about the high concentration of hops and barley on the piece of cloth found at the scene or my theory about Sarah Balowski and Everett Hobbs. Neither bit of information seemed to fit the probable range Morgan was looking for.

"How about Christian Hanson?" Morgan asked.

"No sightings," I said, "and we have every cop in the city looking for the guy. We also know a brothel that he likes to frequent. They will call us if he shows up there."

Morgan nodded. "A whole lot of nothing, again. How about these prostitute murders?"

"Maurice Von Bever came in and identified the last victim. Her name was Pearl Radd," I said. "He also gave us a lead on a pimp named Andre' Du Bois. It appears this pimp came to Von Bever looking for dates for some of his clients. Von Bever provided the girls in a lot of cases as he had with Pearl Radd. The guy we are looking for uses the name of Leonard Fillmore. Von Bever thinks Du Bois has seen the killer. We were trying to reach Du Bois before we had to leave for the Hobbs', but couldn't. That's our next call."

Morgan reacted to this positive news impassively. "Anything else?"

Sam spoke up. "I am of the opinion that this killer has some knowledge of or may be a policeman."

"That's ridiculous," Morgan said. "Why would you think something like that?"

"First we had the killer leaving little gifts on Patrick's doorstep. Next we have these little poems that go and taunt us. Lastly, the hat that was left on Pearl Radd's head. The hat belonged to me. The only place I can think of that the hat might have been stolen from was the precinct house."

"But why a cop?" Morgan asked. "Why not someone who is in the precinct a lot? Why not a janitor or a reporter from the *Tribune*? Why would it have to be a cop?"

"I see your point," Sam said. "It was just an idea."

Morgan rose suddenly and this seemed to irritate his bad back. He reached back with his hand and massaged a spot on the small of his back. His face showed pain. Finally he was able to straighten. "Well, progress in one of three cases isn't bad," he said. "Do your best to keep me posted."

With that he left the conference room and had both Sam and I scratching our heads. Morgan had gone from irritated to not seeming interested in a short minute. Maybe the backlog of cases and pressure were beginning to get to him.

• • •

When I returned to my desk there was a large man standing near it with his back to me. From his height and his girth, I didn't need to see his face to know it was my partner, Gunter Krause. As I got closer he quickly spun and saw me coming. His face broke into a wide grin, showing the chipped tooth from his battle in the alley. Other than that, he looked pretty good.

"They will let anyone walk around in here these days," I said.

Gunter took a big step forward and grabbed me in a bear

hug. If I didn't know better, I would have thought he was trying to crush me. "Let me go you big ape," I complained.

He let me go and stared intently at me. "You look good," he said.

"Thanks, Gunter. Why wouldn't I look good?"

"I thought that something might be bothering you since the last time you paid me a visit was on New Year's Eve. I thought you might be injured or not well."

I shook my head. "Gunter, it's not that," I said. "We've had two new prostitute murders and a kidnapping since I saw you. On top of that, we can't find this Christian Hanson fellow who is behind a rash of murders and your beating."

"Colosimo's thug?"

"We think it's the same guy."

"I understand," he said. "That seems like a decent excuse for not visiting. There are some people who have no excuse." His face reddened at that last remark.

"You okay?" I asked.

He waved at me. "Physically, not too bad, but a bit sore. Not supposed to do too much to aggravate anything. That's why I'll be on light duty for a bit."

"How about mentally?" I asked cautiously.

"That's a different story. I feel very stupid that I let myself get ambushed and beat up in that alley. I think the only way I can regain any confidence as an officer is to find the people that did this to me and bring them in."

I understood this and nodded lightly. This was not what was bothering Gunter. "What else."

He looked around to see who was listening, but the detective area was mostly empty. "It is Margaret. Things between us have not been so great. A lot of arguing. She barely came to see me in the hospital after Christmas. I know we are splitting apart and I think she might be sneaking out on me." He stopped there and looked at me, but there were no tells that I could note.

"I think you're just having a bad row," I said. "You've been gone a couple of weeks. I think the two of you need to discuss things and try and work them out."

"I hear what you are saying, Patrick. I'm just not sure. Have you spoken to her?"

I felt my stomach leap at that. I doubted that Margaret would tell Gunter of the two visits she made to my apartment. I gambled. "I have not," I said.

He nodded. "Maybe you're right. Maybe we just need a little time."

I felt bad for Gunter. I knew his marriage was straining. I also knew he felt somewhat responsible for it. I also knew that he felt Margaret may have cheated on him. Did he have any inclination that it was with me? He got called into Morgan's office to review his temporary assignments and that question would have to wait until later to be resolved or not. I was hoping that the subject would die, but I didn't know.

• • •

It was later in the day and I was the last detective left in our little area of the building. Sam had left to be with his family, still a little nervous about the killer's threat. Gunter had waved to me as he left Morgan's office and headed down the stairs. When Morgan left, I neither heard nor saw him. He made no effort to say good night. I wasn't offended.

With the department quiet, I began to ponder our current

situation. It wasn't long after this that blurry, faded lines started to appear before my eyes. My temples tightened and suddenly I felt nauseous. I was glad no one was around. When the visions and the pain subsided, I made my way out of the precinct and found a cab and headed directly for Soon Lee's.

It took a bit of time in the Chinaman's lower level den and several drags off the long opium pipe, before I began to relax. The pain in the sides of my head was gone, my vision was clear, and I felt free. I could think unfettered thoughts. Even though my thoughts were free they weren't any less confusing.

I thought of Eleanor and how pretty she was and then my last view of her as she lay all cut up next to Bubbly Creek. The bastard that had done that had taken two more lives and was now mocking Sam and me. Was he connected to the police as Sam suggested? I had no idea who he was, but he seemed to want to get closer to us, to get inside of our heads.

Our friend, Christian Hanson had simply disappeared. He was about, we knew that, but no one had seen him or heard from him in a while. A big, blonde haired, mute shouldn't be that hard to locate. This had been pure frustration, but he hadn't done much to draw our attention to him lately. He would pop up eventually and we would find him.

Like Hanson, the Hobbs' twins had also disappeared. It seemed impossible to me that you could actually kidnap one person, not two, and have it remain a secret, but this is exactly what had occurred. We got one clue from the currier regarding the lady with the Eastern European accent, but we needed more. Sam was right. The kidnappers would call again. I still had that vision of Sarah Balowski entering Hobbs' office. Something wasn't right there. As odd as Hobbs had been, would he be behind the kidnapping of his own daughters?

My last thoughts and the most nagging were of Sylvia Pelicanos and her two children playing in the snow. This is the one situation I could control the easiest. All I had to do was confess to killing my father. I wasn't going to do that, but I only had a few days to figure out how to get Frank Pelicanos to escape the hangman. This was the situation where I had the least amount of time. Would I really let him hang and have his family suffer for it? I wondered for a minute what kind of man I was. What would I do if he did hang? I never found that answer. I tried, but the opium overwhelmed me and I slept.

Ten

I had promised to meet Sam early at the precinct the next day for our visit to see Andres' Dubois, the pimp. I arrived earlier than normal, walking into the holding area where they kept the prisoners. The officer who was in charge of the lockup wanted to know if I needed to check my gun before going into see Pelicanos. I told him I had no intention of killing him.

"Probably should," said the young cop. "No one would blame you for shooting the man who killed your father."

I smiled at this comment, but it only made me feel worse. Frank Pelicanos was lying on his cot when I rattled the bars to his cell. There were no other current prisoners in the holding area. This part of the building was akin to a dungeon, cold and damp. Pelicanos' head came off the pillow and he looked hard at me.

"Moment of your time, Frank?" I said.

"I'm done talking about this," he said sharply. "I'm not sorry I killed your father. As I said, he had it coming. I'm not sorry one bit."

I took a second to think over this lie and sighed heavily.

"Why don't you really tell me what happened in that alley on Christmas day?"

Now he popped up off the cot and approached the bars. His eyes showed intense anger. "What do you mean what really happened, Detective Moses? I went to see your father. I was mad. We argued about my monthly fee and why he wouldn't let me in the dance hall any longer. He wouldn't budge and then he threatened me again. That was when I shot him outside the back entrance to the building."

"What kind of threat did he make?"

The anger on his face softened. I could see the lines on his face appeared deeper. He hadn't been sleeping. His long gray hair was gnarled, unwashed. "I don't remember. He made some stupid threat and I drew my gun and shot him."

"And that was it?"

"Well, yeah, that was it. I saw him hit the pavement back there and I got the hell out of there."

"I see, but you took time to toss the gun."

"There were a lot of garbage cans in that alley. I threw it in one, under some rubbish. It happened so fast I couldn't tell the cops who arrested me, or you, which one."

"I saw your family," I said suddenly. "I went by your house to see how they were making out. Sylvia had little Timothy and Stephanie out in the front yard making a snowman."

Now he looked concerned. "Are they all okay?"

"What do you mean are they okay? Sylvia misses her husband and is worried about how she'll take care of her family if he is gone. Stephanie asked me when you were going to be able to come home. Have you thought about any of this?"

"I did what I had to do," he said.

"You need to rethink this, Frank. You didn't kill my father.

You might have shown up after he was murdered and seen him lying back there, but you didn't kill him. You really need to revisit your story. If you stick to it, Judge Kirk is going to have you hanged. Those hangmen don't make many mistakes. You'll get no second chance. If you hang, think about what happens to Sylvia, Stephanie and Timothy."

"Revisit my story," he mumbled.

"You didn't kill him, Frank, and I'm going to prove it, but if I can't just tell the truth and save yourself. I can talk to people about your fee. We can get you into a doctor for help. Will you please just think about it?"

He got a very defiant look on his face. "There's absolutely nothing to think about."

I shook my head slowly. If I did nothing, I was looking at the face of a dead man. This was not going to be easy.

• • •

A bit later, in a cheap apartment on Twenty- Third Street, I was looking into the eyes of a real dead man. He was on his bed in his sleep clothes, lying on his side. His face had been covered by a white pillow with a powder burned hole in it. We had removed it and had discovered Andres' Dubois, eyes staring ahead, with a nice neat hole behind his left ear. On the other side of his head, the hole was much greater and a good deal of his brain matter and blood had stained the bed. We had tried to reach Dubois by phone, but couldn't so we took a carriage to this apartment. When he failed to open his door, his landlord, a Mrs. Connelly, let us in. The first thing to hit us as we entered the unit was the pungent odor of death. Then we found him.

"Now do you believe me when I tell you I think it's someone connected to the police department?" Sam said. We were in the main room now and Sam was puffing on a cigarette. He looked nervous.

"But not necessarily a policeman?" I asked.

"Maybe Morgan is right. Maybe it's just someone who is around the department. Someone who hears things."

I thought of all the people that frequented the detective area during a normal day. The number was rather large. "It could be that the killer knew that we were getting closer. He knew Dubois had seen him so he figured he'd better take him out of the picture."

"That makes some sense if he thought Dubois could identify him, but there's still the poems to us and the bastard stole my hat and stuck it on Pearl Radd's head."

"That he did, so it had to be someone who could get real close to us." I tried to think of all the detectives and cops on the second floor. Then there were the newspaper reporters and the coffee and sandwich boys. The janitors who cleaned the building and kept it running. The number was large. "Don't remember where you left the hat?"

"Usually on top of my coat that I normally drape over the spare chair next to my desk. Went to put it on at the end of the day and it was gone. That was the first time I noticed it missing."

"It might be a cop," but that thought bothered me. Simon Kluge, a doctor, had been a sadist. Did this mean that one that we worked with was also so twisted? It caused my stomach to burn.

When Harold Pinter came out of Dubois' bedroom, he came right over to where Sam and I were standing. "I'm not sure I should get so close to you two."

"Why is that?" I said.

"It seems most people that you talk to end up dead."

A groan came from Sam; I saw Harold smile and I did the same. "What can you tell us?"

"He's been in there a couple of days. I can tell by the amount of rigor mortis present. I'd say two at the least. Surprised it doesn't smell more."

"So somebody shot him not long after Pearl Radd was killed?" I said.

"Somebody who thought we might be able to figure out who he was if we were able to talk with Dubois," Sam said.

"Somebody who has access to the workings of the precinct."

• • •

As much as I wanted to think that the theory of the prostitute murderer being someone from the precinct was absurd, some of the things we were seeing started to make me think it was true. We now had a dead pimp, Andres' Dubois, who had connections to several of the victims. The discovery of his murder came soon after Maurice Von Bever had given us his name. Coincidence or was the killer doing a very good job of cleaning up his recent tracks? I was pondering all of this when we arrived back at the precinct to get our latest bit of news. Riley O'Donnell was standing near the entrance, looking about as distraught as someone could. I was afraid to ask him what was up.

"It's Loftus," he said. "They've got him locked up downstairs."

I didn't know George Loftus all that well. He was a fortyish bachelor, good looking, who wore his hair combed straight back. He was a reasonably quiet guy, who liked a drink and was a good detective. He had helped me out quite a bit with the Marshall Field case. What Riley told us as we went downstairs shocked me. Loftus had been arrested at the River of Bliss, a brothel on Wabash. Apparently he had gotten very drunk, had gone to the brothel, and hooked up with a woman named Maria Farrell. Some sort of argument had ensued, it got very loud, and then it got very quiet. The madam had opened the door to investigate the room the two were in. The room was completely torn apart, George Loftus was passed out on the floor, and Maria Farrell was in bad shape, slashed repeatedly by a big knife that was lying close to the body of Loftus.

"You talk to him?" I asked Riley.

"I did. He told me didn't remember anything."

George Loftus was lying on the cot in the cell, not too far from the space that Frank Pelicanos occupied. When he heard us outside the cell he sat up quickly and then stood. He walked over to where we were.

"You guys gotta get me out of here," he said.

"Talk to us first, George," I said. "Tell us what happened at the River of Bliss." This came from Sam. I was too stunned by what I was looking at.

George's hair which was normally neat and combed to perfection was standing up wildly. His face was sporting a nice knot under his right eye which had begun to show purple. There was a nice scratch on his left cheek. His suit coat was missing. The shirt he wore was ripped in a couple of spots and splattered with blood. Judge Kirk might have sentenced him on the spot.

"I don't know," he said quickly. "I was down at Mother Murphy's having a few drinks and I remember going up to The River. After that, it's kind of a blur."

"What do you mean kind of a blur?" I snapped.

George turned towards me. "Moses, listen to me, I know you're upset. I know you dated that girl Eleanor Winter who was killed, but I didn't do this."

Sam patted my arm. "George, do you remember what girl you went upstairs with?"

George's eyes squinted. He was reaching well into his brain for seemingly easy facts. "She had brown hair, real red lipstick. We were having drinks at Mother Murphy's. She told me she worked at The River."

"How about her name?" Sam pressed.

Loftus shook his head no.

"What about the fight?"

"I don't recall a fight. I barely remember going up those stairs to the upper level. About all I remember is those two cops waking me up and dragging me off the floor."

"What about the knife they found and the blood on your shirt?" I said.

He looked down at his shirt and returned a horrified look to us. "What the hell happened?"

"George, listen to me for a second," Riley said. "The madam said there was a terrific fight in the room and then everything settled down. When she went up to check this morning she found you on the floor, unconscious, and Maria Farrell lying on the bed."

Loftus again looked down at his bloody shirt. "What happened to her?"

"She's at Mercy," Riley said. "Somebody cut her up pretty

bad. They think it was you."

"Me!" Loftus screamed. "Riley, you know me. I wouldn't do anything like that. Come on guys. You've got to get me out of here."

George Loftus looked like a man pleading for his life. I'm sure all three of us seasoned detectives were wondering how he could have cut a girl up so badly and not remember it. It seemed implausible. We weren't given much of an opportunity to discuss it further. There was news regarding the Hobbs' kidnapping.

• • •

A woman by the name of Alice Stewart, a landlord of an apartment building on Twenty- Fourth Street, had called in to report some suspicious behavior in one of her units. It seems one of the other tenants reported that they heard at least one, if not two infants, crying in the apartment next to him. The tenant reported it to Ms. Stewart who investigated the next day, found no one home in the unit, but did find some things that she thought would interest the police. Sam and I were sent to find out what.

The building was a three story six-flat with two units on each floor. The landlord, Ms. Stewart, had one of the units on the first floor. The unit where the tenant had heard the infants crying was one of the two on the third floor. Alice Stewart was a plump, fiftyish looking woman, with gray hair and chipped finger nails. It looked like she had worked hard her whole life.

"I just want my tenants to respect all of the others in the building and follow the rules. In other words, I don't want any trouble," she said frankly with a slight Irish accent.

"Who is the tenant that reported the disturbance?" I asked.

"Mr. Frawley, a nice man, an accountant. He resides by himself in the other unit on the third floor."

"And who resides in the unit where the infants we heard crying?"

"Two brothers, Peter and Michael Kowalski. They have lived here for about a year and a half. They both work at the Schoenhofen Brewing Company over on Eighteenth."

"A brewery?" Sam said quickly.

"Yes, both of them. In the processing area."

"Let us see the unit," I said.

We climbed the stairs quickly, leaving Ms. Stewart a little behind us. When she caught up she produced a key and opened the door. The unit had one main room, two small bedrooms, a kitchen and a bathroom. The place was sparsely decorated, but appeared clean. There wasn't much to see, but Ms. Stewart told us what we really wanted to see was in the kitchen. There we found two bowls in the sink and a large package of baby cereal, the type you mix with milk. In one of the bedrooms we found two unused diapers.

"They were here," Sam said.

"Yes," I said. "These two Kowalski brothers," I said to Ms. Stewart, "tell me about them."

"Like I said, they both worked at the brewery. When I saw them they were polite, not overly friendly. They were both respectful."

"Describe them."

"Both big men, well over six feet tall and broad shouldered. They had dark brown hair. That's about all I can tell you."

"Ever see any visitors to the apartment?" Sam asked.

She smiled. "One female visitor a lot. She has light brown hair, heavy bosom, not very friendly."

"That's the woman the currier described," I said. "When did the neighbor hear all of this?"

"It was last night," she said. "He told me about it this morning. I went up to check and when no one answered I went into the unit. I found the baby cereal and the diapers. I knew the men had no children so I got suspicious. I remembered the elevator man who had his girls kidnapped. I called the police."

"When Mr. Frawley heard the crying what did he do?" I asked.

"At first he said he thought he was imagining it. Then he heard it again, the babies were crying a lot. He told me he went next door and knocked a few times. There was no answer. A few minutes later the crying stopped. He stopped by on his way to the Loop to report it to me this morning. I work nights so he had to wait to report the disturbance to me."

"He knows nothing about the Hobbs' case?"

"He told me he was unaware of any kidnapping."

I thought the whole city knew of the case. "What do you think, Sam?"

"Let's get over to Schoenhofen right away."

• • •

The Peter Schoenhofen Brewery occupied a number of buildings at Eighteenth and Canalport and for the longest time we had difficulty finding anyone who could assist us with the whereabouts of the Kowalski brothers. Alice Stewart had told us the brothers were employed in the processing division of the brewery. There were over ten buildings at the complex and all but one was used for processing. We were finally able to track down a young man, a Mr. Miester, who had a great deal to do with the record keeping regarding the brewery's employees. He found that the Kowalski brothers were employed in building number seven and that there supervisor was a man named Cowell.

Cowell was a man neither short nor tall. He had a massive stomach that pulled at the overalls he wore. He was unshaven for at least a few days and reeked of the cigar that was clamped between his teeth, and garlic. Never mind the prevailing smell of old beer that seemed to be entering our pores. It was one of those times where some smell seemed to take your mind away from what you were there for.

"Haven't seen them boys in about a week," Cowell said. The words came out, but the lips and cigar didn't seem to move.

"They haven't shown up for work?" Sam asked.

"Not at all. I sent a note to the office telling them I didn't think those boys were coming back. So far no replacements."

"Where do you think they went?" I asked.

Cowell put two hands in front of him, palms up. "Who knows? A couple of the fellas say they talked of going back to Poland."

"Do you know if they had any other relatives in the area?"

Cowell smiled. "That I know. Two sisters. One used to come by once in a while and bring them lunch. Good figured woman, nice lookin lady."

This had to be the same woman who had gone to the currier with the pig blood stained pajamas and had them sent to the Hobbs. We thanked Cowell for his time and started back to the precinct.

"What do you think?" Sam said.

"I think they looked at the kidnapping as a way to get some easy money and maybe return to the homeland."

"I agree. I think they quit their jobs, took the two girls and were looking for a payday."

"I also think when Frawley heard the two girls crying last night they got them quiet and then got out of that apartment. God knows where they went, but they can't go back there."

"Patrick, they're starting to panic a bit. Getting the money is not so easy and now someone heard the girls in their apartment."

"What's next?"

"Contact will come soon," Sam said. He lit a cigarette. "They want to get rid of those girls and get the cash before anyone else sees or hears them. It will be soon."

I agreed. Time was no longer on their side. They would make contact with the Hobbs very soon. As I considered this, I thought of Frank Pelicanos. His time was running short. Then the thought of George Loftus, locked in the basement cell for slashing a prostitute, took control. My temples tightened and I saw the flashing lights. I blinked to fight it and that helped. I needed to see a doctor. I was not feeling right at all.

• • •

It had been a long day. With the murder of the pimp, Andres' Dubois, and the findings at the Kowalski brother's apartment, two of our cases were picking up steam. In both it appeared that the crook we were after had noticed that they had been recognized. In return, each had done something hastily. The discovery of the crying babies had sent the kidnappers away from their residence. Further investigation gave us their place of employment and knowledge that they hadn't been in since the girls were taken. Now we had to find them. With Dubois' murder, it was becoming obvious that anyone who saw the prostitute killer would end up dead if he thought they had leaked any information about him. Again, we had to narrow this all down and find him.

I didn't know George Loftus very well; we had spoken a number of times, of course, but I knew little about the man. I did know, even though he had been arrested for slashing a prostitute, that he was not the killer. At least, I believed this. As Sam headed off for his home and family, I headed in the direction of Mother Murphy's.

Mother Murphy's was a nice bar on the far southern edge of the Levee within walking distance of the River of Bliss, the brothel where Loftus had allegedly cut up Maria Farrell. It wasn't that late, but there was a decent crowd in the small bar, mostly railroad types. I walked up to the bar and ordered a beer. When the barkeep, a gray haired, bookish man said it was on the house, I asked if he had worked the night before.

"I was here," he said. "My name's Fred Beckworth. I am one of the owners."

"How did you know I was a police officer?"

He laughed. "I've been in the tavern business over twenty years. I can pretty much tell all types of people by now."

"I would imagine you would see them all."

"Everyone likes to drink," he said.

"Do you know Maria Farrell?"

"Sure," he said. "Everybody knew Maria. She might be a prostitute, but she's a sweet gal. She comes in here quite a bit. I would never turn her out."

"You saw her last night?"

"Yeah. Her and that cop were sitting right over there." He pointed a long, bony finger at the far corner of the bar."

"How'd you know Loftus was a cop?"

He laughed. "Not just by seeing him. George comes in here on a regular basis. Sits in just about the same spot and has a few drinks. I never would have thought he would attack Maria like that."

I nodded. "Did you ever see Maria Farrell with George before?"

Beckworth thought for a minute. "Never. George would just have his drinks and leave. If he talked much it was to the bartenders."

"Why do you think he was with Maria last night?"

"No idea. I just looked over there and they were talking. Next thing I knew they were gone. Funny thing was they never asked what they owed. Just left the money on the bar, more than enough, and they were gone. Next thing I heard was that there had been some type of fight at the River of Bliss, Maria had been all cut up and Loftus arrested. It makes no sense."

"Did you notice what kind of shape Loftus was in?"

"When I went by there one time, he looked very drunk. Maria was kind of holding him up. Then, like I said, they were gone."

The other thing that I was sure about Loftus was that he was a regular drinker. I'd seen this and heard this, but never heard of him being "very drunk". Very peculiar indeed.

• • •

The River of Bliss was one of those longtime brothels that, if it's possible, had a good reputation. It reminded me a lot of The Queen's House where Eleanor was last employed. By a good reputation, I mean the girls wouldn't try and rob you after they had completed their appointed tasks. The place was bustling when I made my entrance and I immediately asked for the madam. As I waited I saw little evidence that a serious crime or two had been committed here the night before. In fact, I'd say it looked a lot like business as usual.

The madam was an attractive woman, by the name of Anne. She was slender with all around nice features and particularly long fingers where each of the nails had been painted a bright pink. This color seemed to match the color of her cheeks as she stood now smiling at me. "How may I help you, Detective?"

"I am trying to make a little sense in what occurred here last night between Detective Loftus and Maria Farrell. I was hoping you might be able to answer some questions."

At the mention of Loftus' name her smile quickly became a frown. "What is there to answer? The lout was very drunk, became angry for some reason, and took it out on Maria."

"I see," I said. "Did you see the two of them enter the house?"

"I did not. I had heard that Maria had a date and would return shortly. We were very busy last night as we are right now. I didn't see or hear much until the fight broke out."

"What of this fight? What did you hear?"

"There was some loud screaming and yelling. One of the girls heard a lamp being broken. Then it was very silent. I went up later to see what had happened and when I opened the door I found Maria cut and bruised and that awful man, Loftus, passed out on the floor."

"Maria was on the bed?"

"Yes, she was."

"Clothed or not?"

"Mostly in a state of disrobe."

"What about Detective Loftus?"

"He was wearing all of his clothes, I believe?"

I found this a little odd, the girl undressed and the customer not. "Where was the knife that was used?"

"Right where the police found it, near Loftus."

I asked to see the room and was led upstairs to the second floor. The room in question had two chairs in it, a bed, a dresser with a mirror, and a stand that held a pitcher and small basin on it. The bed was completely bare of sheets and blankets. On the mattress that remained could be seen a good sized blood stain.

"We have not completed our cleanup," Anne said. "We are waiting for a new mattress."

"And then back to business?" I jested.

"Detective, we are not a charitable institution," she said without a smile.

I noticed that the room had one window that was covered by a single shade. There were some decorative curtains, but they were pulled to the side and held in place by a red sash. I moved to the window and let the shade up. It was dark outside, but I could clearly make out a porch and stairs on the outside. I tried the window and even as cold as it was it went up quite easily. I stuck my head outside into the frosty air. The brothel backed up to an alley. It was dark back there, but I could see foot prints in the snow on the porch. There were many so it wasn't like I'd be able to identify one print over another. I pulled my head back into the window and closed it.

"Who uses that porch and stairs?" I asked.

"The cleaning people mostly. They collect the trash on this floor and use the door at the end of the hall which leads outside to the porch and stairs. They can take the garbage straight out to the trash receptacles in the alley."

I nodded. "No one, not any of your girls, mentioned anything about anyone else entering this room when Maria and Loftus were in it?"

Her face beamed with blush. "That is strictly prohibited. Some places allow that. We do not. One girl and one customer per room."

"But it was busy," I said. "Someone could have entered the room."

"Could have, but didn't. Maria knew the rules."

"I'm sure she did, but is it possible, while you were talking to a gentleman and away from the door, someone could have entered the house and gone upstairs?"

"That is against the rules, Detective."

I put one finger up in the air to shut her up. "Forget the rules. Forget that you think Loftus did this. Is it possible?"

She crossed her arms across her chest. Her look very stern. "I guess that is possible," she said.

• • •

I wanted to visit Soon Lee's and his basement opium den, but decided against it. I opted instead for the quiet respite of Cooper's. I had dinner and a couple of glasses of whiskey. I wanted to believe we were getting closer on a couple of cases and maybe this led me to a bit of calmness and no headache. I decided to stay as alert as possible in hopes that things would move towards settlement of a couple of the cases.

As much as I failed to see that Loftus was the prostitute killer, I did believe there was something going on with the case. With the death of Andres' Dubois and now the slashing of Maria Farrell, the killer was starting to crumble. Someone was behind what happened at the River of Bliss. I was determined to figure this out, first to set poor Loftus free and, secondly, to find the guilty party.

The Kowalski brother's inability to keep Millicent and Holly quiet had led to their discovery in their apartment. They had now fled their place of residence, to another unknown site, but I agreed with Sam. Things were starting to come undone for them. They needed the ransom money and soon. I was confident that we would hear something shortly.

I wondered about Christian Hanson. His whereabouts were a mystery and I thought he might not even be in Chicago. We had every beat cop in the city and the girls at De Sade's on the lookout for him. I hadn't seen or heard from Gussie Black in a bit, but he knew we were looking for Hanson. If he was in town he would pop up. If he was gone, I wasn't sure what we could do.

As I walked to my apartment that night, I felt as good as I had in a while. Maybe things were falling in place. At least, for the shortest period of time, I felt a little hope.

Eleven

I arrived early next day and I felt rested and not tense at all. There was no pain at my temples and my vision was clear. I hoped that I might be free of the problem that had bothered me recently. I hadn't been at my desk for more than ten minutes when Captain Morgan came out of his office and summoned me to follow him. Not another word was said. I looked over at Sam's desk, but he had not arrived yet. I followed Morgan downstairs and then to the lower level where the cells were held. I was behind Morgan as we got to the cells so I was able to slow and look in on Frank Pelicanos. There wasn't much to see; Frank was asleep, but I was reminded that his deadline, and mine, was fast approaching. I looked ahead and saw Morgan turning towards the back cells, the ones that held George Loftus.

Loftus was not asleep and was sitting on the wooden chair in the middle of the cell. He had his elbows on his knees and his head was resting in his hands. He looked up as Morgan unlocked the cell and for a moment Loftus smiled. "Captain," he said.

"There is nothing to smile about here, Loftus," he said

loudly and backslapped George out of his chair. Loftus fell onto his side and looked up at Morgan with a different look, fear.

It was then that I saw the sap that Morgan must have had hidden in his suit coat. He withdrew it slowly and began to pummel Loftus with it. George could do nothing, but cover up and wince out in pain as the sap found its mark.

"Captain," I said, trying to slow down the beating he was giving to George.

Morgan turned towards me and I could see the anger, the rage that covered his face. I had never seen that look in him, or many men. It was an angry animal's look.

"Captain," I said louder. "You're going to hurt him."

Morgan stopped and stood up. He reached back for his constantly inflamed back and rubbed it without thinking. "What have you done, Loftus?"

It sounded to me that Morgan was asking what George had done to the department.

"Did you enjoy murdering all of those women?"

George, in all of his pain, was able to swing around, still lying on the floor of the cell. "Captain, what are you asking me?"

"Don't play stupid with me," Morgan said. "Things will go a lot better for you if you admit your guilt."

"First of all," George said, "I had nothing to do with what happened last night. Secondly, if you think that I had anything to do with the death of those other girls, you don't know me."

"I don't think any of us know you," Morgan said. With that he took to beating Loftus with the sap again. He hit him so many times and so quickly that I lost count. A number of the blows hit George in the head and face. He was soon out cold. Morgan stopped the pummeling and started to exit the cell. His face was beaming with sweat. His eyes were wide. "When Walker gets here I want to see you both in my office."

He left the cell and left Loftus bruised and beaten on the floor. I walked over to the prone body and knelt down. I checked under both of the shirt sleeves on George's arms. There was no indication of any scratch marks as Harold Pinter told us the killer would have as a result of his struggle with Pearl Radd. If she had dug out some skin from her killer's arm then George Loftus was not the killer.

• • •

Before returning to the first floor, I stopped by the little lab and office of Harold Pinter. The small man was huddled over his desk, magnifying glass in hand, staring at some tiny piece of evidence. It took me several callings of his name to get him to look up at me.

"Sorry, Patrick," he said. "I was trying to decide whether my eyes were playing tricks on me or whether this small clue is useless."

He didn't embellish on his comment so I let it pass. "There is a prisoner in cell number one, Detective Loftus, said to be a prime suspect in the prostitute murders."

He raised his eyes at me. "You don't say?"

"I wasn't the one that said it, but we must look into all avenues. You told me that the killer of Pearl Radd would have a scratch from a finger nail, presumably on his arm. I found no marks."

"The murder is not that old. There would still be evidence of the scratch on his arm."

"Maybe it wasn't the killer who Pearl scratched. Maybe she had an altercation earlier in the evening of her death. Maybe she didn't scratch his arm."

"Could be. I wasn't there, you know?" He pushed his glasses back up on his nose; they looked close to falling off.

"Just saying, but there is one thing I would like you to check."

"The fingerprint from Bad Joanie, the one found on the piece of silver jewelry."

"That's it."

"I can check it shortly if you like."

"That would be fine. I don't believe George is the killer, but I want to rule everything out," I said. "When you go over there make sure the guard is with you. Captain Morgan just administered some harsh punishment for the fight Loftus was in at the River of Bliss. He might not be in the best mood."

· · ·

When I got back up to the first floor, I saw that Sam had arrived. He saw me as well and I waved to him to follow me. I also saw Gunter, using a temporary desk. He had his head down in some files so he did not see me. I wasn't ready for another discussion with him.

Morgan was waiting for Sam and me as we entered his office. His face was still flush from the thrashing he had given Loftus; there were still a few beads of sweat on his forehead. "You took a little longer than I thought," he said.

"Sorry," I said. "I had to speak with Pinter about the Hobbs' case. You have heard the latest?"

"I don't have time for that now," Morgan said hastily.

I would say that the look on Sam's face told how we both felt. He looked perplexed.

"I want you two to get over to Loftus' apartment as soon as you can. It's a small place on Thirty Ninth. I want you to go in there and check for any other clues that link him to those murders. If we can, I would like to close this down as soon as possible. If he's behind those murders, he's not leaving any cell soon."

Sam looked down and shuffled his feet. I sighed heavily. "Do you really believe that George Loftus was an accomplice in all of those murders or was the murderer in any of them?" I asked.

Morgan gave me a harsh look. I knew he had been under a lot of strain from headquarters and with our current workload, and I had seen a change in him. For someone who was almost too uninvolved he was now very engaged. "He got caught in the room of a prostitute after he cut her up. What makes you believe that he is not the killer?"

I didn't want to mention the lack of scratches on his arm. "Dancing Walter said the man he saw was taller, hunched over and had a mustache."

"A vagrant, an unreliable witness," Morgan said. He took a deep breath. "Appease me and make a short trip to his apartment. Maybe nothing will come of it; perhaps something will."

"Yes, sir," Sam said quietly.

I said nothing to Morgan as he continued to glare at me as I followed Sam out of the Captain's office.

"You don't think Loftus had anything to do with those murders?" I said to Sam as we climbed into a waiting coach.

"Not at all," he said, "but I am not a Captain. It is my duty to do what Morgan assigns us, even if I find it stupid. Again, Patrick, my family will not do well if I am unemployed."

. . .

Loftus' apartment on Thirty-Ninth was indeed small as Morgan said. It was on the first floor of a two-story brick building. The air was cold and it had snowed during the night, but someone, not the incarcerated Loftus, had shoveled the walk leading up to the building. The landlord had been contacted and the door to the apartment was unlocked. When we walked into the unit we weren't surprised by what we saw. Loftus, a bachelor, kept a neat and tidy little home. There was only one main room, where his bed was located, a small kitchen area and a bath. In the main room was a table.

We looked over the entire apartment, opening drawers and cabinets. We found nothing unordinary. We looked under his bed. Nothing there as well. Lastly there was a small closet near the front entrance. This was wear Loftus hung his suits. There were also a couple of pairs of shoes on the floor. There didn't appear to be anything else until we moved the suits apart and noticed a large wooden footlocker stuck in the corner of the closet. The locker was made of a cheap wood and had seen better days. The wood was splintered, chipped and dirty, but the case had been well made. We slid the box out of the closet. It had a small latch and was easy to open. We both looked inside.

"Jesus," Sam Walker said.

The box didn't hold much, but the significance of the contents was revealing right away. The bottom of the box, which

I will discuss first, was covered with a number of trinkets. There were a few single earrings, a couple of rings, a bracelet and three necklaces that had become tangled together. I also saw at least two women's scarves. This got our attention, but it was the three items on the top of the box that secured it. There we found a floppy, large brimmed hat, a serrated edged bayonet and a bushy, fake mustache."

"Maybe we should look at Loftus a little harder," Sam said as I reviewed our find.

"All of this stuff needs to come back with us for examination by Harold Pinter. Let's see if this could be the knife used on Pearl Radd," I said. With the lack of scratches on Loftus I had my doubts, but this find wasn't helping his cause.

•   •   •

After we dropped the captured items off with Harold Pinter and implored the idea that his research be hasty, I stopped by the cell of George Loftus. He had at least recovered enough to be sitting up on his bed, but when he turned his face towards me I could see the bruises and welts that Morgan had inflicted on his face. His right eye was closed completely, now just a black oval.

"Come on, Moses," he said to me shakily. "You know me. You know I didn't do this."

"That's the problem, George," I said through the iron bars. "I don't know you, at least, not enough. We have had drinks one time and we talked over the Pelicanos case a few times, but that's it. I don't really know you."

"Think about it," he growled. "Your own partner, Krause, would be a more likely candidate for these crimes with his temper."

"I'll give you that Gunter has a bad temper, but he was not caught in the room of a prostitute who was nearly slashed to pieces."

"Then ask the girl," he railed. "She may be the only one who can help me. Morgan is convinced I am the killer."

I thought about Maria Farrell. She hadn't died yet, but I wondered if she would ever be able to tell her story to anyone. "We found some things in your apartment. Women's jewelry, a wide brimmed hat, fake mustache and a bayonet. These items link you to the murders."

He jumped up from the bunk and almost fell, forgetting how depleted his strength was from the beating. He got up slowly and limped to me, grabbing the bars. "There was nothing like that in my apartment. You are in cahoots with Morgan, trying to make me look like the killer. You and Krause botched this case the first time. You're trying to clear this up quickly."

As stupid as the remarks were they stung. I could see how a person in Loftus' predicament could see it that way. "I'll try and talk to Maria Farrell," I said.

• • •

Frank Pelicanos was still asleep when I sauntered past his cell and he did not move when I called his name. He, just like his case, was inert. I envisioned his hanging shortly from the gallows and decided to go over to Mercy Hospital to check on Maria Farrell. I was almost out the door of the precinct when I walked right into Sylvia Pelicanos as she was entering the building.

198

"Detective Moses," she said nearly out of breath. "I must talk to you."

I pulled her into a short hallway away from the hustle and bustle of the main lobby. "What is it?" I asked.

Tears came forth from her eyes. "I saw a copy of the *Tribune* and it said it was likely that this Judge Kirk would sentence my Frank to hanging for the murder he did not commit."

"Yes, that is true." I had already made this clear to her.

"I didn't want to tell you this. I didn't want to admit what I know, but I am ashamed for Frank. I am also worried about the woman who he seeks comfort from. I have heard that her husband is a brute and that he beats her. If he were to learn of her indiscretions he might do worse than beat her."

"If you have any information that will help Frank give it to me now. Time is of the essence. I can make sure the woman is not harmed." I hoped this was true.

She wiped her eyes and looked straight into mine. "Her name is Beth Stokes. She is a neighbor of ours and works at a tavern in Pullman. Her husband works the midday shift at a coal plant. Frank visits her when he is gone. Apparently he was gone Christmas afternoon because that is where Frank went."

"Then I will talk to her if that will prove Frank's innocence."

She grabbed my arm hard. "You must watch out for her husband. His name is Amos. He is a beast of a man and has been known to fight men for simply looking at Beth. She is very attractive."

"I don't think talking to her will be a problem. After all, I am a policeman."

• • •

It was hard to tell that the body that I looked down upon in the bed at Mercy Hospital was a human. It looked more like a mummy. Most of what I could see of her face and throat was covered with thick white bandages. Some of these showed spotting of blood and, I supposed, antiseptics. The rest of her body, that I could see, was robed in a white smock. I knew there were bandages under that as well. The openings in the head bandages where the eyes and mouth would be showed all to be closed. Only the light rising of her chest showed that she was alive.

"As to your inquiry, Detective," the doctor next to me said, "I can't say. She is in grim shape. Fortunately, for her, the assailant managed to not hit any major arteries, but she lost a tremendous amount of blood. We are trying to keep an eye on her and stave off any infection, but for now that is a major battle."

"In the time that you treated her, did she say much of anything?"

The doctor laughed. "If you mean in the way of talking, absolutely not. There has been a lot of moaning and a few screams, some agonizing, but that is it."

"It sounds like any chance of communicating with her would be slim."

"Less than slim, I'm afraid."

I looked down at Maria Farrell again. Her assailant had left her alive, but not by much. "Please contact me if she comes to enough to give us any insight on what happened to her."

• • •

"That is not possible," Beth Stokes said to me. She was, as Sylvia Pelicanos described, a very alluring woman. She wore a tighter than normal dress that showed every curve that she had. Her hair, a chestnut brown, was worn up. Her facial make-up made her look a little cheap, but she was a barmaid. All tips did not come from serving beer.

What I had asked is if she would come down to Judge Kirk's chambers and tell him that Frank Pelicanos had been with her at the time of the shooting of Jacob Fine. Her husband Amos had gone to the coal plant after they had opened Christmas gifts. She would raise a shade halfway in one of her front windows to let Frank know her husband was not home.

"You won't help Frank?" I asked.

"I can't," she said. "I like Frank. He's sweet to me and always brings me little bakery gifts, but if I go down to talk to this judge and Amos hears about it he will not be very nice to me."

"I can talk to Amos about the way he handles disagreements with you."

She laughed so hard that she had to cover her mouth with her hand. "The police have been here twice to tell Amos to stop hitting me. As soon as they were gone he hit me again."

I looked around the modest house with its meager furnishings. They weren't living like kings and queens. "Why don't you leave him?"

"You don't understand, Detective. You don't walk away from a man like Amos Stokes. To him, I am his property. If somebody took his property or it was lost he would come looking for it. You just don't understand."

"So you played this little game with Frank and you'll probably play it with somebody else?"

She shrugged. "You know, just looking for a little

happiness."

I took a deep breath. "If you don't go talk to Judge Kirk, Frank Pelicanos is going to hang for a crime he didn't commit. Are you okay with that?"

I saw a tear run out of one eye and run down her cheek. "Why doesn't he just tell them the truth? Why did he say he killed that man?"

I took her hand. "I think Frank is a sick man. He needs more help than just you, but you have to be first."

She nodded. "Give me a little time to think about it."

"I can only give you until tomorrow."

"I'll come see you at your precinct tomorrow. I promise."

• • •

As much as yesterday had proven to be a day that hoped to provide answers, today had only added to any confusion my mind had. I thought of the two prisoners locked up in the basement, locked up for crimes they might not have committed, and I could only shake my head. I never really thought Loftus was the prostitute murderer, but then when we found the box at his house even I had to wonder. With Frank Pelicanos, I had found a person in Beth Stokes who could prove him innocent. Only thing was, she was reluctant to help and Frank didn't seem to want to help himself. Maybe she would come forward and maybe the doctor would confirm that Pelicanos was sick. Those two items had to help him, if they occurred. We were sure that the Kowalski brothers were the Hobbs' kidnappers, but they had probably gone very deep into hiding. Even if they made a quick next move that didn't mean they'd be easy to locate or to get the twins back safely. As maddening as all of this was, there was nothing more maddening than the disappearance of Christian Hanson. I believed he was gone. It just didn't seem possible that a man with his physical descriptions could remain hiding that long. With all of those thoughts running through my head and Sam off on that never ending burglary case, I was ready to close up for the day when I looked up to see the large presence of Gunter Krause looming over me. He was smiling and smoking a big cigar.

"Gunter," I said. "You look very happy."

He exhaled a large plume of smoke, most of it over the top of my head. "Not really," he said. "In fact I am a bit miserable."

I looked away for an instant, hopefully not showing any of my guilt. "What are you miserable about? You're getting stronger, back to work and things should be getting better."

He pulled up a chair and sat down. "I have spent today fielding any telephone calls that come into the precinct that the desk sergeant cannot handle. It's a bit like being a babysitter. A trained monkey might be able to do the job as well as I."

"That's all temporary until you are healthy. It's got to be better than lying in the room at Mercy or being in your apartment all day."

He took the cigar out of his mouth, tipped an ash onto the floor and pointed the red tip at me. "Mercy wasn't awful. There were some very attractive nurses taking care of me. A man of lesser moral fortitude could have strayed easily."

"It's just until you can get back on your feet all day long," I said.

"Staying at home is another story," Gunter said. "A totally different story."

"What do you mean by that?"

"I know she has cheated on me. I know that Margaret took advantage of my time in the hospital to go out on me. I have no proof, but it's like I can smell it. Things are not like they were."

I swallowed hard. "Have you tried to talk with her about anything?"

He waved his hand at me. "I can tell," he said.

I leaned forward a little bit, lowering my voice. "Things will get better soon around here. I think you have too much time on your hands and you are thinking in the wrong direction. When you are able to return to work and get involved you will feel better about everything. In the meantime, I think you should just focus on getting back to one hundred percent and being reinstated to detective work."

He nodded. "You are right, Patrick. I think too much, but some of what I think about is legitimate. I mean to find those that beat me in that alley and see that justice is done. I promise you that. I also mean to find out if Margaret has cheated. If she has and I find out with who I think they should both pay. Don't you?"

If his look had shown anger, I might have understood his question, but his face was so calm it was unnerving. I could only nod my head.

My streak of trying to behave had lasted all but one day. My caseload, along with the end of the day visit from Gunter, had caused my tension level to escalate and my temples to tighten and throb. It was all I could do to get up from my desk and make it outside without passing out. My vision was blurred as I caught a transom for Soon Lee's. It was barely evening when I made my way down to the basement den. The Chinaman didn't seem to notice or care. He took my money all the same. I spent a good deal of time down there that night, floating to peace and quiet. I didn't notice what time it was when I got home. I didn't notice anything.

Twelve

I slept very well. I didn't hear the usual noises that an apartment building can bring in the night. I didn't feel how cold my little unit was. I might have slept a good deal longer if not for the pounding that ensued at my door. I got up quickly, noting that I still wore my suit pants, shirt and socks and moved to the door. I was still a bit on a cloud when I opened the door and the tough looking face of Sam Walker was standing there.

"Finish getting dressed," he said, assuming I had started getting dressed. "There's been a murder."

My first thought was Loftus, but he was in the cell in the precinct basement. What about the "real" killer? "Who?" I said as Sam stepped into the unit.

"It's that bum that you interviewed after Pearl Radd was murdered, Dancing Walter. Somebody stuffed him into a trash can over on Twenty-Sixth. Somebody remembered he'd witnessed something with the Radd case and connected all of that to us. Lucky us," Sam mused. "Get to start another fucking day with a dead body, albeit a tiny one."

It didn't take me that long to put the remainder of my

clothes back on and splash a little water on my face. I needed a shave but didn't succeed with that as time was important. Once I ran my brush through my hair, I didn't look all that bad. Sam didn't seem to notice in my apartment or in the cab on the way to the murder scene. At least, he didn't say anything.

The small body of Dancing Walter was stuffed head first into a metal trash can behind an apartment building on east Twenty-Sixth Street. He had not been moved. The only reason someone knew it was Walter, other than his size, was the dirty check pants that he wore. That someone, another bum named Lucas Fitch, was looking through the garbage for something to eat when he saw the feet of Walter sticking up in the air. He hailed the first policeman he could find and notified him of the crime.

"Let's be careful not to touch him when we turn the can over," I said, remembering a talk I'd had with Pinter. "We need to be careful with possible evidence."

Sam gave me a sidelong glance; he was still in a foul mood, but agreed. We carefully tilted the can over and, in doing so, were able to slide Walter's now frozen corpse out of the can. I wish we hadn't. Twisted around his neck was a thick piece of rope and it had been twisted so tight that his tongue, now nearly black, hung out of his mouth and his eyes were bulging open. It was a hideous sight. There didn't seem to be any other harm done to the body.

"Somebody probably snuck up on him and was able to get the rope around his neck," Sam said. "He had no chance to get away."

"That part is easy," I said, looking down at Walter.

"What part?"

"The how part. What I am more interested in is the why part. Why would someone kill Dancing Walter?"

"I doubt if he had any money or anything worth a damn on him."

"Then why?"

"Because he talked to you?"

"That's the only reason, Sam," I said as the sun snuck behind a few dark clouds and large flakes began to float from the sky. "Someone who knew he had talked to me about the prostitute murderer. Someone who thought Walter could identify him if he had to."

Sam rubbed at his chin. "Makes sense," he said. "Also, we know it's not Loftus."

"Think about what you said, Sam. You thought that the killer had insight to our discussions and reports, somebody who is a cop or had a lot of access to the precinct. They heard Walter had talked to me and they came after him and silenced him. That is the only motive."

Sam lit a cigarette, shielding the match from the cold wind. "Ideas?"

"Yes. If this bastard is finding out what we talk about then he is still listening. We have to make sure he continues to hear what we say. If we can do that then we need to draw him out; we need to trap him."

The coroner's van was making its way down the snowy alley. I gave Walter one more look, wishing he had never spoken to me.

"I like it", Sam said, "as long as we don't endanger us or anyone close to us."

I knew he was talking about his family. I nodded as the Assistant Coroner exited the van and made his way towards us.

• • •

It was after noon by the time we got back to the precinct. Both of us were cold and tired already. The snow was piling up outside and the air had an Arctic feel to it. Dancing Walter's body was off to the morgue for his last dance. I wondered who would attend the funeral of a bum. Most of the detective squad was out of the precinct, including Gunter, and the place was eerily quiet. It didn't stay that way for long. I had barely sat at my desk when I saw the small figure of Harold Pinter heading towards me.

"You are never here," he said.

"Hello to you, Harold," I said. "You can't solve many crimes in this city by sitting behind your desk."

"Probably true, but I do most of my best work behind a desk and I think I am going to help this department solve a lot of crimes."

I let his remark go. I wasn't sure where we were headed anyway. "Have you solved the case of Detective Loftus?" Sam had come over from his desk and taken a chair across from me; Harold remained standing.

"Yes and no," he said. Sam Walker let out an audible groan.

"Can you do a little better than that?" I asked.

"Of course. I was able to get some prints off of Detective Loftus, particularly the thumb. In no way does his print match that of the one we found on the piece of jewelry removed from Bad Joanie."

"So that should clear him from that murder," Sam said.

"Not necessarily, Detective Walker," Harold said. "The print might not have been put there by the killer in the first place. Bad

Joanie was, as we know, in the business of providing services for men. That print could have come from another of her customers."

I sighed. "Any good news?"

"The floppy hat and the fake mustache are both of the type and quality of material that leave no prints. I did find two hairs inside of the hat which I have preserved. Of course, these will not do us any good until the owner of the hat is found."

"The hairs don't match Loftus?" I asked.

"They do not."

"That sounds better. What about the knife?"

"On the negative side, the handle and the blade were free of finger prints. They had been wiped clean. There were also no blood samples present. On the positive side, from my notes, I can tell that this knife would cause wounds that are consistent with those found on the body of Pearl Radd, but again this is somewhat inconclusive."

"So," Sam said, "we are really no further along than we were."

I ignored Sam. "What colors were the hairs you found in the hat?"

"A dark brown, similar to those of the mustache," Harold answered. "I wish I had more for you, but that's about it."

"That's not insignificant," I said. "We have the hairs and the print on the piece of jewelry and we think the killer had some gashes on his skin courtesy of Pearl Radd. All of this may help to convict him when we catch him."

"If we catch him," Sam said, "and we'd better hurry. Those scratches on him won't last forever, and it looks to me like he is trying to frame our friend Loftus and maybe close up shop for a while until this investigation settles down for a bit."

No one ever said that Sam was stupid. Neither Harold nor I had a reply. We knew that he was right.

• • •

Captain Morgan's reaction to what had been found in Loftus' apartment and what the work of Harold Pinter had revealed was a little striking. To say that he was a non-believer in what the evidence told us would have been an understatement.

"The fact that the knife, the weapon used on Pearl Radd, was found in his apartment is a strong indictment," he said. He was sitting behind his desk. Sam and I occupied two of the hard, wooden chairs in front of him.

"According to what Harold Pinter told us the thumb print found on the piece of jewelry worn by Bad Joanie does not match Loftus. Pinter also said that Pearl Radd inflicted some severe scratches on her killer. There was no evidence of scratches found anywhere on George. Lastly, two hairs were secured from the hat found in the apartment. They are dark brown. George's hair is black, with some hints of gray. Three pieces of physical evidence. None seem to match up with Loftus."

Morgan leaned forward, resting his elbows on his desk. His look was one of concern. "Patrick, I don't want all of this work by your new friend, Mr. Pinter, to influence your good detective work. How often are you delivered the murder weapon on a silver tray? The fact that none of the evidence matches Loftus does not mean he isn't the killer. You said so yourself. The knife appears to have been the one used to kill Pearl Radd."

It was evident to me that Morgan was unwilling to drop

Loftus from the status of suspect number one. "Pinter did say that the wounds on Pearl Radd would be consistent with those made by the knife that was found."

"There," Morgan said, sitting back and slapping his two hands together, causing a loud clap. "I think we should press Loftus for some sort of confession, implying of course that this will go better for him at the time of prosecution."

"He's going to deny it," Sam said.

"Then we'll press for more evidence," Morgan answered. "Now what about the Hobbs' girls?"

We would press for more evidence because we weren't convinced that George Loftus was our killer. We also made no mention of our plan to set a trap for the killer. That would remain only between Sam and me until the plan could be conceived.

"We have narrowed the kidnappers down to these Kowalski brothers," Sam said. "One of their neighbors heard the girls crying and complained to the landlord. When the landlord went to visit the brothers the next day they were gone. We were then called in and saw the evidence of two babies being held and taken care of in that unit."

Morgan nodded like a learned professor. "What do we know about these Kowalski brothers?"

"Not much," Sam continued. "Two good tenants who both worked for the Schoenhofer Brewery. They quit their jobs right when the girls were kidnapped. Patrick and I think they saw the heist as their potential big payday so that they could move onto something else."

"No idea where they are?"

"None," Sam said. "Everyone in the city knows we are looking for two men taking care of two small girls. Our best guess is that we will hear from them before they hear from us. They know they are found out and will need to make a move for a ransom before they are caught."

"That's probably true," Morgan said. "Headquarters has been quiet, and I have no other reports of Patrick assaulting anyone from the victim's family." He smiled over at me.

"Not for lack of wanting to," I said, drawing a dirty look.

"And your other friend, Patrick, the elusive Christian Hanson?"

"Again," I said, "everyone in this damn city knows we are after the guy, but he appears to have gone deep underground. He may have left the city for all we know."

Another clap of Morgan's hands seemed to startle Sam. "All we can do in our shorthanded state is press on and work harder. Of course, I expect to be kept abreast of all three cases as I doubt that the people downtown will remain quiet forever."

This signaled the end of the meeting, another with Morgan, with us saying a lot and him not understanding much of what was said. Sam and I left his office to do what we had been doing a lot of lately, waiting.

• • •

I was at my desk waiting for the next move in my life to be determined when a very tall and skinny man made his way over to me. He was well in excess of six feet tall and looked almost underfed. He wore an impressive gray suit, red tie and had a nice gold chain hanging limply from his vest. The hat he wore on his head was not from a cheap haberdasher and the spectacles he wore gave him the look of a scholar. He looked down at me for a while and I wasn't sure if he was ever going to speak.

"May I help you?" I finally asked.

"Detective Moses, I am Doctor William Ely. I was contracted by the Circuit Court of Cook County to administer an examination of a prisoner of yours, Mr. Frank Pelicanos."

"Oh, I see," I said. This skinny physician was one piece that I needed to help me clear Pelicanos of any charges brought against him. "What have you found?"

"May I sit?"

"Of course." Doctor Ely took a seat to the side of my desk.

"It was reported to me that Mr. Pelicanos might be suffering from syphilis. This is not the easiest disease to pinpoint without a blood test and I can tell you that I was unable to confirm one way or the other whether Pelicanos suffers from this affliction."

I felt my shoulders slump. I didn't know if Ely had seen my mood dampen.

"Even though my findings for the disease were not proven," he continued, "I did find enough, in talking to the man, that there is something mentally deficient about him. He is a very confused man. His answers to simple questions are inconsistent. He seems to have to search his brain for every response. I have no doubt that, even though he may not be physically sick, he has some severe mental limitations. Any testimony he may have to give, any questions that he may have to answer would need to be scrutinized immensely."

I was a tad confused by the doctor's rambling dialogue. "So what are you going to report to Judge Kirk?"

He looked insulted. "The truth, Detective Moses. I find Mr. Pelicanos extremely addled and I think he is a bigger concern to himself than others. He is delusional. I think that he has given himself a position of power by admitting to the murder of Jacob Fine. I don't believe he had anything to do with that killing and that is what I'll report to Judge Kirk."

I smiled with the knowledge that Doctor Ely finally confirmed what I knew all along. Frank Pelicanos was not of right mind. This was important. His oration to Judge Kirk that Pelicanos was not the killer was more important. I just needed Beth Stokes to come forward and admit that he was with her at the time that he was supposed to have killed my father.

• • •

I was about to leave the precinct for a break in the early afternoon when the call came in that the kidnappers had contacted the Hobbs' family attorney, Thomas Mallory. We were wanted at once at the Hobbs' home. I tried to find Sam, but all that I knew for sure was that he was out following up on the old robbery case that seemed to be taking up more and more of his time. I would make the trip to the Hobbs' on my own.

I donned my coat, gloves and hat and secured a police vehicle to take me to the Prairie Avenue residence. As I waited for the patrolmen who would take me to the home, a familiar figure came walking up the street towards me. It was Margaret Krause. The immediate reaction I had was to become invisible, but that was not an option. Hiding behind a horse might have worked, but there were none of those in sight. I smiled at the pretty lady as she got closer.

"Margaret, you are looking well," I said. She was bundled for the cold as well as she could be, but her pretty face reminded me of her overall astounding beauty.

"Patrick, have you seen Gunter?"

In my time in the building that day I had not seen him. That left me no reason to be alarmed. "I have not seen him today."

She immediately looked anguished. "He did not return home last night and I am very worried that something bad has happened to him."

Now she had my attention. "What do you mean he didn't return home? Was he at home at some time during the evening?"

She suddenly reached out and grabbed my arm. "We had a terrible fight, a silly one if you ask me, and he stormed out of the house. That was around eight o'clock. He didn't return at all. I was hoping that he came to work."

"I was fairly busy and did not see him. What was this fight about?"

"I took on a new client. She commissioned me to make several dresses for her. I thought we could use the extra income."

Margaret was a dressmaker with a stellar reputation. "Why would he get upset about something like that?"

She hung her head when she answered. "The woman is Victoria Colosimo, Big Jim's wife."

Now I could see Gunter's reason for anger. "Margaret, I think you know that Colosimo's men were probably behind the attack on Gunter. We think one of his henchmen is responsible for several murders in the city. These are not the people you should be associating with."

She looked up at me and now there was anger on her face. "It is just a dress commission, nothing more. I tried to do what's right, but that is difficult when Gunter will barely talk to me."

It was then that the automobile and my driver pulled up to

the curb. I wasn't sure where Gunter was, but felt he'd be okay. I also knew the Hobbs' situation was far more important at this time. I had to get to their house. "I have to go Margaret, but I promise to look in on Gunter when I return. I am sure he is in no danger."

"You don't know that, Patrick."

I pulled away from her grasp. "I must go," I said. As I got in the car it was hard to leave her standing on the chilly curb. She looked lost. She was also right about one thing. I wasn't sure that Gunter was in no danger.

•   •   •

The usual group was waiting for me in the library of the Hobbs' home where the maid led me. Thomas Mallory looked calm, dressed in a dark blue suit. Alicia Stone stood near him; she did not look so calm. The Hobbs, Susan and Everett, took up their normal spot, seated in front of the fireplace that had a nice, roaring fire going in it. They both looked at me as if I was guilty of something. I stood facing this small group.

"You have some news from the kidnappers?" I said.

"He acts like he doesn't know," Everett Hobbs said.

"Where is Detective Walker?" Mallory asked.

"He had another matter to attend to," I answered. "Due to the immediate nature of the case I have come on my own."

"Convenient," Hobbs said.

"Is there a problem here?" I asked. I wasn't getting a warm feeling from anyone in the small room.

"It's the demand that the kidnappers have made," Mallory said. 'It's a bit unusual."

"May I see it?" I asked.

"It wasn't received in writing. It was called into my office."

Mallory was calm, but his look was a bit accusing. "You spoke to the kidnappers?"

"No. One of my secretaries took down the message, had it repeated for accuracy, and called to give it to me."

"Well," I said, tiring of all the secrecy, "what was said?"

"They want the Hobbs to place twenty thousand dollars in cash into a bag. This bag is to be entrusted to you. The kidnappers will contact you; they didn't say when. When you deliver the money to them they will call here and tell us where Millicent and Holly can be found."

I was stunned. "They want me to hold onto the money until they contact me."

"How convenient, I said," Everett Hobbs repeated.

I turned to him. "I don't understand what you are implying."

"You don't? Nothing has turned up for days on our girls and now they make a demand that the money be given to you to hold until they find you. Seems a bit odd."

"I don't see it that way. We happen to know who the two kidnappers are. We know where they lived. They know we are onto them and they know that Detective Walker and I are investigating. They are getting nervous. We thought they would make a play and they have."

"You don't find it unusual," Hobbs said, "that you are being asked to be the conduit?"

"I hadn't thought about it, but I don't think anything in a kidnapping is unusual?"

"What do you suggest, Detective Moses?" Mallory asked.

He would be the more practical of the two men in the room.

"I suggest that if you have the money you give it to me. When they contact me we will get the girls back. After we get the girls back we will find them."

Hobbs stood quickly; his face was a bright red. "You actually expect us to believe that?"

I turned to face him. "I do. The kidnappers have been found out. We don't think they want to hurt the girls. Indications are that they were caring for them. They just want some money. Give it to them and we'll get the girls. Then we can go after them."

"And if we don't give them the money?" This question came from Alicia Stone. She looked almost as upset as the usually inconsolable Susan Hobbs.

"I think they are getting nervous and would like to return the girls. They've gone this far. Like I said, they are getting nervous. Don't give them the money and we all take a chance."

"A chance of what?" Susan Hobbs blurted out. She quickly buried her head in her hands and began to cry.

"If you'll give us a minute by waiting in the lobby we can give you a quick answer," Mallory said.

I nodded and excused myself from the library. I found a nice chair in the lobby area and plopped myself into it. I understood the stress of the situation. I also understood that Hobbs didn't care for me. For him to imply that I might somehow be involved was ludicrous, but I guess a reasonable thought, coming from him. I leaned back and closed my eyes. I suddenly realized how tired I was.

I wasn't sitting there long and perhaps I dozed for a moment when I heard my name being called, almost whispered. I opened my eyes and was looking into the attractive face of Sarah Balowski, the two kidnapped girl's day nurse.

"Detective Moses," she said. "Are you alright?"

The look of concern on her face was almost comforting. I held this young lady in a bit of contempt as I was sure she was in some kind of partnership with Everett Hobbs, but for the moment I enjoyed her company.

"Thank you for asking," I said. "The family is having a meeting in the library. I have been asked to wait out here. I am actually quite well."

"Is there anything that I can get for you? Perhaps a drink?"

I may have stated this before. Sarah did not possess overwhelming beauty to the degree of Margaret Krause or Alicia Stone, but what she had on them was a bit of purity. Her beauty was simple and natural. "I am fine. I do not believe my wait will be long."

She stared at me for a moment with her beautiful, blue gray eyes and simply walked off in the direction of the kitchen. Those eyes of hers were so unique. I hadn't ever seen that mixture of colors. There was something mysterious and haunting about them.

I tried to close my eyes again, but that didn't work and I was left staring at the library door and hoping to resume my duties shortly. Whatever discussion was going on was going on quietly. I heard nary a peep. My thoughts shifted to the likes of Beth Stokes and if she would help Frank Pelicanos. I also thought of Gunter. I hoped he hadn't done anything stupid.

It was another good ten minutes before the library door opened and Mallory stepped into the hall. "We are ready for you, Detective."

I got up from the chair and followed him back into the small room. The appearance on the faces of the others did not project their earlier gloom except for Everett Hobbs. His looks for me never changed.

"The family has decided to give you the money to hold in the event the kidnappers contact you about an exchange," Mallory said.

"I think that is wise," I said.

"We are to burn a candle in the center window tonight indicating that we agree to their terms. When they contact you they are to give you a yellow slipper that Millicent wore on her feet. This will indicate that they are genuine. When you give them the money they will contact this house with the whereabouts of the girls."

"That sounds simple enough," I said.

"They did say emphatically that if there was any interference with the person that meets with you the deal would be off."

I nodded. "Do you have that kind of money in the house?"

"Of course not," Everett Hobbs said loudly.

Thomas Mallory raised a hand to quiet his client. "I will have the money in my office after one o'clock. Please come by and get it. We will make sure the candle is in the window tonight. We don't expect any contact until after that so the earliest would be later tonight."

"I will be in your office sometime after one o'clock."

After retrieving my coat and hat and preparing to leave, I was stopped near the front door by Alicia Stone. She still looked very sad, and I could see the ordeal was wearing on her.

"Miss Stone," I said. "Everything okay?"

"I just want you to know that I know you are doing everything you can to get the girls back to us safely and that I am sorry for my brother's outbursts. He is used to getting his way regardless of the situation. He is just frustrated."

I wasn't that interested in her explanation of her brother's behavior. "I will do my best to get the girls back to you and to find the kidnappers."

"We just want the girls returned safely."

"They will be."

"And when this is done, Detective, I must talk with you about another matter."

Before I could reply she turned from me and headed back into the library, leaving me to wonder what on earth that was about.

. . .

I asked the patrolman who drove the automobile to hurry back to the precinct as quickly as he could. This was accomplished in a short period of time that included a number of slips and slides on the wet and icy surface. It reminded me of my trip to Blue Island with Gunter where we discovered the horror of The Ranch. I shivered when I thought of that day. Now I was faced with another problem. What was Gunter up to?

The first thing I did when I got back to the precinct was to inquire about messages. The Desk Sergeant Casey advised that Beth Stokes had stopped by to see me. She also left word that it would be better if I went to see her at the bar where she worked instead of her home. I hoped this was good news as I plodded upstairs in search of Gunter. He was at his desk busily looking over a large stack of files.

"You look like you've got enough to do," I said.

He was smoking his customary big cigar and leaned back in his chair showing me the red glow of the tip. He pulled it out of his mouth and exhaled a vast quantity of smoke in my direction.

"Like being an over trained babysitter," he said. There was no humor in his voice.

"It's only temporary until the doctor clears you for full duty."

"I'm as fit as any of the men here and probably in better shape than most."

I couldn't argue with him. A lot of our good detectives and patrolmen were a bit heavy. Some were downright fat. "Like I said, it's only a temporary thing."

"Most commonly referred to as bullshit."

Again no argument from me. "I saw Margaret this morning. She came by the precinct looking for you."

"I suppose to tell you what a bad person I am?"

"No. She told me that she was worried about you. She said you went out and that you never came home last night."

He waved his cigar at me. "Did she tell you about her new friend?"

"She told me that she was making some dresses for Victoria Colosimo."

"That doesn't strike you as a little strange."

"She said she was just trying to make some extra money for the family."

"By accepting commissions from the wife of the man who tried to have me killed?"

"We don't know that Big Jim was behind that?"

"Patrick, please," he sputtered. "The blonde, mute man that everyone is looking for works for Colosimo. He was behind my attack."

"You saw him?"

"Didn't have to."

"Okay, I understand that you are upset. I also asked you to

try and work things out between you and Margaret. Running out and staying out all night is not a good thing. At least think about your two children."

For the first time I saw a little look of guilt on his face. "It's just that she drives me crazy. I don't trust her right now. She is up to something and then she goes off to do work for that pig, Colosimo."

"His wife."

"Same thing."

"I just think you are overreacting. I think you should talk to her and don't run out on things. Your children, and Margaret, need you."

He inhaled deeply on the cigar, nodded his head lightly and again exhaled smoke at me. "I'll think about what you have said, Patrick."

• • •

I caught up with Sam who was sitting at his desk viewing a report. Like many of the people I had seen early in this day he didn't look very happy. "They said that you had to run out to the Hobbs' house."

"They were contacted by the kidnappers."

This got a raise of his eyebrows. "A demand?"

"An offer. I will be given twenty thousand dollars later today and I am to hold onto it until contacted. Once I turn the money over to the kidnappers the girls will be released."

"Legitimate?"

"Think so. They have a slipper of one of the girls that they will give to me. I give them the cash and they tell the family the safe location of the girls."

"Then we need to follow you."

"No. Any show that I am being followed or that their messenger is traced will cause the deal to fall apart. Once we have the girls we will find the kidnappers. I am convinced. We already know who they are." I pointed at the report he had been surveying. "Your robbery case?"

"It is done as far as I am concerned. The robbery boys have taken it over completely. Where will the kidnappers contact you?" he asked, shifting topics.

"That's the fun part. They are going to contact me when they feel like it, nothing prearranged."

"Kind of smart on their end."

"Anything new with Morgan?"

"He wants us to press Loftus for a confession or find more evidence that links him to the crimes. He is most delusional that George is the killer."

I nodded. "Maybe we should try and set up our trap for the killer sooner than later."

"No. We have to wait. Too close to Loftus' arrest will raise a lot of suspicion. I think we need to wait."

"And do what?"

"Just wait. Loftus didn't do this," he said emphatically. "Morgan just wants an arrest to get headquarters off his back. George can cool off in his cell for a couple of days. He won't be indicted."

"Speaking of indictments, I have woman who I think can clear Frank Pelicanos. I am going to see her later."

He stared at me for a moment. "I don't get you, Patrick. This guy admits to the murder and you're running all over trying to prove he didn't do it."

"Like Loftus, I don't think he did it."

Sam shrugged. "And Christian Hanson?"

"You know something I don't?"

"Absolutely nothing."

"Then we agree on that."

· · ·

Beth Stokes worked in a nice bar in the Pullman District by the name of Days End. The tavern was as long as the sixty foot mahogany bar in its front. There were no more than twelve round tables scattered in front of the bar. It was mid-afternoon when I got there and there were only a few loyal patrons sipping on cold beers. Beth Stokes, looking quite pretty in a colorful dress, was standing behind the bar. She also wore a big smile. It disappeared when she saw me. She immediately pointed to the end of the bar where no one was sitting.

"Nice place," I said.

"It's a bar, Detective. The men here, fed enough booze, are just like men everywhere else."

I didn't need her to go into details about what she meant. "There was a message at the precinct that you wanted to speak with me."

"It's about Frank," she almost whispered.

I looked to my right. There was no one within thirty feet of us. "Will you speak to the judge about where he was on Christmas day?"

"I'll do it, but I need your promise that not one word about my helping Frank will get out. If Amos hears about it I will be in a lot of trouble."

"No one will find out. I'll go with you to the judge's chambers and you can tell him you were with Frank at the time of the murder."

"I can do that." She looked very nervous. "Amos can't find out."

"What time is good tomorrow?"

"About ten. That is usually when I run my errands and Amos is sleeping. Can I meet you somewhere?"

"In front of the Cook County Courthouse. Will go up to the judge's chambers and you can tell your story."

"They'll let Frank out? I don't understand why he's doing this, but I'd feel awful if he were punished for something he didn't do."

"They'll let him out," I said confidently. "Just don't wear that dress," I said, pointing to the plunging neckline and ample cleavage.

She smiled for the first time. "The judge might like it."

I couldn't deny that. "Where something a little less…"

Another big smile. "Showing?"

• • •

It was after four o'clock when I got to the law offices of Thomas Mallory. Mallory and Associates was located on the fifth floor of a newer building on LaSalle Street. In the past I have often mentioned my great fear of elevators. Seeing that I had fully recovered from my injuries from the altercation with Horace Langley, I walked as quickly as I could up the five flights of stairs to Mallory's office. I might have recovered from the physical injuries, but my personal physical condition was questionable. I was puffing hard and my heart beat was audible as I hit the fifth landing. The thought of less booze and opium crossed my mind, but only briefly.

As expected, Mallory's office was top notch. All of the decorations and furnishings were first rate. The people who worked there were young and vibrant looking, dressed in the top fashions, whether male or female. I was led back to Mallory's private office by a young woman, not very attractive, but dressed in an expensive manor.

"Judge Hathaway's daughter," Mallory said when the girl had led me into the office and I was seated in front of his massive desk.

"A little politicking, Mr. Mallory?"

He smiled. "It takes place in all walks of life."

"You've done rather well for yourself. Dealing with irascible people like Everett Hobbs must pay pretty well."

"I think you misunderstand Everett."

"No, I don't. The man does not care for me in the least."

"You accosted him in his office."

"He infuriated me with the nonchalance that he has exhibited with respect to his daughter's kidnappings. I can't understand several of his actions. He doesn't seem to care."

"That is where you are making your biggest mistake, Detective Moses. Everett Hobbs cares too much. He cares too much about his work which causes a lot of conflicts on the home front. He is only irritated, especially since he can't solve the puzzle of finding his girls. It frustrates him."

Alicia Stone had told me a similar tale. "How could he possibly think that I had anything at all to do with the kidnappers?"

Mallory laughed. "He really didn't. In that case I think he

just didn't like you."

I didn't find it funny. "Do you have the money?"

He grabbed a small, brown leather satchel which was on his desk and flipped it to me. "The candle will burn tonight, all night. They are to give you the yellow slipper or its no deal. Once you have given them the money call me. They are to contact the house with instructions on where the girls can be found."

I nodded. "You know, I think your client is sleeping with one of the help."

He wasn't laughing now. Instead he gave me a stern look. "Is that germane to the case, Detective?"

"No," I said. "That is purely conversation between two gentlemen."

"A conversation piece that I think, if it is really true, should be kept quiet, especially since Everett Hobbs is not being investigated for anything."

I could only nod. "I think that is wise advice."

• • •

When I returned to the precinct, money tucked safely away, I made a quick visit to the two prominent residents of the cells on the lower level. I wanted to visit George Loftus and let him know that we didn't think he was involved in any of the prostitute murders and that we were trying to get him out. I also wanted to see Frank Pelicanos and let him know that I had someone who could prove that he hadn't killed my father.

Loftus was standing in his cell, looking out through the iron bars when I approached. His face was puffy and there were a number of bruises from the beating Morgan had given him.

Other than that he looked fine.

"Moses, come down here to give me more bad news?"

"Not really, George. Came down to see how you were doing."

"Why do you care? You stood there the whole time the Captain was pounding on me."

"George, I had no idea that was going to happen and really wasn't sure what the hell was going on."

He stared at me through one and a half open eyes. "I didn't have anything to do with what happened in that brothel room and nothing to do with the other dead whores."

"We know that, George."

"You know that?" he blurted. "Then what in the hell am I doing still locked up down here?"

"Morgan is looking for an arrest for the prostitute murders. When you got arrested for whatever happened he figured he had one. Give Sam and me a little time and we'll get it straight."

"That little guy came down here and told me he was a friend of yours. He took my fingerprints."

"That's Pinter and he is a friend of mine. The prints didn't match anything we had, but they didn't exclude you yet."

"I heard that Morgan is pushing for an arraignment."

"Hopefully, we'll get it taken care of before then," I said. "Remember anything else about that night?"

He thought for a moment. "I was with her in the bar, we had a couple of drinks and I remember feeling a little fuzzy. That's about it until I woke up here."

"Just hang in there a little longer. We'll get you out soon."

"Don't let anything bad happen to me, Moses. I didn't kill those women."

"I know, George."

. . .

I found Frank Pelicanos lying on his bunk. He was barely moving and, after the guard let me into the cell, I had to make sure he was alright. I poked him a few times before his eyes popped open. It took him a minute to adjust his vision and figure out who was there to see him.

"What do you want?"

"I came by to tell you that I found a witness that will claim they were with you at the time that you were supposedly killing my father." I didn't tell him what Doctor Ely had said.

"She is lying."

"I didn't say if it was a he or a she."

He sat up abruptly on the bed; I stepped back hurriedly, thinking he might swing at me. "Whoever it is, Detective Moses, they are lying. I don't understand what it is about you. I killed your father and am prepared to pay the penalty for it."

"And end up leaving your wife and children behind with no one to take care of them?"

"If that's what it amounts to."

This was too much to bear. I grabbed Pelicanos by the front of this dirty shirt and lifted him up so that his face was inches from mine. "Listen, you little maggot, this city has enough rotten people in it who truly do nasty things to other people. Why are you in such a great rush to be one of them?"

"I must pay for the crime that I committed. Why can't you understand this?"

"It's impossible for me to understand that."

"Why? You're a smart man."

"Because, Frank." Now I pulled his face even closer and I spoke in a quiet whisper. "I killed Jacob Fine on Christmas day. I shot him in the head behind Freiburg's. It wasn't you. It was me."

I'm not sure how my face looked, but I could see his. His eyes looked ready to burst and I was pretty sure that he thought I was going to dispatch him right there. I put him down lightly on the bunk, but he never took his eyes off me. "We're going to see the judge at ten tomorrow morning. This misunderstanding will be straightened out then. You will be a free man. You'd better get used to that feeling because this little charade will be over."

I called the guard and when he came, I turned quickly and left his cell. I don't think I could have climbed the stairs any faster than I did.

• • •

Whether foolishly or not, I felt that we were gaining on a couple of our cases. This thought hit me as I drank my third beer of the night at Coopers. Dinner had been roast chicken and vegetables, and I had hoped the beer would help with the dry feeling the chicken had left in my mouth. The beer took care of the dryness, but was a bit stale. Didn't stop me, though. The first two went down easily and the third would probably follow suit.

I felt strongly that the Hobbs' kidnappers would contact me soon. This would lead to the cash exchange for the girls. After that we could focus on catching the kidnappers.

I knew the pressure that Morgan felt in making an arrest regarding the prostitute murders. I knew this had led him to a hasty decision regarding Loftus. Sam and I felt Loftus was innocent. Our decision to trap the killer seemed logical as well, as long as he was someone, as we thought, who had a lot of access to the precinct or was a cop himself. We just had to come up with something that was convincing enough to draw him out. That plan had not yet been decided.

Gunter was right. Every cop in the city was looking for the blonde haired mute man named Christian Hanson. He had been very lucky he had not been spotted or he had left town. My guess was he was gone. I don't think even Jim Colosimo, as slippery as he was, wanted anything to do with Hanson. He was too hot. Anyway, it was a wait and see thing with this case. If Hanson showed we would catch him. If not, several murders would go unsolved. Not the first time for this.

As I drained the glass the thought hit me that I should try and stay sharp. The thought of Soon Lee's was in my mind, but that was not a good idea. It was to be home for me and early to bed. Before I left Coopers I thought of Frank Pelicanos and the last night he would spend in jail. The man had problems and they would not be solved by me freeing him. I didn't think they'd even go away. I only hoped he tried to do a better job with his family and tried to get well.

Lastly, as I paid my bill, I thought of Gunter and Margaret. She seemed like she wanted to work things out with Gunter. He was a hard person to live with and he was probably the reason they weren't smoothing things over. The always present thought about Gunter crossed my mind. I only hoped he didn't do anything stupid.

I had the carriage driver run me up Prairie Avenue before returning me to my apartment. I called out to him to stop in front of the Hobbs' house. It was a clear and cold night and easy to see. There, in the front, center window, burned a large candle. The kidnappers were being told that their terms had been agreed to and that I had the money they were looking for. I expected something to happen very soon.

Thirteen

It was a bitter cold morning when I met Beth Stokes on the steps of the Cook County Courthouse. It was a little before ten and I had no contact from the Hobbs' kidnappers. Beth had arrived before me and her face was pink from standing out in the cold. She gave me a warm smile as I approached her, but there was apprehension on her face.

"Are you okay?" I asked.

"I'm only doing this because I really like Frank. He was always nice to me when I went into his bakery and he always treated me like a lady. That's more than I can say about Amos."

I wasn't sure I was an expert on why people treaded into infidelity. "I understand."

She grabbed my arm roughly, even through my thick coat. Now there was fear on her face. "Amos can't find out that I came down here and talked to this judge. We have to be clear on that."

"He won't find out."

"If he does it's not going to go well for me."

"I promise you that Amos will not find out about this

discussion. The judge will be discreet."

With that confirmation, Beth took my arm more gently and we made our way up to Judge Kirk's office. I had called ahead the day before and asked that the judge see us. His secretary let us into his office as soon as we arrived. We caught the fat judge eating some kind of enormous pastry. Powdered sugar had fallen onto his suit lapels and frosting and fruit filling smeared his lips. He quickly wiped his lips and stood to greet Beth. As promised, she had worn a conservative dress, but she was still attractive. The judge seemed overly friendly towards her. She smiled and played along.

"Mrs. Stokes," I reminded the judge, "has a story that she would like to tell you, your honor."

Kirk settled into the chair behind his desk, the legs straining against his girth. "Of course," he said. "This is about Mr. Pelicanos?"

"It is," I said.

Kirk eyed the pastry on his desk, but didn't pick it up. "Doctor Ely sent me a letter. It said that he was unable to positively test Mr. Pelicanos for any type of illness, but was definitely convinced that the man is not credible. He's convinced the man is delusional."

From what I knew of the Jacob Fine case, I also knew this to be true. "Mrs. Stokes can offer physical evidence that Mr. Pelicanos was not at the scene of the crime when it occurred."

"Did you host some sort of holiday party that Mr. Pelicanos was a guest at?" the judge asked Beth.

She smiled demurely. "I suppose you can say that."

A slight frown from Kirk. "You were with Mr. Pelicanos?"

"I was."

"Can you tell me, Mrs. Stokes, what time you were with Mr.

Pelicanos?"

"My husband Amos had to work on Christmas day at four o'clock. It wasn't long after that, maybe four-thirty, that Frank came over. He was at my house until about eight o'clock."

"So you're telling me that Mr. Pelicanos was with you from four-thirty until eight o'clock on Christmas day?"

"Yes, sir."

"The body of Jacob Fine was discovered at just past six," I said.

"I'm aware of that, Detective." Kirk eyed Beth warily, and I thought for a moment that he doubted what she was telling him. "Mrs. Stokes, you will give this version to Miss Cromwell, my secretary, and you will sign it once it is transcribed. Do you understand this?"

Beth swallowed hard. "I understand."

Kirk turned towards me. "Detective, based on what Mrs. Stokes has told us and the information that I received from Doctor Ely, I believe that what Mr. Pelicanos has admitted to can be discredited. I will have him further evaluated by a specialist and then he will be released, pending some additional treatment."

"Thank you, your honor," I said.

"Mrs. Stokes, thank you for coming forward with your story. You have served the court well and have done a good deed today."

Beth Stokes looked uncomfortable. I wasn't sure she felt as if she had done anything that was that special.

I felt I had done as much for Frank Pelicanos as I could. It was clear that the man was not mentally stable. Trying to admit to a murder you hadn't committed was the craziest thing I had ever seen. At least I gave him a chance to return home and seek some help for himself. At least that was what I thought.

. . .

When I walked into the door at the precinct, the large desk Sergeant, Conners, called out my name. There were a lot of people in the lobby area and I could see he was trying to be discreet. "There's been a little bit of a problem in lockup. They told me to send you down there as soon as you came in."
My first thought was that Morgan had lost his temper again and had paid Loftus another visit. I hurried down the stairs to my left.

The first groups of cells that you saw as you came down these stairs were the ones that held George Loftus. I could clearly see Loftus sitting on his bunk with his head hanging low. He didn't look happy, but didn't look worse than the last time that I saw him. It was then that I heard the commotion coming from the other end of the lockup area was. The cells that housed Frank Pelicanos.

When I got to those cells I could clearly see Morgan, Sam Walker and the cell guard, Ed O'Malley standing outside of Frank's cell. My view of him was blocked by the three of them. None of them were smiling.

"Justice sometimes has a way of taking care of things on its own," Morgan said.

"He got what he deserved," Sam said.

They parted as I got closer and I was able to walk into the cell. Little Harold Pinter was in the cell staring up at a body that was hung from the top of the iron bars. The body was that of Frank Pelicanos. "Son of a bitch," I said.

I moved into the cell for a closer look and could see Frank

hanging from a belt from top of the bars where there was an opening before the ceiling. The belt was wrapped tightly around the bars and looped completely around his neck. His eyes were bulging and his tongue, now almost purple, was hanging outside of his mouth.

"Crazy bastard hung himself," Pinter said. There was a chair on its side under Frank's body.

"Why would he do this?" I asked aloud

"Probably to atone for his sins," Morgan said as he came up behind me. "Sure did rob the hangman, and didn't do that bad of a job of it."

I turned quickly towards Morgan. "The biggest sin he had to atone for was infidelity. This man didn't kill my father. I have just come from Judge Kirk's office where a woman named Beth Stokes told the judge that Pelicanos was with her at the time of the murder. He was to be freed, probably within days."

Morgan took another look up at Pelicanos. "Well, either way, it's not our problem any longer."

I felt my face flush with anger. "So, Captain, whose problem is it to tell his wife and children that he did this to himself? Who is going to take care of that family now?"

Captain Morgan looked a bit startled by my statement. "I believe you are becoming a little too emotionally caught up in this act, but if you feel all that strongly about it, Patrick, than I suggest you see the woman and tell her yourself."

I wanted to punch Morgan and I think Sam sensed this because he stepped between us. "Relax, there, Patrick. Let's go back upstairs why they clean this mess up."

I turned from Morgan as Sam led me out of the cell and back to the stairs. "I really should go talk to his wife," I said. "I can't believe this."

As we walked the stairs to the detective area, I felt the now familiar tightening at my temples. My vision blurred for a second and I saw little wavy lines crossing before my eyes. I took a couple of deep breaths and blinked my eyes furiously and that helped a little. The sides of my head weren't getting better. They hurt.

"You okay, Patrick?" Sam asked. "You look a little pale."

"I can't believe it," I said. "What would make him do that?"

"I think that guy was not right. Who knows what was going on inside that head?"

I nodded. What was there to disagree to?

"What made you think he didn't kill your father?" Sam asked. We were near our desks and I took a seat.

I looked up at his face and I thought I could read suspicion in his eyes. "I don't know. He just didn't seem like the type to shoot someone in the head in cold blood."

Sam nodded. "I'm surprised you can figure any type based on the number of people who we see who have so little conscience."

I was about to respond when Gunter came barreling up to our desks. His face was beet red and there was sweat on his forehead. "He's out there, Patrick."

I knew who he was, but I took a deep breath to clear my head and stood up. "What are you talking about, Gunter?"

"Hanson," he blurted. "I just received a call that he is gambling and drinking at Missed Fortune. We have to go now."

The Missed Fortune was a gambling parlor on Clark. I didn't know much about the place. "Who is your source?"

"Patrick, we have to go now. He's losing and he might not be there long."

I looked at Sam. "Let's go," he said.

•   •   •

Just like that, the death of Frank Pelicanos and what happened to his family got filed away as something to be dealt with later. That was the way of life in the Levee. We gathered some shotguns and commandeered an auto to get us over to Missed Fortune. Sam and I seemed relaxed. Even my head felt a tad better. Gunter looked like a fighting dog on the end of a leash.

"Gunter and I will take the front; Sam you go through the back," I said.

"This bastard is crazy, Patrick," Sam said. "Don't think about who's in the way if he starts shooting at us."

"Just don't shoot us," I said and Sam nodded.

We got to the Missed Fortune and allowed Sam two minutes to work his way to the alley in the back of the place before we entered. It was freezing cold out but the shotgun felt warm in my hands. "Remember, Gunter, you can't just shoot this bastard on sight."

Gunter groaned something and then we opened the door to the gambling parlor and burst in. There might have been nine or ten men gambling at the time of our entry and all of them instantly sobered up when the two of us came through the door leveling shotguns in their direction. I wasn't sure what they thought. Maybe they thought it was a robbery.

"Hands up where we can see them," Gunter yelled. Everyone in the small group complied.

Sam came in through the back as I surveyed the crowd for Christian Hanson. He wasn't there. "Police," I said. "Who is the proprietor?"

A tall man, dressed in a fine dark suit, came out from behind a dice table and approached up. He didn't look very happy. "What is the meaning of this? I have always paid my fees promptly to Bathhouse John and Hinky Dink."

A familiar response to a police raid. Paying the two ward aldermen their juice seemed to make people feel they were immune to investigations.

Gunter stepped forward and jammed the barrel of his shotgun into the owner's chest. "Hanson, where is he?"

The owner's eyes were now a bit crazy going from the shotgun to Gunter and to me. "I know no such man."

"Big guy," I said. "Blonde hair, parts it down the middle. Can't speak."

"He was here," the owner said, "but you missed him. Not more than ten minutes ago. He was not winning so he left. I didn't care for him. He looked dangerous."

Gunter took the gun from the owner's chest. "Son of a bitch."

"Was he with anyone?" I asked.

The owner shook his head. "I don't think so. Came in early, played some dice, didn't win very much and left. He had a few drinks. When he didn't speak it scared me. He looked surly."

"He can't speak. He is a mute," I said.

"I am sorry, officers. That is all I know of this man. The first time I have seen him and hopefully the last."

I wondered at that moment and on the quiet ride back to the precinct whether we would see Hanson again or not. I was convinced he was out of town, but apparently he wasn't. I looked over at Gunter, but he only stared ahead, the rage in him at a low boil.

. . .

The day settled into a normal routine if that is possible. I couldn't get my head to understand the Frank Pelicanos suicide. The more I thought of it the more frustrated I got. I was sure that Gunter felt the same way about our unsuccessful attempt at catching Christian Hanson. He didn't stay put for long once we got back to the precinct. He left and I didn't see him the rest of the day. Sam felt like I did about Hanson. "Slippery as grease" he mentioned to me before leaving the precinct for the day. There was nothing new with the prostitute murders. Someone wanted us to believe Loftus was the killer; Morgan wanted to indict him, but that was on hold. No new murders took place. There were no new leads. No one had approached me about the money I held in my suit as ransom for the Hobbs' girls. I wasn't worried. Something would happen soon. It was late afternoon before I could get out to see Sylvia Pelicanos. I stopped at home and grabbed another two hundred from the Field case.

. . .

It was very cold as I walked up the steps to the small house. I could see lights on within it so I knew they were home. With all of the garbage that we processed in the Levee I seldom found myself nervous or uneasy. I think you just got used to it. This was new for me. Telling Sylvia that she was now a widow with two small children had my stomach jumping around.

I knocked on the door never thinking for a minute that Sylvia wouldn't answer. When the door was opened by little Stephanie I might have well have seen a ghost.

"Hello," she said, her little brown eyes staring up at me. "Did you bring my daddy home?"

"I, no, he's not with me," I said. I almost decided to turn and walk away.

"He's not coming back, is he," a voice behind Stephanie said.

I looked up from the girl and Sylvia was standing there. She wore an apron and looked as if she had been preparing dinner. "Stephanie, go check on your brother," she said. She waited until the little girl was out of the room before she spoke. I stepped into the small area and closed the door behind me.

"Answer me, Detective Moses," she said. Her eyes were alive, aflame.

"He is not coming back," I said quietly. "He took his own life this morning."

"That is a lie," she said. "Frank wouldn't do anything like that. You said he would be back and now you tell me he isn't coming. What has your police department done with my Frank?"

I tried to take a step closer to her, but she held up both hands, telling me not to come any closer. "I am telling you the truth," I said.

Her shoulders drooped and the truth hit her. She was all alone. What was she to do with her two small children? "I am sorry," I said.

"You have killed him," she blurted out.

"Me," I said meekly.

"You and that criminal father of yours. It is all because of your family that my Frank is no longer here. What am I to do?"

I was at a total loss for words. Jacob Fine was my father, but we weren't family. How totally twisted was Sylvia's understanding of the situation.

"Please go, Detective Moses. Please leave my home and do not return."

I nodded and reached into my pocket for the money I intended on giving her. I held it out for her. She laughed. "You kill my husband and now you want to give me blood money to make it all seem better. You and your Goddamn father." She took two steps closer to me and spit right into my face. "I don't want your money. I don't want anything to do with you."

Alone, on the walk in front of the house, I turned back to look at it. I understood her anger at the situation, but not at me. This confused me and brought back the pain in my temples. I heard one short scream come from the house, but I was not alarmed. It was a scream of grief. I felt awful. I had wanted to stay sharp until I was contacted by the kidnappers, but I couldn't. My body, my mind, all of me craved whiskey and then Soon Lee's.

• • •

The whiskey did the trick. It's always the case that the first couple of sips burn and then they soothe. After that there is a numbing feeling. It's still good at that point. You just need to know when to stop. I was at Cooper's and I had four or five and I knew the time had come for me to quit or I would be useless. So much of my day so far had been a waste. I had lost Frank Pelicanos despite my efforts to free him and his wife, Sylvia, wanted me to rot in hell. The same was true of Christian Hanson. Gunter got a tip that he was at the Missed Fortune, but he wasn't there. Sam was right. Hanson was a slippery character. I wondered if we'd ever catch him. Not tonight, I thought.

I moved to Soon Lee's. The night was still somewhat young when I entered the chop suey restaurant; there were still patrons there who were actually eating. Soon Lee gave me a funny look and then pointed me down the stairs to the left that led to the opium den.

This is where things became a little fuzzy. I don't know how much opium I smoked, but I was certainly feeling good. I was as hazy as the rest of the room, covered in a cloud of smoke. I was completely somewhere else, drifting in and out of sleep. For once, no evil clouded my thoughts. There was only peace.

I awoke one time and there was a beautiful woman in front of me. I was lying on a cot and she had taken a seat right by me. She wore a light colored dress and I could see that she was well endowed. She had light colored hair. I couldn't make her eyes out clearly.

"Detective Moses," she said quietly. "Can you understand me?"

She was talking to me and I understood her, but I wasn't sure if this was a dream or a real person. I reached out with one hand and slipped it into her dress caressing a very large breast.

"Not now," she said. There was a bit of an accent. "You need to wake up and understand what I am saying."

I tried to rise off the pillow, but that was not wise. My head, due to the whiskey and the opiate, wouldn't function well enough. "What is it?" I asked.

"I am your connection," she said. "I am here for the money for the release of the Hobbs' twins. If you will give me the money a call will be made to their residence tomorrow at ten o'clock informing them where the girls are. Do you understand this?"

My head cleared for a bit. The smoke in the den also cleared and I had a better view of her face and those eyes. I had seen them before. "I understand," I said.

"The money, detective."

I was able to rise off the cot and reach into my pocket for the package that contained the twenty thousand dollars. When I handed it over to her I could read the look of relief on her face. I am sure it was due to the thought of the ordeal of hiding two kidnapped girls was about to end.

"Thank you," she said. "The call will come at ten o'clock." She got up to leave but I grabbed her arm firmly. She looked startled.

"You have something for me," I said.

"Oh, yes. In my haste, I almost forgot." She reached into her purse and removed a little, yellow slipper, the kind that would be worn by a small infant. She gave it to me. "Ten o'clock."

I grabbed her again and she looked frightened. "You have the money. I want those girls and they'd better be safe. When this transaction is done, tell your friends that I am coming."

She got up from the cot and left the den in a hurry. I closed my eyes and was asleep almost instantly. When I awoke it was nearly two in the morning. I felt groggy and hung over. Then I remembered my nighttime visitor and I got up. My head hurt, but I was fine. I looked at me feet and I saw the yellow slipper. It had been no dream. They had the money and we'd get the girls. I remembered something about telling the woman I would come for the kidnappers. That had not been in a dream either. I was going to find them.

Fourteen

I was awake and ready to go by nine the next day. It was a bit of a struggle to get up and get moving, but I managed. I walked to the police call box on the corner and placed a call to Thomas Mallory's office. An assistant there told me that she would get a hold of him and that he would meet me at the Hobbs' residence. I caught the first carriage that I saw and proceeded to the house. It was going to be a sunny day and I could tell it was going to be warmer. Snow and ice in the streets had begun to puddle.

Being that it was early I caught most of the Hobbs' clan in their bedtime attire. Both Susan Hobbs and Alicia Stone wore heavy robes over their night clothes. Everett Hobbs was not at home and I was told he had already gone to his office. I also didn't see Sarah Balowski, but I knew she was around since it was not her day off.

"Is there news?" Alicia Stone asked.

"There is," I said. "Contact was made last night and I have delivered the money to the kidnapper's messenger. We will get word of the location of the girls at ten o'clock."

At this, Susan Hobbs began to cry; she was immediately

comforted by Alicia. I felt good, but it was an awkward setting. "Will you be calling Mr. Hobbs?"

"He had an important meeting," Alicia said. "We will try and call him, but it may be difficult to reach him."

I felt a surge of anger and wondered how Hobbs could place anything ahead of the plight that his girls were going through. I let it go for now. A few minutes later Mallory showed up at the house.

"You're confident that the woman you gave the money to is connected with the kidnappers?" He didn't seem like he believed this.

I pulled the yellow slipper from my coat and handed it to Susan. "Is this the slipper that belongs to Millicent?" I was careful of what tense I phrased the question.

Again this brought forth a rash of tears and only two subtle nods of her head.

"That is the slipper," Alicia said. "Thank you, Detective Moses."

I noticed the look of sincerity on her face. "Don't thank me until we have found the girls and they are safe and well."

We all waited in the small library. The black maid, Amelia Johnson, brought us all hot coffee and it tasted great and felt like a savior for me. The night before had ravaged me a bit. The coffee helped to get my feet back on the ground.

The minutes slowly, and painfully, crept past ten o'clock. There was a large clock on the fireplace mantle and those of us that could see it watched it closely. Everett Hobbs' office had been notified of the happenings, but he had not arrived yet. I pulled out my pocket watch, hoping that the mantle clock was wrong. They both said the same thing.

At ten minutes past the hour, Mallory spoke. "Are you sure

you got the right time?"

"The woman said ten o'clock," I said calmly.

Someone rang the front doorbell and it turned out to be Sam Walker. I had left word at the precinct for him and he came as soon as he could. He must have noticed how tense we all looked because he said nothing.

"Are you positive that the woman you saw was from the kidnappers?" Mallory asked again.

A dumb question from a smart lawyer. "She gave me the slipper."

Mallory nodded, realizing his blunder. I knew it was all due to tension.

At quarter past ten the telephone on the small table in the room rang. I looked at Mallory, but he made a hand motion indicating I should answer. I walked to the telephone and picked it up. "Detective Moses."

"Listen carefully," a muffled voice said. "The two girls are in a carriage in the house wares section of Marshall Field's near the Washington Street entrance." The line went dead.

I hung up the phone. "They're in Marshall Field's, house wares section." I picked up the telephone again and dialed the central police number and told them who I was and to have a patrolman get to the store and find the girls. We would be along shortly.

The two women, not caring how they looked, found winter coats, hats and shoes and we were soon all piled into two carriages Sam had found. We were quite a ways from the great store of my former employer but the drivers made excellent time as we tore through the streets towards the Loop. I found it funny that the kidnappers had picked that locale to drop off the girls. When we reached the store and entered the Washington

Street entrance there was a crowd gathered. We forced ourselves through and found two patrolmen, each holding a little, smiling Hobbs' girl. The smiles I saw on the faces of Alicia Stone and Thomas Mallory were precious. Sam, a good father, grinned from ear to ear. I felt relief. Susan Hobbs, upon seeing that her two daughters were safe and healthy, promptly fainted.

• • •

Back at the Hobbs' house there was much joy and celebration. Everett Hobbs had arrived and actually seemed happy that his two girls were home safely. I won't say that he congratulated Sam and me because he didn't. He wore a smile for the first time that I had known him. Sarah Balowski also made an appearance and she fawned over the two twins. She stayed completely away from Everett. Mallory was there and he looked relieved, sipping on a glass of red wine. Susan Hobbs had been revived and she was between tears and smiling broadly. I can't imagine the stress that must have left her body. Alicia Stone was near her side and held her hand from time to time; she looked a very different person, smiling broadly. A number of neighbors and friends appeared during the little celebration, some bearing small gifts for the girls. Sam and I did manage to stay out of the way, but we did sneak a fair amount of wine.

"Only half done," I said.

"What do you mean?" Sam responded.

"We should try and find the kidnappers."

Sam waved a hand around the expansive, well-furnished dining room. "We got the girls back and this bastard, Hobbs, has the money. Does it matter?"

I thought it did, but I said nothing. I also had a very good idea where my next lead was going to come from, but not today. Sam finished his glass of wine and said he had to go to the Cook County jail. I was still drinking my third glass when Alicia Stone made her way over to me. Both she and Susan Hobbs were still dressed in nightwear.

"May I have a word with you, Detective Moses?" She had suddenly taken on a very serious tone.

"Certainly," I said.

I followed her out into the hall and into a small room, a storage room near the kitchen. She closed the door. "I must talk to you about a matter that I have discovered," she said.

"Is this about your brother?"

The look on her face showed mild shock. "It is, I am sorry to say."

"I will listen to what you say and hold it in confidence between us unless it involves a crime."

She heard this and her teeth came out and bit her lower lip. She was clearly struggling with this matter. "I may have mentioned to you or you may know that Everett has an office on the second floor. He has the only key to this room and, to my knowledge, was the only one allowed in there."

I sipped my wine, saying nothing.

"Two nights since the ordeal had started, well after Susan had gone to bed, I have heard noises from this office. I have waited around as secretly as I could until someone exited the office. Both times it was past midnight and both times it was Sarah Balowski. I am afraid that my brother has been having an affair, an illicit one, with Sarah."

I nodded and took another sip of my wine. "And why are you telling me this?"

Her lips quivered a bit. "I don't know what it is, she is a nice young woman, but I suspect that Sarah is somehow behind the kidnappings. I can't hold my brother blameless, but I think she has used herself to help manipulate Everett. I know some of this may sound completely ridiculous, but I had to tell you. The whole thing just didn't feel right." She lowered her eyes and appeared to be tearing up.

I took her hand in mine and she looked up at me. "I intend on finding the kidnappers," I said. "I will leave no rock unturned. If Ms. Balowski is involved I will find out."

"I only ask one thing," she said. "Please do not embarrass my brother. Do not embarrass my family."

Again, I could think of only one proper response. "Your brother and I have failed to build much of a relationship, but I will do my best to not embarrass anyone, but can't hold that promise if there's any chance he had anything to do with a crime being committed."

She looked up at me with wet eyes and nodded her agreement.

• • •

I was genuinely happy for the first time in a while at the recovery of the Hobbs' twins. I probably had a little more wine than I should have and it was mid-afternoon by the time that I got back to the precinct. I felt a little lightheaded. This cleared up as soon as I walked through the doors and was told that Maria Farrell, the prostitute that George Loftus allegedly slashed, was awake at Mercy Hospital. I was told to hurry once I got the message since she was "in and out". I rushed back outside, grabbed a nearby coach and told him to travel quickly to the hospital.

The same young doctor who had met me before when I visited Maria was on hand at the nurse's station when I arrived. He looked a little upset. "I left that message for you over an hour and a half ago, Detective Moses." The nurses in the station all stared at me.

"Sorry," I said sheepishly. "I really did have some other pressing matters."

"Miss Farrell has been in and out of consciousness all day. She was awake a few minutes ago when I checked on her."

I followed the doctor, whose name was Taylor, into the room that held Maria Farrell. When I looked down at the poor woman in the bed it reminded me so much of the day that I was forced to look down upon Eleanor, dead in that dirty snow near Bubbly Creek. Some of the bandages had been removed, but her face was still a mixture of colors, bumps, cuts and bruises. My heart sank.

"Maria, this is Doctor Taylor. You have a visitor to see you," the doctor said to her as he held her right hand. Only her heaving chest gave any proof of life.

She moved a little and there was a small groan. A moment later her eyes opened. The light in the room must have hurt them because she blinked furiously. Her head was propped up by a couple of pillows and the doctor gave her a small sip of water. "You have a visitor, Maria," he repeated.

"Who?" she asked and even in this small syllable there was pain.

"It's Detective Moses. He is here to ask you about that night. He wants to help find who did this to you."

"Help me," she said and then she smiled.

I walked up next to the doctor where she could see me. "Hello, Maria. My name is Patrick."

"Hello," she said quietly. It was a struggle to hear what she said.

I knelt down beside her bed, my knee touching the hard floor; Doctor Taylor moved a bit to the side. I took her hand gently. "Do you remember much from that night?" I asked.

She thought for a moment, coughed a little and Taylor gave her more water. "Was at Mother Murphy's with that cop," she said.

"George Loftus?" I said.

"His name?"

She wasn't understanding me. "Did the cop make the date with you?"

She closed her eyes for what seemed like an eternity and I thought she might have drifted off. She was on laudanum and I had seen its effects before. Her eyes came open again. "Big man made the date."

"What big man?" I said a little quickly and I startled her. She looked at me funny for a second or two. "Take care of cop. Get him drunk." Again her eyes closed, but they opened quickly.

"This big man, he told you to get the cop drunk and knocked out?"

"Gave me powder for his drinks. Thought the man was going to fall asleep. Got him up to my room. Fell asleep on the floor. Couldn't budge him."

She paused and I thought we might lose her. "Then what happened?" I said loudly.

"Door opened and big man came in. Hit me in the face couple of times. Almost knocked me out. Felt knife..." The conversation was all getting the best of her. There were tears running out of her eyes.

"I think we'd better stop for now," Doctor Taylor said.

"One more question," I said. "This big man. Describe him."

"Bent over, brown hair, mustache. Big hat."

"Get his name?" I asked.

Her eyes closed for a moment. "No name."

I got up off my knees. I was sure I had all that I needed to free Loftus. I felt Maria Farrell touch my hand once more before I left her room. "Yes," I said.

"Hurt him like he hurt me," she said and now the tears came freely.

I knelt again by her side. The man who did this had killed at least three women that we knew of. My Eleanor was one of them. "I will make him pay," I said.

• • •

"It is the same man who killed Dancing Walter who cut up Maria Farrell." I was telling this to Sam Walker outside of the precinct on Twenty- Second Street. We had decided when talking about the prostitute murders that we would only do so in privacy. We were becoming more certain that the killer was someone who had access to the precinct or was a cop. We knew we had to keep things to ourselves. "I think we should let Morgan know this so we can get poor Loftus out of that cell."

Sam was quickly smoking a cigarette, drawing on it and puffing the smoke out of his mouth as if he needed it to breath. "We should wait on that," he said.

"Wait? We know that Loftus didn't do this."

Sam flicked away the spent smoke and quickly lit another. "I want to hold off until we spring our trap. I don't want to give anyone, including Morgan, any clues about what we know."

I wasn't in agreement with this. "What do you suggest?"

"I am going to make it public through Morgan and others here at the precinct that I have been contacted by someone who wants to meet me privately and who can tell me the identity of the killer. We will indicate where the meeting is. If nothing else it may draw out the curious and maybe, if the killer is around the precinct, then him."

I thought for a moment. "When do you think this meeting should take place?"

"Sooner the better. The killer tried to frame Loftus. What was his reason behind that? It's simple. He wants to go away for a while. Too many people have seen him. Even if Loftus is freed, which he will be, there has been enough of a diversion to take the attention from the killer. He can take some time off; he might not ever be found."

• • •

"What did the whore who got cut up tell you?" Morgan asked this as he sat at his desk. He had heard that there was a call from the hospital saying that Maria Farrell was alert and speaking.

"Nothing much," I lied. "She was so in and out from the laudanum that it was hard to get anything out of her."

Morgan nodded. "Poor woman. Do you think she'll make it?"

"I don't know. The doctor says she's still in a very guarded condition. It's not day to day, more like hour to hour."

Morgan stretched his aching back; you could hear some crunching. "There's not much there. What about Loftus? Do we have enough to indict him?"

"Nothing more," Sam said, "but there has been a development in the case."

Morgan gave Sam a serious look. "What kind of development?"

Sam took a deep breath. "It might be a hoax, but I got a call this morning from someone who told me that they would contact me later in the week and let me know where we could meet. This person told me he knew the identity of the prostitute murderer. He said he would only meet with Moses and me and it would be a location out in the open."

Morgan shook his head. "I'm still betting on Loftus, but everything in this case needs to be followed up on. Headquarters is constantly after me to close this mess."

Sam looked over at me and I shrugged. His ploy to draw out anyone who knew something of the killer wasn't that strong, but you never knew.

• • •

When I returned to my desk there was a message that there was a woman in the lobby to see me. My first thought was that it would be Alicia Stone, but when I walked down the stairs I saw Beth Stokes pacing madly about. When she saw me she rushed over to me. She had a newspaper in her hand.

"Have you seen this?" she yelled.

I looked down at today's *Tribune* that she held. "I don't usually read the papers," I said. "What's wrong with you?"

"Thanks for keeping what I told you a secret, Moses," she said. "Some idiot guard in your cells here claims you said that you had a witness, a Beth Stokes, who could prove that Frank Pelicanos was with her at the time that Jacob Fine was murdered, clearing Frank of any charges related to that crime."

I looked down at her and saw nothing, but anger. I recalled my conversation with Morgan, Sam and others in the cell block after Frank Pelicanos had hung himself. A guard had been present and he had repeated what I said to a *Tribune* reporter who was covering the Jacob Fine case and then the Pelicanos suicide.

"What do you have to say for yourself, Moses?" Beth yelled at me. Several people were looking our way.

"I will talk with your husband. Nothing will happen to you."

She tossed the paper in my face. "You stay away from Amos. I don't want your help. I've seen what you can do. I will deal with Amos on my own." With that she turned on her heels and was quickly out the door. I knelt down and picked up the paper. I wouldn't read the article. It sounded like the reporter had covered what happened accurately.

• • •

With the recovery of the Hobbs's twins you would think that a celebration would be in order, but that was not the case. After drinking wine with the family earlier in the day, everything else that happened after that had gone downhill. I was in Cooper's trying to lighten my mood, but not getting very far. I was tired and I had a bit of a headache. I thought it might be from the wine drinking or maybe it was the somewhat constant problem I was having. Either way, the whiskey I drank was easing the pressure at my temples.

I twirled the cold glass in my hand, the condensation wetting my fingers. Why I bothered thinking about these things was a mystery to me. I knew better. Once you figured something out in the Levee something else would come along and switch your view point. We had accomplished our goal of getting the Hobbs' girls back. This was a good moment. This had been followed up by a visit to see Maria Farrell, not such a good time, and an angry visit from Beth Stokes, a worse moment. There was never anything down here that stayed consistent.

As I finished my whiskey and contemplated the challenges that faced us, I felt myself on the verge of giving up. Maybe there was something else out there. Maybe trying to solve crimes in such a lawless area as the Levee was just a big game, a game you could never win. When I came to this realization, I suddenly felt a bit relaxed. Everything that went wrong in the Levee didn't fall on my shoulders. I could only do so much to correct so little of it. I paid my bill and headed for home.

The night air was cold as I trudged along the sidewalks trying to make sure that I didn't slip on any hidden ice. I sucked a bit of the frozen night air into my lungs and it felt good. I could only do so much, I thought again. I was just about to enter my building when a police vehicle pulled up in front. Sam Walker burst from the front seat.

"Evening, Sam," I said. I knew this was not a social visit.

"Let's go, Patrick," he said. "It's your friend, Krause. Somebody got him over at the Bucket of Blood. He's not doing very well."

I hopped into the automobile with Sam and the driver, a young patrolman. We sped through the late night streets to the Bucket of Blood, a lowdown brothel on Bed Bug Row. Sam's information had been a little wrong. Gunter's problems had not occurred inside the brothel, but in the alley beside it. This had been the scene of his first beating, the one he had survived. This time it didn't look so promising.

There was a crowd packed into the alley, a number of them policemen. Sam and I got out of the vehicle and pushed through the mass. There was enough light in the small space to make out Gunter's large frame lying in the old snow in the alley. He was lying face up and he was fully clothed. All I needed to see was his face. I couldn't tell from it that it used to be human. There was so much bruising and blood it was almost impossible to tell it was Gunter. His mouth hung open and it showed that most of his teeth had been knocked out. There were no signs of life.

I stood up. "Who saw anything here?" I said.

There were some mutterings in the crowd, but no one came forward with anything of value. "Anyone see what happened?" I repeated.

This time there was less chatter. A big cop came up to me. "Someone called it into the precinct. Said there was a body back here. We checked his wallet. When we saw who it was we called it in. They called Detective Walker who went looking for you."

I nodded and looked back one more time at Gunter. He could never leave things alone and then he would go after things on his own. This time it had cost him.

"Nothing to do here, Patrick," Sam said. "Looks like our friend, Hanson, is in business again."

"I wonder why Gunter was down here," I said. I would find this out shortly.

It took a while for the door to be answered at Gunter's apartment. I couldn't believe that Margaret and the children weren't home. Finally, after the third time that I pounded on the door, it was opened. Margaret stood there, hair down, dressed in her night clothes. She took one look at me in the door and broke down. She knew Gunter was in trouble.

She invited me in and we were in their small kitchen drinking tea. She had sent her children back to bed after they had been awaken. She would tell them later what had happened to their father. Now, we sat in near silence, sipping the hot tea and listening to the steam rattling in the radiator.

"I can't believe he's gone," she said.

"I am so sorry," I said.

She let out a big sob and tears rolled from her eyes. "I never got a chance to work things out with Gunter. We were both mad at each other and now he is gone."

I wanted to take her hand, but I didn't. She sipped her tea and wiped her eyes. "What happened tonight?"

She looked at me. It was amazing how sorrow made someone look so unglamorous. "It was late. The children were asleep, I was in our room and Gunter was reading. We'd had a quiet night. No fighting. I was ready to go to bed when the telephone rang. I came out of our room to see what it was. All Gunter said was that he had a lead on something and that he had to go into the Levee."

"That was all he said?"

More tears streaked her face. "That was it. Those were the last words he spoke to me."

"He didn't say who called or where he had to go in the Levee?"

She shook her head. "No, Patrick. Just that he had to go into the Levee."

I nodded. Someone had called Gunter and told him something important. My guess is that they told him where the mute, blonde man, Christian Hanson could be found. That was one thing that would get Gunter out the door late at night. As Sam Walker had stated, Hanson was back in business and he didn't want Gunter interfering with him. That was why he had decided to take him out.

• • •

I didn't want to be around any people so I avoided taverns. It was much easier to be by myself and drink at home. It was only whiskey. It tasted the same regardless of where you drank it. I drank a lot and I lost track of time. There was something about watching families disintegrate. It was different when it was just some slug that was dead. Most of the time no one cared, especially the police. With people like Gunter, and even Frank Pelicanos, it wasn't the same. Here was the husband, father and bread winner suddenly gone from the picture. The money could possibly be replaced, the women might find another husband, but the children involved would never have their fathers again. I was an orphan. These thoughts tore me apart. I punished myself with Canadian whiskey.

Fifteen

How much I drank I will never know. It's not important. The sleep came and went with fleeting dreams that tormented me. There was nothing sound about it, but one thing was clear when I awoke. Today had been exactly one week since I had seen Sarah Balowski enter the offices of Everett Hobbs and spend an hour and a half in them. Today was her day off again. The thought hit me as soon as I awoke. It was two o'clock in the afternoon. It wouldn't be long before I thought she would return to see her lover. I quickly cleaned up and dressed and was out the door. I didn't bother with the precinct. I was sure word was out that I would not be in.

When I reached the tavern down and across the street from Hobbs' office I finally realized just how awful I felt. It didn't stop me from ordering a double from the bartender. The whiskey soothed me and made me feel alive as I took my seat in the front window. It was three-fifteen. She had come right about four the last time. If things went the same way, she would arrive before long.

I had two more whiskeys before the grand carriage rolled up

in front of the office building. I watched as it stopped, the coachman got out and opened the door. Out into the cold air stepped Sarah Balowski. She kept her head down as she walked the several steps into Hobbs' building. It was four-ten. I settled back and waited for the carriage to return to take her back home. I knew it would be at least an hour. I ordered more whiskey.

It was just past five- thirty when the carriage rolled by the windows of the tavern and pulled to a stop in front of the office building. I had already paid for my drinks and I got up quickly. Maybe too quickly for I wobbled a bit. I righted myself and headed out the doors. The cold air hit me and I felt fresh and ready to go. I walked up the side of the street of Hobbs' building across from the carriage. Soon I saw the doors to the office building open and Sarah step outside. She waited a minute for the driver to open her door and let her in. Once she was in the carriage and the driver had gone back to his spot I quickly ran to the carriage, opened the door, climbed in and took a seat beside Sarah. It happened so fast, she was too startled to make any sound.

I was lucky because this was an entirely enclosed cab and the driver had no idea that he had another passenger. Sarah looked at me passively, saying nothing. I wondered if she expected a visit from me at some time.

"Did you have a nice visit with Mr. Hobbs?" I said. I don't know if I was angry or upset, but I was tense.

"You knew?"

"Not just me. Alicia Stone reported some visitations you had in Mr. Hobbs' study. I saw you leave his office a week ago today after I had visited him."

"He doesn't love his wife," she said curtly. "Now that the

girls have been returned and are safe he will seek a divorce. This will all be proper very soon."

She was looking directly at me and the cab was well lit. "I don't care about your love life," I said. "You have her eyes. That smoky gray blue color is too unique. You have to be related. Sisters?"

The look on her face registered shock, but she quickly tried to cover it up. "Who are you talking about? I don't know what you mean."

"Sure you do," I said. "The woman who brought me the ransom money and who gave the blood soaked pajamas to the courier to deliver to the Hobbs. She has the same eyes as you and nearly the same colored hair." I slid my hand inside of her coat and felt a small breast. "She did make out a little better on the top."

She quickly pushed my hand away. "You are crazy," she said.

"Not so crazy to take you down to the precinct and get some answers out of you. You knew they were coming for the girls. You unlocked that bedroom window."

For the first time I saw some resolve in her eyes. "You don't understand," she said.

"I just want to recover the money and catch the kidnappers. Depending on what you say will determine how we treat you. Would you like to come into the precinct and tell us what you know?"

Instantly, there were tears in her eyes. "I never wanted the girls to get hurt. I knew they wouldn't be."

"We'd better get to Twenty- Second Street and you can tell me your story."

She grabbed my hand. "Does Everett have to know?"

I only shook my head.

I pounded on the cab to get the driver's attention and had him take us to the precinct. I gave him a couple of dollars so that his story would be that he had let Sarah off in the Loop to shop. He gratefully accepted the tip and quickly got us to the station house.

. . .

The precinct was no place to be the day after one of our own had been killed. I could feel the somber silence the moment we walked through the doors. I could feel the eyes watching me as I led Sarah Balowski up to the second floor and into a meeting room. I saw Sam at his desk and motioned for him to join us. I closed the door behind him as he entered and sat at the long table. Sarah's eyes shifted from Sam to me and back again like a wild animal.

"You don't understand," she said.

Sam looked to me. "Maybe you should tell us what you know about this kidnapping. Maybe you should help us understand," I said.

She nodded and took a couple of breaths to calm herself down. "We came here about ten years ago. My sister, Anna, and my brothers Michael and Peter. They are much older than us and they controlled us. We tried to do everything that we could to build a better life, to live like normal people, but we were nothing. We were just more immigrants from off the boat. As Anna and I got older, one way to make a little extra money was to sell us off for services."

"Wait a minute," Sam said quickly. "Your brothers were

selling you out to service men?"

She nodded and I noticed the buildup of tears in her eyes. "I was about seventeen the first time; Anna is a couple of years older. They would sell us to men from the brewery. We would go to where they lived and service them. The money would go to my brothers. This went on for about four years until I heard about the job with the Hobbs. I took the job and moved into their house, but..."

"What happened?" I asked.

"Michael followed me on my day off and demanded that I send him half of my earnings or else he would tell the Hobbs of my past as a courtesan. If they found out about this they would fire me instantly."

"So you're paying your brothers half of your pay to keep some of your past from the Hobbs? What led to the kidnapping?"

She looked at me. "I saw Anna from time to time. She was sympathetic but my brothers controlled her. She told me they wanted to return to Poland, but needed money for the trip and money to buy a farm when they got back there. They wanted me to help them with the kidnapping."

She looked at both of us; we said nothing.

"They promised me that the girls would not be harmed. They would only take them and hold them until a ransom had been paid. Then the girls would be released unharmed. They would leave the country and I would be left alone."

"You believed them?" Sam asked.

"I believed Anna, and I had fallen in love with Everett. I knew he would leave Susan for me. I knew I had to get my brothers out of the country. I agreed to help them."

"What were you to do?" I asked.

"You know, Detective Moses. I was only to unlock the nursery window so that they could raise a ladder up to it and get the girls out. I knew not even my brothers would harm those little girls. I knew once they got the money that we would get the girls back."

I nodded. "We need to find them and quickly. I am sure they are planning their departure."

"You mentioned," she said, "something about my eyes. That was how you connected me."

"I met your sister just once when she brought me the ransom. She is a bigger girl, fuller figure, close to the same hair color, but the one thing about her that was identical were those smoky, blue gray colored eyes. Too much similarity for the two of you not to be related."

She smiled. "Same mother, different father. We only share the eyes, my mother's eyes, and that's how you caught me."

• • •

Anna had led it leak out to Sarah where they were staying after we'd found their apartment. They had rented a two bedroom unit at the Fister Hotel, a modestly priced place at the south end of the Loop. The building had five stories and they had taken a unit on the fifth floor. There was an elevator and there were stairs that led up to the room. There was only one door and one way out. When we knew this we armed ourselves with shotguns and Sam and I went upstairs using the always dreaded elevator.

Room Five-oh-One was in the corner of the building and there didn't appear to be anyone on the floor at all. The place was deathly quiet. We walked up to the room, guns ready and Sam knocked with the stock of his weapon. There was no sound for a minute and we thought the room was empty, but the hotel management had told us they were in. Sam knocked again. We heard some voices and then someone was by the door.

"Who is it?" a male voice said.

"Management," Sam said. "We got a call that there was a disturbance coming from this room."

Quiet for a minute. "No disturbance here," the voice said.

"Can we just come in and check for a minute to make sure all is good?"

More silence and then we heard the door chain being rattled. Sam stepped to the side of the door, gun pointed at what would have been head level. I was on the other side. When the chain came loose and the handle moved the door opened about three inches. It was then that my foot slammed into it, knocking the Kowalski brother onto the floor. Sam was on him quickly, barrel up under his chin. The other brother and Anna were seated at a small table, eyes about a foot wide. I leveled my shotgun at them.

"Hello," I said. "The three of you are under arrest for the kidnappings of the Hobbs' girls. Come along peacefully and things will go well. Cause a bit of trouble and most of you will end up on the wall behind you."

Sam had cuffed the one brother and moved to cuff the other. I was surprised when Anna got up and moved towards me. I still had the gun pointed at her.

"Detective Moses," she said sweetly. "I could tell from the first time that we met that you were attracted to me. I think that it is possible that we could work something out. After all, my part in all of this was very small."

She was attractive and she had a fabulous figure. There were also those beautiful eyes, alluring. She gave me an amorous look. The shotgun was in my left hand. I thought of the Hobbs' twins, so little that maybe they never missed their mother, but they would have been scared. I thought of my own daughter. With my right hand I swung as hard as I could, open fist, of course, and knocked Anna Kowalski flying across the small space. She hit the wall and crumpled. When she recovered she looked at me. She was no longer smiling and probably knew the mood I was in.

They weren't the smartest crooks; that was for sure. They had booked a train for New York the following day and a steamer to France after that. In the hotel room, we found the balance of the cash. I wondered if Everett Hobbs would complain about the small loss.

• • •

It was later in the day after we had booked the Kowalskis. We were holding Sarah Balowski, but weren't quite sure what to do with her. It was true that she had aided the kidnappers, but based on what she had told us some of this was done under duress. She would cool herself for a while in the cells with her brothers and sister.

Sam had volunteered to do most of the paperwork with the arrest. I told him I would return the unspent money to Hobbs and tell him of the arrests. I also told Sam that I had never apologized for assaulting Hobbs and now was as good a time as any. I called Thomas Mallory and told him what had happened; I told him to meet me at Hobbs' office in thirty minutes. The night was dark and cold by the time that I climbed into the cab and had it take me back to where my day started.

I was told that Hobbs and Mallory were waiting for me in Hobbs' office. I was led back there by the same receptionist as before. The office was empty and there were only lights burning in the one, large office. Mallory was seated in front of Hobbs desk; Hobbs was standing behind it when I entered. Mallory stood and shook my hand when I entered the office; Hobbs stayed where he was.

"Congratulations are in order, I should say," Mallory said. He was smiling broadly.

I removed the money from my suit coat and placed it in the middle of the desk. "It's not all there. The Kowalskis spent some of it planning their return trip to Europe. We'll have to see if that can be recovered."

"Excellent," Mallory said. Hobbs remained silent.

"I have also come here to apologize for my behavior the first time that I visited your office. I was completely out of line." I said this directly to Hobbs. He nodded his acknowledgement.

"I also want to say that I misunderstood your manner of behavior and may have acted out of line in that regard as well."

Hobbs finally spoke. "I don't understand."

"I accused you of being aloof and detached in your behavior during the time of your daughter's kidnapping. I think that I viewed your handling of it as an inconvenience. I was wrong."

Mallory was staring up at me from his seat. Everett Hobbs gave me a sidelong glance.

"It wasn't that it was inconvenient or that you were aloof," I said. "I have spoken to Miss Balowski and know of your relationship with her. I also understand your nonchalant actions. She explained to you about the kidnappings and she told you that her brothers and sisters only wanted the money to get out of town. They would not harm the girls. It would totally free Sarah from her abusive brothers. You played along with this, even if it meant putting the two girls into harm's way. You went along with this and understood the girls would eventually come home. You did all of this to avoid any scandal about Sarah's past and so it wouldn't look like you just paid the brothers off. That was why you never seemed too distressed about the whole mess."

"You are absolutely crazy, Moses. You are a sick man," Hobbs said. His face had gone a crimson red.

"No, I don't think so," I said. "I promised your sister, Miss Stone, that I would not embarrass the family or you and I won't. My true purpose for coming here was to tell you what a complete piece of shit you are."

Hobbs looked to Mallory. "None of this is true, Thomas." The lawyer wore a shocked look.

"We are holding Miss Balowski. Her entire story will be transcribed. I don't think she wants to hurt you so there is a good chance your name will not appear anywhere, but she did tell me and that is all I needed to hear."

Hobbs was trying to say something and he may have, but I was out the office door and headed for the stairs. I was exhausted. With Gunter's death the night before and this day long end to the Hobbs' case, I needed whiskey. Maybe after that, Soon Lee's. That was the only thing that mattered right now.

• • •

Oh, how I wanted to relax. I just wanted to be left alone and to be in peace. It hit me hard now that Gunter was gone. I was down. The discussion with Hobbs and Mallory, one that I needed to clear my conscience, did not help. I felt more unease as I left the office. I went to Cooper's. It was late, nearing eight o'clock. My temples were tight. The whiskey was having little success in loosening them. There were no lights or faded vision, but I just didn't feel right. I needed a break from this and soon.

I had finished several drinks and was on the verge of ordering another when my sight fixed on a small figure that had entered the tavern. I hadn't seen him in a while and he looked better, but not much. It was clear that he was here to find me. He waved when he saw me over in the corner near the bar.

"Moses. You are far too predictable," Gussie Black said. His face looked fuller with no welts

"Because I like to come to the same place for dinner?" I asked.

He noticed no food in front of me, only a couple of empty glasses. "I hear you have been drinking quite a bit."

I felt a rush of anger wash over me. "I should just shoot you, Black."

"That would make it all better?" he asked.

I took a sip of my latest drink. "What do you want?"

"I have a message for you, but I'm not sure looking at you that it will do you any good."

I bristled. "Who gave you this message?"

"I have recently been making some deliveries to the Palace De Sade. I have gotten to know Madam Claire and a few of the girls. Anyway, as you asked, I have inquired about the mute, blonde man. They told me you were asking about him as well."

"Get to the point, Black."

He sighed and took a deep breath. "He has a date tonight with Colette Vitriol at ten o'clock. Her room is the last one on the left, east side of the building, second floor."

I stood quickly. "You are sure of this?"

"I have just left that brothel and knew it was a little early for you to be at Soon Lee's. I came right here."

I had an hour and a half to get myself together and find Sam. I figured he would be at home. "You've done well, Black. Maybe we can catch this son of a bitch."

•   •   •

As I readied myself to pound on Sam's apartment I remembered my earlier invitation from him to visit his home. This wasn't a social visit; I wasn't going to meet the wife and kids. There was a sense of gloom over me. I hoped this wasn't the last visit I made to the apartment. Also, I knew that Sam looked down upon my drinking and visits to the opium den, so I made sure I washed up, ate some minted candies and rinsed my mouth out. I didn't feel too bad. I hoped I didn't reek of booze.

"Patrick," Sam said, peering through the opening in the door. I knew his gun was at his side. The killer's threat was still on his mind,

"I got a tip from Gussie Black. He was told by Madam Claire, at Palace De Sade, that Christian Hanson will be there tonight after ten o'clock."

He gave me a quick once over. I must have passed. "Then we shall pay him a visit," Sam said.

He invited me into the apartment where I waited in the small foyer as he got ready. I didn't meet Mrs. Walker or the kids; they must have been asleep. It took Sam several minutes to get ready. The last thing I saw him doing was strapping that knife to his calf and covering it with his pant leg. "You never know," he said.

We were both quiet and calm on the short carriage ride to Palace De Sade. It was cold out, but clear and dry. It was just after ten when we got to the brothel and the place wasn't that busy when we entered and met Madam Claire.

"She is upstairs with him in her room," the madam said.

"Anyone else upstairs?" I asked.

"Only Marcelle, but she is on the opposite side of the floor. Colette's room is the last one on the left. Take a right at the top of the stairs."

We removed our overcoats, suit jackets and hats and left them downstairs. We moved as quietly as we could up the stairs and waited a second on the second landing. The hall was well lit and we could see Colette's room three down on the left.

"I'll go in first," Sam said. "Hopefully he is engaged with the young lady, or she is whipping him, and this will be easy."

I laughed, remembering Christian Hanson's odd sexual behavior. "If he makes a move for his fucking gun, shoot him. He can't answer our questions, anyway."

"No problem there, Patrick."

No problem there, Patrick. This is the answer to the question that Mrs. Walker would ask me later. What were my husband's last words? I didn't know if Hanson thought about who would come through that door first, but I later presumed that he thought it would be me. It was Sam. As soon as the door was opened and Sam stepped into that room the shotgun blast came and it took a good part of Sam's head off. I was trailing behind Sam and got a few pellets in my left shoulder. It felt like a bee had stung me.

Sam was blown back towards me and knocked me over. There was blood, bone fragments and any other piece of the human body you could think of all over that hall and me. Somehow the door closed on me, but there were three more shotgun blasts. I stayed down. I heard some screams from other rooms, but this ended shortly. When all was quiet, I looked up at the door and it had been riddled with buckshot. I looked over at Sam, pushing him away from me. There wasn't a question of life or death. His head was gone.

I found my gun and with my foot kicked open the door. Just as I expected, the window in the room was wide open and Hanson was long gone out of it. I got up and entered the room. Poor Colette Vitriol was on top of the bed, fully clothed, throat slashed. I walked to the window. It led to a staircase on the outside. I poked my head cautiously out of it, but all was quiet. Hanson was gone again. My partner, the second in two days, was dead. Another prostitute, this one by a different killer, was gone as well. My quiet night was not ending all that well.

• • •

Somehow, like in a dream, I found myself outside. The air was cold, below zero, and someone had wrapped a blanket around me. I couldn't remember where I'd put my coat and hat. The blanket smelled of old perfume and I caught myself thinking of the whores and their bizarre trade at the Palace De Sade. I thought of Sam Walker's missing head and the blood and guts and I vomited in the street. Then I had a cigarette in my hand and I was puffing on it. I didn't smoke. I was shaking, but not from the cold. I was, at least for a moment, in hell on earth.

There was so much noise at that time, so much confusion; I didn't know what was going on. I saw the girls who worked in the brothel flowing out onto the street, looks of horror across their faces. There were normal citizens, curious onlookers, wondering what had taken place at the Palace. Then there were cops, lots of cops, some milling about like patrolmen will do and others actually working. Many were walking all over the area looking for the elusive Hanson. I knew this was useless. He had killed two cops in two days. He would get as far away from Chicago as he could.

Riley O'Donnell was the first person I recognized. (George Loftus was still jailed in our basement). I was starting to calm down and flicked away the half smoked cigarette. Riley walked up to me and grabbed my arm. I turned towards him and could see the look of deep concern on his face. "You okay, Moses?" the old detective asked.

"I'm fine," I said. "Getting better every minute."

This comment brought forth an odd look. "Sorry about Walker."

"He never felt a thing," I said. "The first blast took most of his head off."

"Jesus," Riley said. "Somebody will have to talk with his wife."

I nodded stupidly. Does this grim discussion always fall to the ex-partner?

"Hey, you know that barmaid, Beth Stokes, the one who provided the alibi for that Pelicanos fellow?"

Beth Stokes' name caught my attention. "I know her."

"I was over at Mercy, trying to interview a stabbing victim when they brought her in on a gurney. Somebody beat the hell out of that poor girl. Her face was just one mass of bumps and bruises."

With that Riley turned and headed into the Palace De Sade. The coroner's vans had just showed up and were getting ready to remove the bodies of Sam Walker and Colette Vitriol. I thought of the position I had put Beth Stokes in and my already shitty mood darkened. I knew who had done this to her.

The little criminalist, Harold Pinter, came out of the brothel and he looked as if he'd seen a ghost. He walked up to me without saying anything.

"Find any clues, Harold?" I asked.

"Sure," he said."One victim with no head, one with a cut throat. So many finger prints and loose hairs in that room we'll never be able to figure it out. You okay, Patrick?"

"I see a lot of death."

Captain Morgan emerged from the crowd in front of the brothel and found us. He wore a grim look on his face. "We'll find this bastard, Patrick. We've got the whole city looking for him. There is no way for him to get away."

I only listened. Harold Pinter moved towards the coroner's vans as one of the bodies was being taken out.

"I heard you will need some treatment for your shoulder," Morgan said. "You should get over to Mercy and have those pellets removed. Infection is an awful thing."

"Yes," I said. "I will go soon."

"Late this afternoon I received a telephone call. It was a man calling me. He gave a similar message to me that he gave to Walker. He told me that if I met him at the old Sherman's Warehouse building on Thirty-Ninth tomorrow at eight o'clock he could give me the prostitute killer. He told me to come alone, but I think you should come along with me. Do you think you'll be up to that task?"

Morgan was staring intently at me. I was still coming out of my dreamlike state, but I was coming out quicker now. Someone had called Morgan the same way they had called Sam with an offer to give up the prostitute killer. The only thing wrong with this scenario was that no one had ever called Sam.

"What do you say, Patrick?"

"I will meet you in front of the warehouse at eight o'clock tomorrow night."

He placed his hand on my good shoulder. "Take the day off tomorrow. You have earned it." He turned and walked into the crowd. I felt my shoulder burn for the first time and went in search of medical help.

Sixteen

I did go in search of medical help, but not to Mercy Hospital. That was where too many people I knew went to die. I went to see my old friend Doc Mitchell on Wabash Street. He was never too pleased to see me and tonight was no different. Luckily for me there had only been four pellets that hit my left shoulder. I was glad I had removed my overcoat and suit jacket. The pellets had missed my vest and had only torn through my shirt which was spotted with blood. Doc Mitchell cut away the shirt and removed the pellets, cleaning the wounds carefully. Then he gave me some laudanum for the pain and I slept.

When I awoke the first person I saw was the Doc. He was peering at me and for a minute I thought something was wrong. "Am I going to live?" I asked.

"For my sake, I'm afraid so," he said. "Everything looks good with the wounds. My biggest concern, Moses, is that you look like shit."

"Thank you, Doc."

"You look bloated to me. Too much whiskey and opium, I would think."

"Probably not enough to deal with the Levee."

He smirked. "You have a visitor."

"I do?" I was surprised.

"Yes. That man you called last night, Pinter. He is in the outer room."

I didn't remember calling Pinter. I also didn't deny it. "Send him in."

Pinter came into the room that I was resting in and smiled. "You look well, Patrick."

"Not bad for somebody who's been shot."

"A few pellets in the shoulder is not being shot," he said. "Anyway I brought over what you asked for."

"What did I ask for?"

An inquisitive glance. "Walker's gun and knife and a protective vest that I thought of."

The light in the room was bright; I squinted up at Pinter. "I'll be honest. I don't remember calling you. What did I say?"

"You told me to gather Walker's weapons, which I did, and that you were going into a meeting tonight where there was sure to be gun fire."

My meeting with Morgan. "What kind of protective vest?"

"It's here," he said, holding up what looked like a lumpy garment. "The French have developed it and have been experimenting with it. No promises, but it might help stop a bullet. It is made of silk. You where it under your suit."

"What do you mean experimenting?"

"It has stopped a seven caliber bullet. It can't hurt to wear it, you know." He looked hurt.

"I suppose not," I said. "I'll give it a try. You didn't tell anyone about my meeting tonight?"

"You told me not to. Are you going to be okay, Patrick?"

I thought for a moment. Something was up with Morgan, something I didn't like. "I hope so," I said. "Has anyone seen Mrs. Walker?"

"Captain Morgan went by there this morning. Very sad, I hear."

I nodded. It was very sad. It was also the least that Morgan could have done.

 • • •

I was well rested and alert when Morgan approached me from the west as I stood in front of the old Sherman's Warehouse building on Thirty-Ninth. The place had once been used for storage for equipment for the meat packing industry, but had been closed for some time. It was cold out and the wind had started to blow. I was dressed with an overcoat, hat and gloves. Under my suit was the silk vest Pinter had given me for protection. I didn't know if it would stop a slug, but it was helping to cut the cold wind. I was armed with my gun, Walker's piece and his knife, a six inch hunting blade strapped in its scabbard to my right calf.

"We need to get inside," Morgan said without any further greeting. "If we are seen out here the whole meeting might fall apart." I watched as he casually opened the door in the front of the building and walked in. I followed behind.

He walked deep into the building, dark as it was, and it led me to believe that he had been here many times. The building was cold and the roof had caved in many spots. Moonlight provided decent light in rooms where the roof had collapsed. Morgan led me into one of these, a smaller room with a table in the center of it. I could only make out ropes on the floor. He stood about fifteen feet from me and stopped. I stopped as well. His head was down, but when he raised it I could see the silhouette of a taller man, slightly stooped, wearing a wide brimmed hat with a bushy mustache on his face.

"What is this meeting about, Captain?" I asked. I wasn't nervous or scared. Maybe stupid.

"This meeting, Patrick, is about understanding and disclosure," he said. He sounded like one of the old priests at Holy Trinity delivering his Homily. "When I came onto the police force it was with the idea that I would be doing something good. I wanted to help clean up the bad in the city."

"I think we all have those thoughts when we join the force."

"Exactly," his voice boomed. "We all have those thoughts and then there is so little we can do. We can deal with all of the theft and robberies and murders as well as we can, but some things we can do little about."

"What things, Captain?"

"The sins of the flesh like prostitution."

"Prostitution is legal."

"In whose eyes, Patrick? Certainly not in God's eyes. I am surprised to hear you say that, especially with your upbringing at Holy Trinity."

At that moment the moon shone through the roof and splashed on Morgan's face. I could see his eyes, full of fire. "So what do you propose?" I asked.

He laughed. "I propose nothing. I am only here to tell you that you and Krause made so many mistakes when trying to capture Doctor Kluge. How could you not see that more than one person was involved in those murders? How could you also not see that some good was finally being done with the killing of those whores?"

"Why would I see any good in that?" My thoughts went to Eleanor, anger rising.

"I have seen it in your behavior. You are so hypocritical, but you kill without remorse. You see evil and you can dispatch it, but talk about how bad Doctor Kluge was."

"What are you talking about?"

"I could hear it in your voice when we talked to that man, Pelicanos, about your father's murder. I could hear you doubting him and so strongly. There was only one reason for your attitude towards him. You had killed your father."

I took a deep breath. "So we erred that there were two killers. We did eventually figure this out."

Morgan laughed. "After more bodies turned up."

"You spoke of revelation, Captain. I can only expect that you plan to reveal something to me."

"You were digging and getting closer. Clues were coming together. It wouldn't be long before a number of them were strung together. Doctor Kluge and I shared the same dream, to eradicate the prostitutes. You caught him; I felt you would catch me. I have Loftus and enough evidence to hang him, but not with you in the picture. Walker did me a favor by having Hanson kill him. It's you, Patrick. You are the only piece left in my way."

We stood for a moment looking at each other. He wore a heavy coat, open. The sleeves were long and I could not see his hands. He raised his right arm and a barrel protruded from the sleeve. I could barely think before the barrel exploded and the shell hit me in the shoulder, same spot as my wound from the night before. It struck right on top of a heavily padded part of the vest that Pinter had given me. Vest or not it stung like hell and the force knocked me down onto my back. Before I knew it, Morgan was straddling me, a large knife in his hand.

"I felt bad about Eleanor Winter," he said. He was leering down at me. "A lovely girl and she did ask for you right before I cut her. It was a shame, but it did get the message across."

"What message?" I managed to say. My shoulder was throbbing as I reached my right hand along my calf for Sam's knife.

"Why the message that we were not done with our mission. I am sorry, Patrick, but the time has come. By the time they find you, Loftus will be gone and I will take a short vacation." He got a strange look to him; his eyes gleamed. He raised the knife, a serrated bayonet.

He was standing over me, his crotch right over my stomach. The target was too easy; the knife now in my hand. I made one quick lunge and drove the knife completely into the area where his privates were housed. The look in his eyes went from gleam to horror. The scream that came from his mouth sounded like a wounded animal.

He reared back and I pulled myself out from underneath him as he fell to the floor, trying to remove the knife from his crotch. I managed to stand and draw my revolver. I would not make the mistake I had made with Kluge. I walked to him as he drew the blade from his body, agony on his face. I pointed my weapon and can say today that I never heard it fired. I emptied the entire gun into the head of Captain Morgan. If he'd ever left a live witness they would have been unable to recognize his face.

• • •

After shooting Morgan, I sat on the floor of the warehouse not more than ten feet from his body. I probably sat there several minutes. It was cold and my shoulder ached. I needed to get back to see Doc Mitchell. I also needed to figure out what to do with Morgan. My first thought was to abandon his body and let the rats have a nibble at him, but I was better than that. I finally got up off the floor and made my way out of the warehouse to the nearest call box and placed the call. I was a police detective. There had been a shooting. I had been the shooter and had killed a police captain. This call was sure to get some attention.

As sick as I knew Morgan and Kluge were, I couldn't figure out why Morgan had left the little poems for Walker and me; why had he stolen Walker's hat and left it on Pearl Radd's head? I asked Pinter about this later and his thought was that Morgan had wanted to be caught.

"You must be kidding me," I said.

"Not really," the criminologist said. "He was sick and he believed that he was doing some good by killing those prostitutes, but deep inside he knew he was evil and he was hoping to get caught so the killing would stop."

"What about all of that nonsense with George Loftus?"

"Another sick attempt to maybe stop himself. If Loftus somehow got convicted and executed maybe Morgan thought he could stop himself."

"What a sick mind."

"An understatement, Patrick."

Of course there was all of the physical evidence that needed to be tied up and this proved to be simple. The knife that Morgan was going to use to carve me up matched up with the types of wounds that Pearl Radd had. The hairs that were found in the hat at Loftus' apartment were from Morgan's head. The print on that piece of silver jewelry from Bad Joanie perfectly matched the Captain's right thumb. The print on the two notes for Sam and I matched Morgan's writing. Lastly, at the morgue, Pinter saw a final puzzle piece when they removed Morgan's clothes. On Morgan's right arm were two deep gashes that were a gift from Pearl Radd. The two red hairs in the vial matched the hairs on Morgan's arm.

In my earlier documentation of cases in the Levee I had mentioned trinkets from the murders that had been left on my doorstep. It seems that Morgan was the collector of such items from the victims. His small apartment on Sixteenth was like a museum of souvenirs from the murders. He was the second prostitute killer. The case was officially closed.

Seventeen

I slept most of the day after the shooting of Morgan. This had followed a long night of inquiry and a trip to Doc Mitchell. The shot that Morgan had fired at me had been stopped by the vest that Pinter had given me. The bullet had done a nice job of bruising my already tender shoulder, but Doc said I would be in good shape in a few days.

I don't know what it was that I realized after killing Morgan, but I was certainly overcome by thoughts that evil was everywhere. I couldn't stop it and I was becoming part of it. I needed to get away from the Levee and the evil. I had an idea where to go.

• • •

Later in the day I found myself at Gunter's wake, a solemn affair. I consoled Margaret and felt absolutely sick when I saw his children and the pain on their faces. It twisted the knife in my belly more and more as I thought about Christian Hanson, walking around out there a free man. Sometimes things have a way of working themselves out and I took what happened next to be my sign of that.

I was about to leave the wake when I saw Jim Colosimo and his wife Victoria enter the funeral home. Both were dressed magnificently and both looked somber. I wasn't too surprised to see them there since Victoria had hired Margaret to make dresses for her. I was surprised when Big Jim left his wife's side and walked over to me.

"I am sorry about your partner, Detective Moses." There was a warmth in his eyes I had never seen before.

"Do you mean you are sorry since one of your former employees did this to this family?"

The sadness never left his face. "He is not my employee. I told you that before."

"That makes everything better."

"The last time we spoke, I didn't answer one of your questions."

"What question was that, Mr. Colosimo?"

"Where Christian is?"

I felt the excitement surge in my body. "You know where he is?"

He nodded. "I have heard that he left town to return to his home in New York City. He has returned there to work with The Black Hand."

"New York, you say?"

"I have it from a very good source that he left town for New York."

I thanked Colosimo and turned and left the funeral parlor. Was it a coincidence that Hanson was in New York? I saw it as a sign. My uncle, Irving Fine, had told me that the last known residence for my mother was New York City. I needed a break and that was where I was going to go. If I was going to try and find my mother, I was sure there would be down times in that search. I could fill those times by trying to find Hanson. I had a few more things to do before I left town.

• • •

I remembered that Beth Stokes told me that her husband, Amos, worked the middle shift in the day. I knew that when I got there at two o'clock in the morning that he would be fast asleep. Their door lock was easy to slip and it was very quiet in their small house as I made my way through it. I found the bedroom near the back of the house and entered it quietly. The only noise I could hear was coming from the fat, bloated body of Amos Stokes, snoring away as if he had not a care in the world. I had checked on Beth and she was still in very serious condition at Mercy.

I watched Amos for a bit and saw my chance when he rolled onto his back and was looking right up at the ceiling. He was a fat slob and he farted loudly as I took a step closer to him. I shook my head and then I stuck the small barreled pistol under his chin, poking it into his Adam's apple. His eyes popped open.

"What the fuck?" he said. He tried to raise his head, but I pushed it back down with the gun.

"Quiet, Amos," I said.

"Who are you?"

"Patrick Moses."

"You're that cop who Beth told the story of being with that fucking Greek on Christmas day."

"The same," I said.

"What the hell do you want?"

"You feel pretty big and bold when you beat up a woman?"

"Come on. You would have done the same, your wife telling the whole world she was fucking somebody else. Especially on Christmas Day. She deserved it in my eyes."

"Too bad that I don't agree with what you think she deserved."

"So you've come to arrest me in the middle of the night?"

I shook my head. "Not to arrest you."

He turned his head and in the soft light I could see fear cross his face. "Then what?"

I shoved the pistol into his Adam's apple again. "Justice."

Now he seemed to understand what I was saying. "But you're a police officer."

"Not any longer." I pulled the trigger and there was a muffled blast and there was actually more noise as Amos writhed on the bed and made sucking noises through the hole in his throat. He finally died. I didn't know if Beth Stokes survived if she would have been better off without him, but I guessed and hoped I'd made the right decision. I also knew then that I had crossed the line into the darker world of Kluge, Morgan and Christian Hanson. I was becoming an animal, bred in the streets of the Levee.

·   ·   ·

Later that morning, I was in the downtown office of Lieutenant Shipley. I had called ahead and asked for a moment to speak to him privately. It wouldn't take long. I had a train to catch for New York. He still looked a bit astonished as he looked up at me.

"You're sure you want to do this, Detective Moses?"

I placed my badge on his desk. "I need a bit of a break."

"I understand that, but New York."

"My mother lives there and there is an old friend I would like to try and catch up with."

"Well, you know how much we respect you here, regardless of some of our differences. If you should happen to change your mind, please come see me. I will see that you are immediately reinstated."

"Thank you," I said.

Shipley stood and shook my hand. His was small, his wrist bony. "Watch out in New York. They breed a nasty sort of people."

I nodded. I was from Chicago's Levee District. New York did not know what they were getting in me.

• • •

I stopped at the bank and cleaned out my accounts. I had enough with me to get a good start and took some of the remainder of the funds from the Marshall Field case and had a bank draft written to Sylvia Pelicanos. I posted an envelope and mailed the check to her house. Hopefully it would hold her over until things settled and she could find her own way.

• • •

At Union Station as I waited for my train east, I felt relaxed. I heard the newsboy yelling something and then he said it again.

I walked over to the stand and looked down at the stack of *Tribunes* on the floor. Jumping out at me in a bold headline confirmed what the newsboy had said:

Marshall Field Dies in New York

It appeared that the retail mogul, and my former employer, had gotten sick after playing golf with the son of Abraham Lincoln. It turned out to be pneumonia and he had succumbed. How strange that it had happened in New York and on this day. After all, most of my realization of who and what I was becoming had started on that day that Field had hired me to find out how his son had died. Odd that his life had ended on the day I hoped my life would begin again.

The End

Purchase other Black Rose Writing titles at www.blackrosewriting.com/books

and use promo code PRINT to receive a 20% discount.